Praises are in for *D.R.T. - Dead Right There*

"Ray Ellis's D.R.T. (Dead Right There) is one of those rare crime novels that not only keeps you teetering on the edge of your chair, but reminds you that the jagged line between good and evil is as narrow and painful as the razor's edge. Penned with blood red imagery and the haunting grace of an old poet, this young author is sure to thrill legions of fans for years to come."

VINCENT ZANDRI
Bestselling author of *The Innocent* and *Scream Catcher*

DRT is a police code that stands for Dead Right There, a message used by police to tell paramedics, detectives, and the coroner driving to the scene that the victim is dead. No need to hurry.

Nate Richards, detective for the Treasure Valley Metro Police, is about to use DRT a great deal.

A serial killer is on the loose, but the murders aren't normal. Assassination seems to be the best word. And the victims all have one thing in common. They are all listed as registered sex offenders. Someone in the Treasure Valley, Nate discovers, is on a personal crusade to rid the world of those who abuse others.

Nate is torn by the idea of protecting those who've molested children in the past, and his duty to protect those who've paid their dues to society in prison. But for Nate, the law is the law, and his job is to stop the murders.

But juggling his career and his personal life is growing difficult. Prepared to date again after his true love, Amber, abandons him, he tentatively takes a woman out for dinner, and the evening is a hit. His choices grow more difficult, however, when Amber returns from her sabbatical.

But the mystery is cleared somewhat as Nate and his partner discover who is next to be murdered, and they scramble to save her life. But the killer won't give up easily, and the attempts for assassination grow in complexity, giving credence to the idea that the murderer could be a woman.

DRT is fast paced novel that puts the reader in the seat next to Nate Richards. The author's in-depth police knowledge gives the sense of standing in the private meetings of the detectives, as well as in the station with the investigators as they sort through evidence. But be prepared to dodge bullets and chase bad guys.

Gritty, but not excessive, Christian, but not preachy, DRT is a worthy second in the Nate Richards series. If you're a fan of modern police shows and love tension in life and death decisions, as well as plot twists and turns, DRT is for you.

PETER LEAVELL
Author of Songs of Captivity
Winner of the *Jerry B. Jenkins Operation First Novel Contest*

"D. R. T. (Dead Right There) is Ray Ellis's intriguing second book in the Nate Richards series. Ellis once again grabs hold of the reader and won't let go in this intense book. A serial killer is targeting registered sex offenders in the Treasure Valley. Richards and his partner, Mac, must stop him before he completes his list. Ellis takes the reader into the killer's mindset where he believes God is directing him to take out the registered sex offenders. Ellis draws from his own experience as a detective to illustrate the difficulties of life in law enforcement. Richards and Mac miss Thanksgiving dinner with their families because they're called out to a crime scene. Richard's love life becomes complicated when he finally decides to start dating again, and Amber, the woman he professed his love to just before she left town, returns. Richards again feels his faith being tested in both his professional life and his personal life. Ellis gives the reader enough insight into the murderer to remind the reader that there is a human being who was once hurt himself somewhere inside the monster committing the crimes. With characters who are multilayered rather than caricatures of good and evil, D. R. T.: Dead Right There exposes the raw truth that even the most righteous have sinned and that it is human nature to see one sin, especially someone else's, as worse than others."

T. L. COOPER
Author of *All She Ever Wanted*

Ray Ellis

A Nate Richards Novel - Book Two

D.R.T. (Dead Right There) – 2nd Edition
By Ray Ellis

First Edition eBook: 2011
First Edition Paperback: 2011
Second Edition eBook 2012
Second Edition Paperback: 2012
ISBN: 978-1-938596-02-5

Cover and Book design by Michael Sloane
Photos and Imaging by E(xploratory) Photography, Meridian, Idaho
Cover Model: Raymond Ellis II

Boycott typeface: Copyright 2008 Flat-it type foundry
    (http://flat-it.com/)
Francois One typeface: Copyright 2011, Vernon Adams
    (vern@newtypography.co.uk)

Published in the United States of America
NCC Publishing
Meridian, Idaho, USA
www.nccpublishing.com

10323820120921

This book is dedicated to Mike & Debbie Sloane, Cathi Gonzalez, and Sharon Ellis, without whose help, prayers, and constant belief, this project would have failed. Thank you.

"And be not afraid of them that kill the body, but are not able to kill the soul: but rather fear him who is able to destroy both soul and body in hell."

Jesus
Matt 10:28 ASV

"A man who does not have something for which he is willing to die is not fit to live."

Dr. Martin Luther King Jr.
Civil Rights Speech
Chicago Tenement

D.R.T.

CHAPTER ONE

WET SNOW looked like a spilled cherry snow cone spreading from beneath the man's downturned face. Detective Nate Richards, of the Treasure Valley Metro Police, looked down at the body stretched out on the ground at his feet. A quick glance suggested *a single blow to the side of the man's head* had ended his life. Nate shook his head, dislodging snow from his loose curls, the white flakes contrasting against the coffee-colored tone of his skin. He shivered. *I hate winter.* Nate looked up momentarily, drawn by the halo that encircled the streetlight as its russet glow illuminated the night sky.

His partner, Detective Chris MacGilvery, worked a short distance away, talking to the on-scene patrol officer. The unbroken surface of the snow, pristine in its whiteness, made the whole scene eerily bright. MacGilvery cupped his hands and blew into them, attempting to thaw them out, his gray-blue eyes reflecting the light from the snow. He had been assigned as Nate's partner when Nate's previous partner, twenty-year veteran Sabrina Jackson, retired after being shot in the line of duty by a rogue cop.

Looking up with the memory, Nate flexed tight muscles in his jaw and stooped to better examine the body. Remembering his scripture reading from that morning, *Hebrews 9:27*, *"And it is appointed unto men once to die, but after this the judgment."* Nate wondered where this man's soul was now.

He looked over the crime scene trying to decipher its secrets. Shaking his head from side to side, he considered the snow. It was not helping, no footprints led to or away from the body. *The snow will have to be collected and sifted for possible evidence.* He rubbed gloved fingers across his chin.

"Mac," Nate called out, "witnesses?"

"None. A man walking his dog found the body and called it in."

Nate made his way over to Chet Baraza, the patrol officer in charge, and looked in the direction of the sirens sounding in the near distance. "I guess we can tell the paramedics to downgrade," Nate said, extending a hand to Baraza.

The group of patrol officers laughed. Baraza chuckled and shook Nate's hand. "He's DRT. Dead right there, man, this one's not going anywhere on his own. He must'a dropped like a sack of potatoes. Farrumph!" the officer said and gestured as if dropping a heavy load.

Wheels crunched in the snow as the paramedic van pulled up and rolled to a stop just outside the crime scene. The overhead lights flashed brilliantly against the snow perforating the velvet drape of the night sky. The already too bright landscape sparkled like an oversized diorama as the red and white lights of the van played against it. The driver, a middle age balding man, stepped from the van. "What'd'ya got?" he asked nobody in particular.

Nate dipped his chin toward the body. He looked back at the driver and shook his head from side to side in a slow sweep.

Pulling on rubber examination gloves, the paramedic bent over and examined the four-inch gash in the temple of the victim, paying particular attention to the jagged edge. He stood and whistled, blowing air through pursed lips. "Wow, that's...," he began. "That's—that's bad." He looked over his shoulder at his partner who was quickly pulling gear from the van. "Bag it, Jeff, this one's DRT. Better call the coroner, Nate."

***

Mac finished talking to the witness and, after getting his contact information, released him to leave. Turning to face the group of officers, he jogged-skidded his way back across the thin sheet of ice on the street to join Nate and the others near the body.

Nate locked eyes with Mac before they both turned to face Baraza. The veteran street cop pulled his note pad from his breast pocket and frowned as he prepared to check his information against what the detectives already had.

"The old guy," he said, indicating the RP (reporting party) "called in a medical-assist-man-down at about 2015 hours...just after the first call came into dispatch about what sounded like a single gunshot being fired."

Nate looked back at the body of the unidentified man lying face down in the snow. "Anybody pull I.D. yet?"

"Naaa, it was obvious he was dead. Thought we'd wait for five-one to call it, and of course, you guys."

"So you're a doctor now, Baraza," Mac chided.

Baraza frowned, feigning injury. "You don't need a M.D. in front of your name to know you can't live with a hole like that in the side of your head. I'm thinking long gun, .22 caliber, maybe."

"That much damage from a twenty-two?" Mac asked, arching a brow.

"Heavy load, low velocity at close range," Baraza finished. "Maybe a tumbler. Of course, it's just my guess. But I'm only a lowly street cop, not like you bright boys up there in Criminal Investigation Division." He smiled sarcastically and, with a tap of his fingers, tucked his pad back into his jacket pocket.

Nate cupped Baraza on his shoulder and pushed him, causing him to slide on the ice, barely managing to keep his balance. "I'll see you in the morning, wise guy."

Baraza laughed. "Heck, we'll be back for morning briefing before you even finish your paperwork."

The men laughed, and Nate turned his attention back to the dead man belly down in the snow. Looking up, Nate saw the coroner's van pulling into the intersection. The deputy coroner, a tall dark haired man in his mid to late twenties, got out and prepared to bag the body.

"Hold on there, cowboy," Mac called to the deputy coroner.

Nate waved a hand to get the coroner's attention. "We haven't finished here yet; crime scene's still mine."

"Works for me, I'll wait in my wagon. Too cold out here for me anyway," he said and hefted his bulk back into the van.

Flipping open his cell phone, Nate called the on-call crime scene tech. Rosie answered on the second ring. "Hey, sorry to bother you this early…"

She cut him off. "I'm already en route. Got in late and heard the call go out. I should be on scene in about…now." She honked her horn as she parked her van across the street from the crime scene. Rosie, a fifty-something Hispanic woman, was almost as tall as she was round, with a personality just as big. She was a no-nonsense, fresh-off-the-streets type girl.

Bumping the van door closed with her hip, Rosie opened her bag and began to set up her camera. "What do you want?" She asked over her shoulder.

Nate and Mac smiled knowingly as Rosie sorted the varied baggies and evidence containers. "Better get everything. We don't know what we have yet," Nate answered.

"You can get me the heck out of here," MacGilvery added sarcastically and glanced over at Rosie.

As Rosie began to create a photo log of the crime scene, recording the location and placement of items of interest, Nate and Mac stepped back to consider what they had discovered. A half hour passed, and Rosie signaled that she had finished with the preliminary photos and was all set to begin evidence collection.

"Ready?" Nate asked.

"Nope," Mac said joking.

"Oh, shut up," Rosie cut in. "We're ready."

"Okay," Nate began, "I'll walk the route. You watch Mac and Rosie you—"

"I'll stand by for collection and tagging. It's not my first ride on this train you know"

Nate smiled.

Standing near the head of the body, he looked at the scene again. Studying the body's position, Nate moved around it trying to determine the victim's direction of travel at the time of attack. Beginning at the corpse's feet, taking slow steps moving in a spiral search pattern, he progressed outward from the body. Nearing the head again, he stopped, feeling something hard beneath the toe of his shoe. "Mac...I think I got something."

Nate knelt down and retrieved a small rectangle shaped piece of plastic from beneath his right foot. Reading the writing on the side of the object, he recognized it to be a 16-gigabyte thumb-drive.

Holding the thumb-drive between his index finger and thumb, Nate dropped it into a small evidence bag held by Rosie. She cut her eyes at him. "Next time use rubber gloves, Sherlock."

He exchanged glances with Mac. "What'd'ya think?"

"I think you should wear gloves." He cleared his throat and chuckled. "I don't believe in coincidences," he answered. "Let's get it back to the lab and see what the boys in cyber tech can do with it."

Rosie didn't smile. "Let's just get it dried out and see if there's anything on it."

Nate nodded and continued the swirl pattern outward to about ten to twelve feet from the body. Mac tracked his progress from the side, looking for anything that Nate may have missed.

Nate positioned himself near the shoulders of the body, directing Mac to the opposite side near its knees. "Okay, let's roll this fellow over and see who we have here."

Aided by the cold and rigor mortis, the body rolled easily and rocked onto its back like a saucer settling into place. Its hands and arms splayed, frozen above his head. Blue eyes stared unseeing through ice crystals into the night sky.

"Whoa," Nate said, "you know who this is?" He reached into the dead man's pocket and retrieved his wallet. Opening it, he passed the ID to Mac.

Mac forced air through pursed lips. "So justice finally caught up to old Bobby."

"When did he get out of prison, anyway? I thought he got fifteen to life on his last jaunt to State."

"Yeah, fifteen, but only two fixed. He must have made parole."

"Only two years for child rape." Nate shook his head. "Maybe he should'a stayed in prison."

CHAPTER TWO

T HE NEXT MORNING, Nate, from behind heavy eyelids, sat listening to his portable police radio. With a slow deliberate motion, he picked up his coffee mug and, holding it against his face, rubbed it across closed eyes. He sighed. Across the table sat Mac, his head back and eyes closed. The morning crowd at the Library Coffeehouse was just starting to thin out, and the back room was warm, dark, and quiet.

Nate eyed his partner through the wafting veil of steam, and swallowing a mouth full of the sweetened dark liquid, winced. "We should probably check that out," he said, indicating the radio traffic, a teasing tone in his voice.

Mac leaned forward and stirred lazy circles in his coffee, clinking the spoon against the sides of the cup, "Yeah, probably, huh?"

Neither made a move to get up.

Nate looked out the window and sighed as wet snow fell in silent clumps, accumulating on the grass and dirt while leaving the paved surfaces relatively clear. For now, *I hate snow.*

The dispatcher's voice came over the radio again, disturbing the stillness of the coffeehouse's sense of peace, rows of books lining the walls giving the Library Coffeehouse its name. "Ten-fifty, P.I. Main south of Fairview. Available units respond. Repeat: ten-fifty with personal injuries. Main at Fairview. Respond!"

Jackie, the morning shift manager, placed two cups of steaming coffee in front of the men. She tilted her chin, listening to the radio traffic. "Looks like another accident, personal injury this time. The snow's winning again, I guess," she said smiling.

They looked up in surprise then smiled at the attractive brunette. "What? You feeling generous all of a sudden?" Nate asked and then chuckled.

"Now, boys," she said in playful flirtation, "you know you two are my favorite customers, but this came from the lady over there leaving with the group of students. Says it was for the two officers."

They looked up to see a woman in her mid to late thirties ushering a group of feisty teenagers out the door. The laughter and teenage boy-girl-conversation rose and fell as the adolescents collected their beverages and poured out into the snow. As the door swung shut, the petite woman turned and pushed her small framed glasses back up the bridge of her nose and offered a shy, but focused, smile at the two detectives.

"Who is she?" Mac asked, pushing his cold cup of coffee aside in favor of the fresh cup.

Nate watched as the woman wrapped the scarf around her neck and pulled her head lower into her collar against the wind. He couldn't hear her, but judging from the way the teens were responding, Nate could see the power and connection she had with them.

Nate smiled at the woman through the frosted glass and looked back at his partner. "You know, that's what I love about this job—this town, the people are real nice." He stood and grabbed his coat off the back of the chair and picked up his handheld. "Let's have a look and see what this is." He pointed the radio toward Mac who was still slouched in his chair.

"It's a patrol call; let 'em handle it."

Nate tucked a dark curl behind his ear and lifted the collar of his jacket, his coffee-colored skin dry in the cold morning. "Who knows? Maybe it's one of the guys we're looking for. Let's just drive by."

Mac drained his cup and rubbed his eyes. With an audible grunt, he lifted himself from the chair, locking his legs into a standing position.

"You're too young to be grunting like that," Nate said.

"Oh yeah, let's see you try and keep up with a three month old who hates sleeping and likes the sound of her own voice, and we'll see how well you do." Mac grunted again, looked over at Jackie, and then back at Nate. "Besides, you're too young to be living on just a memory."

Nate stopped. Staring at his partner, he arched a brow and sighed.

"How long since you even heard from Amber, anyway? Three, four, five months?" Mac asked, his voice taking on a softer tone.

Nate looked away, returning his gaze to the snow-covered landscape. For a minute, he sat lost in thought, his mind on the only woman he had ever truly loved. He remembered how for years he and Amber had denied their feelings for each other only to confess it once it was too late. Amber had left Treasure Valley confused and hurt. She needed *time,* she'd said. She had not only left the valley, she'd left him. And that had been much too long ago, longer than he'd cared to admit.

Almost 15 months had passed since Amber had been caught up in one of Nate's homicide investigations and kidnapped by the leader of a local street gang. Barely escaping, her faith had been badly shaken. Her once confident assurance in her ability to handle the dangers inherent in Nate's job eroded. She fled to give herself some time, she had said. Nate shook his head against the memory.

"She talks to my mom and dad—"

"Yeah, your parents," Mac said, stuffing his arms into his jacket. "But when was the last time she called you?" He placed a hand on Nate's shoulder. "Look, man, Amber's gone," Mac sighed, "but Jackie's right over there, and she's all woman." Mac tilted his head toward the manager of the coffee shop who smiled when she noticed the men looking at her.

Nate turned and walked away. Mac followed him out, the door swung shut with a soft swoosh. Nate's cell phone rang as he settled in behind the steering wheel, "Richards."

Mac rolled his eyes and settled his head against the neck rest. "Who is it?" he mouthed.

Nate looked at his friend and held up a finger before fishing a notepad out of his breast pocket. He began scribbling.

"Who is it?" Mac asked again, leaning over trying to read the note. "Who is it?"

Nate smiled and flipped the phone shut, passing the note to Mac. "Got a report of an assault at the high school; we'd better roll."

"Man," Mac sighed, "this stuff never ends."

***

Parking his green Jeep Cherokee along the yellow painted curb, Nate closed the door behind him and ran toward the ramp leading to the second floor of Meridian City High School. "You coming or what?" he called back to Mac who was still moving slowly. "We need to check with the librarian, she's the RP."

"The library ain't going nowhere. Besides it's nice out here." He tilted his head back allowing snow to fall onto his face.

Nate stopped at the top of the ramp and turned to watch his partner playing in the snow. "Will you come on! Morning break isn't until ten." He looked at his watch. "She only has twenty minutes left on her break."

The two men made their way into the upstairs hallway, stamping wet snow from their feet as they did. The bell rang just as they entered the hall, and the passage quickly filled with the noise of students hurrying to their next class.

"Come on," Nate said, "we can hide in here." He pulled Mac after him toward the lounge against the flow of students who were making their way out the door.

After a few minutes, the noise died down and the throng thinned. The detectives stepped out of their alcove and ventured back into the hall. "Hey, look, is—" Mac began.

"—Isn't that the woman that bought us the coffee this morning?" Nate finished for him.

From down the hallway, Nate watched the woman laughing freely with her students as they exited her classroom, and the new ones entered. He and Mac headed toward their benefactor just as a straggling couple made their way around the corner into the main hall.

"Stop! Come on, Josh! Stop already!" the female student said smiling, despite the irritated tone of her voice. The male, ignoring the girl's complaint, draped himself over her, continuing to try to kiss her.

The girl smiled weakly and elbowed the boy in the ribs, but the blow lacked any real conviction.

The boy laughed, and again, paying no heed to the girl's protest, began to force her face around to kiss her, his hands taking liberties with her body. Before Nate could respond, the teacher left her doorway and zeroed in on the couple.

With a violent jerk, the teacher snatched the boy's arm from around the girl's shoulders and, grabbing him by his collar, pushed him back against the wall. "She said no, jerk! Which part was too hard for you to understand, the vowel or the consonant?"

In stunned silence, the teen hit the wall with a dull thud. "I ah…I was—"

Grabbing him by the shoulder, the teacher pulled him forward and then shoved him down the hall. "Get to the office and you'd better be there when I arrive, Mr. Stanzel. Now, get out of my face!"

"Ms. Higgins…it's-it's okay. He didn't mean anything. Please," the girl said, pulling her blouse closed and brushing away imaginary debris from her face. Her cheeks colored.

Ms. Higgins turned to the girl, her shoulders tense, and hands on her hips. "And you…. You let him treat you like trash? Don't be so weak, Karrie. Get in the classroom. We'll talk later."

Nate and Mac exchanged glances and mouthed, "Wow", to each other.

"You see that?" Nate asked.

"What? I didn't see anything." Both men smiled, walking toward the teacher.

"Ahem," Nate cleared his throat as he and Mac approached the teacher. She turned and faced them. "Ms. Higgins, is it?"

"Yes," she said, looking directly into his face.

"Ah, I'm Detective Richards and this is my partner Detective MacGilvery," he said, expecting that she would remember them.

"Yes." She looked at them nonplussed.

The men exchanged embarrassed glances.

"May I help you?" she asked.

Taken aback by the fact that she did not recognize them, Nate stumbled over his words. "Well…I…ahh…."

"That was interesting the way you handled that little incident," Mac said, tilting his head toward the end of the hall where the belligerent student had disappeared.

"And?" she said.

"Well, not that we have a problem with it or anything, but we were here at the school and thought we'd stop by and say thank you for the coffee this morning." Nate said, finally finding his voice.

"Oh, that. You are welcome, of course, but now is hardly the time to celebrate that small gesture. I do have a class to teach." She stepped toward the open door.

"Of course," Nate said and extended his hand.

She took his hand and shook it firmly.

"So, what do you teach?" Mac asked.

"Social Studies," Ms. Higgins said and turned to face him, shaking his hand as well. "Gentlemen, while I have really enjoyed this visit, I do have a job to do." She smiled mordantly.

She turned away from the men and walked back into her class closing the door softly but firmly behind her.

Both Nate and Mac looked at each other in surprise, and again, mouthed a silent, "Wow."

***

"Darn kids." The slow drawl came from near the main entrance where Nate and Mac had entered the hallway. The janitor, a tall, thin man, pushed his bucket and mop from one side of the hall to the other, collecting small piles of melted snow and muddied water.

Nate walked back to where he'd left a mess of snow and dirt near the door. "Ahh, sorry Mr.?"

The middle-aged man turned to face Nate, looking at him as if he hadn't noticed him until that moment.

Nate noticed the name badge. "Mr. Jackson, sorry about the mess. I'm afraid that's me—my partner's fault." He smiled. "The kids were clear on this one."

Mr. Jackson chuckled as if it were a regular response. "Well maybe this time, but they make mess plenty enough for all of us. Be sure of that." He grasped Nate's outstretched hand firmly and laughed easily.

Mac waved at Nate from the door of the library. "Fifteen minutes, partner."

Nate acknowledged Mac with a tilt of his chin and then slapped the janitor playfully on the shoulder, turned and walked away.

***

Leaning on the handle of the mop, Mr. Jackson watched the retreating backs of the officers. Then shaking his head, he turned back to cleaning the mess in the hallway mumbling to himself as he did.

CHAPTER THREE

"RICHARDS! ANYBODY SEEN RICHARDS?" Lieutenant Brown called over the pods in the CID workstation. The middle-aged man stood just inside his office doorway with his arms folded loosely over his bulging gut.

"Just look at those veins sticking out on your neck." A slow southern drawl floated up from beside Brown, drawing his attention back into the office. "You gonna kill your fool self with all that yelling you doing," Lieutenant Donald Haynes said, as he squeezed by the slightly older man and looked out into the pod. "Larry, come over here, and sit down and use your phone like a civilized person. Your neck is starting to turn red, and you know how that scares an old Southern black man like me."

Lieutenant Brown harrumphed while turning from the door and sauntered back to the desk covered with files. "You know, Don, sometimes you really get on my nerves," he said and dropped into the chair behind the desk.

"I do try," Haynes said and poured himself a cup of coffee. "And hurry up and get out of my chair. I don't want Gwen calling me wondering where you are."

Brown looked up and rolled his eyes at his friend. "You and Brenda still coming over this weekend to watch the game?"

Brown asked, while dialing the phone. "BSU's playing Fresno, and the Bulldogs are looking for revenge for last year."

"And the year before that, and the one before that one too, if memory serves. It's been a while since the Bulldogs beat us on the blue turf. Yeah, we'll be over, but Brenda will probably want to play a board game or something with Gwen, so let her know." Haynes picked up the day-sheet and began reviewing the calls for service from the last twenty-four hour period.

"Whew," Haynes whistled, "a shooting last night...."

Brown turned to his friend. "I was trying to get Richards in here to give me a brief before you came on, but as usual—"

"You looking for me, L.T.?" Nate asked, holding onto the doorframe and leaning his chest in through the open doorway. Behind him the noise volume of the CID, ringing phones and several conversations carried on at once, rose and fell like the swell of a wave.

Lieutenant Brown looked at the receiver in his hand, and then to the ringing phone still clipped to Nate's waist and slammed the phone back into its cradle. "Where have you been? You know, Haynes needs that update before p.m. shift begins."

"Sorry, got stuck at the lab."

Mac ducked under Nate's arm, and sat on the corner of the desk. "Got any more of those sunflower seeds, L.T.?" he asked, while moving papers aside and rummaging the desktop.

Haynes looked up and grinned at Mac but didn't comment.

Brown turned his attention to Mac. "Get off my desk. Between you and Richards, it's amazing anything right ever gets done around here."

"Come on, Lieutenant Brown, it's not that bad. I think you kind of like us." Mac's voice had a teasing quality.

In the doorway, Nate lowered his head and shook it from side to side, smiling. He was still amazed at how well Mac fit into the unit. Replacing Sabrina Jackson had been a large order, but Mac had done it and then some.

Haynes looked around his desk and moved a stack of folders, uncovering a square pink dish fashioned in the head of a pig wearing a blue policeman's cap. Mac removed the policeman's hat and retrieved a handful of barbeque-flavored sunflower seeds.

"I don't want to see those shells on the floor," Brown said, as Mac spit the chewed hull toward the trashcan and missed.

Brown closed his eyes and drew his hand roughly across his face.

Haynes chuckled.

Mac stooped to pick up his expelled shells.

"Brief Haynes, so I can go home," Brown said, rubbing his eyes with the backs of his knuckles.

Nate folded his long arms across his chest and leaned his shoulder against the doorframe. "Well, we know the dead man was Robert Monarch," he began.

"No loss there," Haynes said, looking up from the clipboard.

"...a single shot, small caliber long-gun caught him in the temple just above the right ear," Nate finished. "He apparently was up to his old tricks. He had these in his breast pocket," Nate said, as he dropped a small stack of ten contact sheets of digital photos. All the images portrayed prepubescent children in seductive poses, either partially clothed or nude.

"Well, Nate, that one's gone to that Hell you're always talking about, huh?" Brown said, a slight smile pulling at the corners of his lips.

Nate didn't look at him, but said, "Well, sir, that's between him and God, but I'd say so."

"You can't believe your God would have anything to do with an animal like Monarch, do you? My god man, he raped babies!" Brown slammed his palms onto the desktop.

"The value of a man's soul can only be—" Nate began but stopped.

"Tell him about the thumb drive," Mac said. His interruption had the desired effect, stalling yet another of the well-known religious debates between Brown and Nate.

Nate caught his breath and refocused on the stack of papers in his hand. "Yeah," he muttered, "the thumb drive contained approximately fifty-thousand images just like the ones you have there…. Oh, and that includes videos."

"Which is why," Mac added, "we want a search warrant to go toss his house."

Haynes kicked his feet up onto the corner of the desk and rocked back in his chair, lifting the two front legs off the floor. "It's days like this that makes me want to retire. Maybe Sabrina got it right: 'It's time we all just got out of here.'" He dropped the chair back on all four and stood up. "Okay, Larry, I've been briefed. You go on, get out of here, and give Gwen my love."

Brown clearly didn't want to leave now, just as the investigation was starting to get interesting. Haynes saw the look on his face, grabbed the file from Nate, and tucked it firmly under his arm. He smiled at Brown.

Brown started to speak, "I could always—"

"Nope. Don't need ya. Go home." Haynes said and waved his hand in the direction of the door as if to introduce Brown to the rest of the CID office.

Lieutenant Brown walked slowly toward the door. Frustrated, he turned to look at Nate. "I wonder what your daddy would say about you telling people that God's taking a baby raper to Heaven."

"As a matter of fact, my father is starting a new series on the doctrine of Hell this week at the midweek Bible study. Want to come?" Nate said, unable to resist firing the barb.

"It'll freeze over first," Brown said and slid past him.

"I'm gonna tell your daddy," Haynes said, catching Nate's eye and smiling.

"But I didn't start it this time," Nate said and looked to Mac for support.

Mac put up both hands, palms out. "Leave me out of this. I'm just the newbie." He sat down and continued eating sunflower seeds.

"So you need the on-call prosecutor to get a judge to sign a search warrant." He looked at the clock hanging on the wall. "It's only six-thirty. You might be able to catch a magistrate still in chambers."

Mac took a break from the seeds. "Might want to call patrol and get them to sit-up on the house and keep it secured until we can get there."

"Good idea," Haynes said and reached for the phone. "You're gonna make a good investigator before it's all over, MacGilvery."

Just as his hand touched the receiver, the phone rang. Haynes picked it up. "Lieutenant Haynes, CID."

For the next few minutes, he didn't speak, just nodded his head and made notes on a sheet of paper in front of him. He looked up at Nate. "Yeah," he said into the receiver, "he's standing right here."

Haynes hung up the phone and leaned back into his chair while locking his fingers behind his head.

Nate and Mac stared at him.

"That was Lieutenant Cypress in patrol. They just found another body. Single gunshot wound to the side of the head."

Nate turned and exchanged glances with Mac. "Any idea who the victim is?" he asked.

"Yeah," Haynes said, "it's Reginald Willaby."

"Who's Reginald Willaby?" Mac asked, seeing the obvious recognition on Nate's face.

"Another registered sex offender," Nate stated matter of fact.

CHAPTER FOUR

THE KILLER KNEW what was being said in the press. Knew that they thought the hands were wrong, that the hands were the animal. But they were wrong, all of them.

The rifle, trembling in the gloved hands, seemed to quiver with a life of its own. The hands polished the barrel, finishing the cleaning cycle making sure that as the *sword of God,* they would be ready when the next opportunity presented itself.

The hands closed the folder on the desk and looked at the photograph of the next subject. Of the fifteen subjects, the first two had been targeted and destroyed. Judged. The next, the only female on the list, would have to go soon. This one would have to pay. She, who had been designed to be a nurturer, had become the very object of evil.

The hands clenched themselves into fists until they shook with rage. Relaxing, the hands picked up the photograph of the woman, Crystal Johansson, and again studied it. The hands knew that the woman, like all the rest of the offenders, would have to die. The hands trembled with the weight of their responsibility. They had not wanted the obligation, but had been chosen. The voices—the voice had demanded it of him. It was the duty of the hands to bring them all to judgment.

***

The coroner's report lay open on the lieutenant's desk. Lieutenant Haynes read the file and sighed. "What do you think? The papers finally got one right? You think we got a serial killer in the city?" He'd asked the questions quickly, not allowing space for an answer. He leaned back in his chair, propping his feet on his desk.

"As much as I hate to think so, but yeah, I think they got it right," Nate said in resignation.

Haynes shook his head again. "Looks like Monarch was actually your second victim. Willaby had been dead for a few days by the time they found him."

"At least the heat in his apartment had been turned off," Mac said, coming through the open door. He waved his hand beneath his nose scrunching his face, and furrowing his brow, as if smelling a foul odor.

"The bad part about this is that we actually do have a sicko out there targeting RSO's," Nate said, acknowledging his partner.

Lieutenant Haynes leaned forward resting his elbows on the desk, positioning his chin in his palms and exhaled long and deep. "Talk about your ironies. We've got a freak in town killing our registered sex offenders, and it's our job to keep 'em safe."

Both Nate and Mac pulled up chairs and sat down in front of the lieutenant's desk. Nate grabbed the file and turned it around, reading the fifteen names on the list. "Willaby and Monarch had the two earliest dates of original offenses. Think our killer's moving in chronological order?"

"Sounds reasonable," Mac said, looking from Nate back to the lieutenant.

Haynes dropped his coffee-colored finger to the list stretched out in front of him. "That would mean, aaah," he said, trying to read upside down, "...that Crystal Johansson should be our next possible victim."

"Our only female on the list," Nate said.

"Where's she at?" Haynes asked.

"Ooo-o-o...Mac said thinking, "over on that little tip-out on Sugar Creek on Cherry Lane Golf Course," Mac said, checking his notes.

Lieutenant Haynes dragged a finger across his brow. "You guys better be—"

"Already moving, sir," Nate said, getting up and heading out the door.

Mac pushed his chair back, grabbed his pad off the desk, and tucked it inside his breast pocket with a tap of his finger. "We'll let you know how things turn out."

***

Nate walked up to the front door of the one story English Tudor with ivy trimmed windows and manicured walkway. Off the back of the property stretched the fifteenth fairway; the famous water hazard as it was known by the locals. He rang the bell.

Mac joined him on the small porch. "Nobody moving out back," he said, looking through the leaded windows.

Through the glass of the front door, a shadowy figure made its way toward them. A petite blonde in her early thirties with dark blue eyes and classic, yet exotic features opened the door. "May I help you?"

"Hi, I'm Detective Richards, and this is my partner Detective MacGilvery. Crystal Johansson, may we come in for a minute, please?"

She looked beyond the men and down the walkway as if expecting that someone else might be accompanying them. "Yeah, Maryann, my parole-officer, said you'd be dropping by." She opened the door, allowing the men to enter the expensively furnished living room. "Can I offer you something to drink; tea, coffee, sparkling water?" She asked in a pleasant voice.

"No thank you," Nate said, taking the offered seat.

Mac waved away the offer, but instead walked toward the inset fireplace and studied the huge oil painting of a mother and child hanging above the mantel. The rich colors of the oils stood in vibrant contrast to the muted brasses and wood tones that dominated the room. "You live here alone?" he asked.

Crystal turned and focused intense blues eyes on him. "Why? Not the sort of house you'd expect a child molester to live in?" she asked, her voice laced thick with sarcasm.

"Well, that too," Mac said, matching her tone, "but I was thinking that the décor was rather masculine and you were registered as living here alone."

"Well, I do entertain occasionally," she said.

Both men focused their attention on her.

Stiffening, she matched their intensity. "My business, gentlemen," she said and squared her shoulders, "sometimes requires that I have client meetings here for my computer networking company, and most of my clients are men. Maryann knows all about it." She rolled her eyes and sat across from them, bending her sensuous legs at the knee and crossing her ankles.

She folded her fingers in her lap, considered her manicured nails for an extended moment, and looking up, she took a deep breath. Seemingly centering herself, she exhaled. "Look, I messed up and had an affair with a teenaged boy. I was in a bad place in my head—in my life. I did some bad things, made some bad choices. But that was a long time, and I'd like to think a different person ago." She focused her brilliant eyes back on Mac. "And if it's okay with you, I'd like to leave that person in the past."

"Well, that might not be up to you," Nate interjected.

Crystal leaned forward, dropping her face into her hands and brushing back golden bangs as silent tears first pooled, then dropped delicately from refined lashes. "Why? I've met the terms of my parole." She gripped the arms of the chair, her knuckles turning white. "I'm working and I haven't hung out with anyone under eighteen since I got out of lockup."

"Maybe you've heard about the killings in the valley?" Nate paused and allowed her to change tracks in her thinking. "We think the killer may be targeting RSO's in the valley."

The color drained from Crystal's face as the gravity of what was being said settled on her. "You think he'll be coming after me? But-but…why me?"

"Because you're next on the list," Mac said.

She turned to face him. "List? Look Detective, I'm sorry if I came across harsh earlier, but it gets old sometimes with people always judging me for something I did over ten years ago."

Mac didn't respond, but returned her gaze with a cold expressionless face.

"Look," Nate said, "we think the killer is choosing his targets based on when they first offended and the date of their registration. And that places you next on the list."

Crystal stood abruptly. "I need a drink. I'm going to make myself a cup of tea. Can I get you something…anything?" Her voice trembled. Then catching Mac's expression, she added, "I gave up alcohol along with the old life."

Mac surprised everyone when he said, "Yes, a cup of coffee, please."

"Nothing for me," Nate said cordially. "Tell me, Crystal, have you noticed anything strange lately? Have you been aware of anybody following you around or anything unusual happening here around your house?" Nate finished and gestured toward the expanse of the room, taking in the grounds with his gesture.

Crystal stood in front of the over-sized bay window overlooking the golf course, selecting dried herbs to brew her tea. Shaken by the news, she rested her hand on the cool surface of the granite countertop, steadying herself. She bent forward; her eyes closed and rested her forehead against the inlaid glass of the pantry door.

Nate noticed how the stainless steel appliances stood in stark contrast to the deep reds of the mahogany-faced cabinets and the rich tawny creamed-colored porcelain floor tiles. He exchanged an approving glance with Mac.

Muted sunlight filtered through the thinning trees and reflected from the surface of the gray-green waters of the lake, which bordered her backyard. The few remaining red and gold leaves dotted the snow-covered foliage that surrounded the lake's near edge. The water's reflection danced off the beveled edges of the window, causing a soft prism like reaction, sending washed out colors swimming through the kitchen's interior.

Mac walked over to Crystal and placed a consolatory hand on her shoulder. "Let me help you with that," he said and lifted the packages of herbs from her hand.

She stood and faced him, brushing honey golden strands of hair from her now ashen face. "Thank you," she said in a shaky voice.

"Where's your teapot?" Mac asked.

"Ahh, let me get that. I suppose you think I'm a terrible person," Crystal said, retrieving a porcelain teapot from the china cabinet.

She turned to bring the pot back to the sink when the window shattered, and the teapot exploded in her hand. She screamed as shards of glass and porcelain flew through the kitchen like miniature missiles, slicing through flesh and impaling wood.

Knocked to the floor by the shock of the explosion, Crystal rose slowly trembling on weakened arms and pushed up to her knees. Shaking, she peeked over the counter's edge.

A second shot exploded through the remaining glass, skipped off the granite surface, nicked her face, sending her into a spin and knocking her backwards.

"Get down!" Mac dove on top of her and covered her with his body.

Snatching his Glock .40 caliber handgun from his holster, Nate rushed to the sliding glass door and with quick bird like actions, looked out into the backyard and across the lake. "Stay down," he called over his shoulder. "Mac, get back up out here. Post uniforms on the north side of the lake," he shouted as he disappeared through the open door.

***

Mac dug his cell phone from his coat pocket and dialed dispatch requesting the assist. Almost immediately, the wailing cry of sirens could be heard converging on their location. Beneath him, Crystal began to cry.

With a series of short hurried scoots, Mac got to his knees and pulled Crystal, who was unresponsive, out of the kitchen.

Crawling on all fours, he dragged the petit woman by her belt into the interior of the house away from the exterior windows.

Once in the living room, Mac rolled over until he was sitting on the floor and then pulled Crystal's shoulders across his lap. "Let me see your face," he said, picking fragments of window glass and flower patterned porcelain from her hair.

She moaned and reached a hand reflexively toward the gash in her forehead. Mac trapped her hand, pushing it back down to her side. Taking his knife from his belt, he cut off part of his t-shirt and pressed it to her face. "Hold that there. We'll get you to a doctor as soon as possible."

***

After completing the area search, Nate came back through the patio door looking annoyed and frustrated. Seeing the question in Mac's eyes, he shook his head from side to side.

"Nothing?" Mac asked, walking toward his partner.

"Not quite. We did find casings, .22 caliber. Looked like self-loads," Nate said, looking around at the damage. "How's Crystal?"

"A concussion and her nerves are shot," Mac laughed. "Pardon the pun."

Nate smiled and walked into the dining area observing the Crime Scene Technicians as they began to unload their gear preparing to work the fancy kitchen turned crime scene. Already they had photographed the area and were starting to pry the expended rounds from the walls where they had lodged.

Several figures in jumpsuits swarmed the property, and Nate could see white-suited figures on the far shore of the lake working that area as well. White suits on their knees searching for any evidence overlooked in the first sweep. Others with yellow tape and orange plastic markers with numbers or block letters on them marked the possible location from where the shots had been fired.

Frustration clawed at Nate's gut. They had almost been too late. Finally, he turned back toward Mac. "Where's Crystal?"

"St. Luke's West. Don't worry, uniforms are with her and ordered not to leave for any reason. If she goes pee, somebody in uniform will be in the loo with her. Come on, let's get out of here, and let the techs do their job."

"You hungry?"

"I already called Sara. She says she's got dinner on the table, so we can stop by the house and get a bite. I figured we'd be working late."

The two men headed back down the cultured path they recently entered by. Nate's Jeep looked out of place in the barrage of CSI vans, police cars, and news trucks parked along the otherwise quiet lane.

One news truck sat off from the rest. The fluorescent number six in the familiar blue and orange swoosh identified it as belonging to Channel Six News. Nate knew that this meant, of course, that newsman, Butch Jensen, was somewhere inside his crime scene.

As if on cue, Jensen stepped in front of Nate's Jeep. "You know, it's not really a crime to run over you if I can swear I didn't see you until it was too late," Nate said.

"Besides," Mac said, as Jensen lowered his face into the driver's side window, "all the judge will give you is three months community service because he's media."

"Richards, MacGilvery, how are you guys? What'd-ya got?" Jensen asked in his 'I'm your best friend' voice.

"Go away," Mac said.

"Whatever happened to the days when the rookie sat quiet-like and let his elders do the talking?" Jensen said to Nate, trying to ignore Mac. Then turning his attention back to Nate after eyeing Mac, he asked, "What happened in there, Nate?" his digital recorder in hand.

Nate laid his head back against the headrest and closed his eyes, a smile tugging at the corners of his mouth.

"You talk to your momma with that thing on?" Mac asked pointing to the recorder.

Jensen rolled his eyes at Mac. "The only difference between you and me is I tell people when I'm recording them."

"That just means you're stupid. That's not something I would brag about Butchie-Boy," Mac said.

Nate could tell that Mac was enjoying himself, and normally he would have allowed the playful banter to go on for another few minutes, but he was hungry. "Look, Butch, it's too early to tell anything yet. As soon as we have some facts, I'll call ya," Nate said, lifting his head from the backrest and shifting the Jeep in to drive. He revved the engine for emphasis.

Jensen pulled his face back but maintained his grip on the window opening. "Look, Nate, I know there was a shooting." He paused at the look on Nate and Mac's faces. "Don't ask me how I know," he said, waving a hand at their unasked question. "But what I don't know for sure is why."

Nate exchanged a look with Mac. "We don't know either. We heard the call and responded just like everybody else," Nate said matter fact.

Jensen stood up, a puzzled look on his face. Nate used that moment to drive away, leaving a confused looking Jensen staring after them.

"Ooooo, you lied," Mac teased.

"No, not a lie; a tactical deception," Nate said and pulled out into the traffic on Cherry Lane.

"Oh, I wish you had kids," Mac said.

"Why is that?"

"Because I'd love to watch you explain the difference to a four-year-old." Mac slouched down in his seat and closed his eyes. Then as if talking to a chauffeur, he said, "Home Charles and don't spare the horses."

Nate looked over at his friend and laughed. "Yes, sir."

CHAPTER FIVE

"I HEARD ABOUT THE SHOOTING yesterday. That woman…is she going to be all right?" Sherri Richards asked, as she poured Nate a cup of coffee. The afternoon sun poured through the box-window over the sink, bringing out the red highlights in her blond hair. A petite woman of fifty-nine, she had retained her youthful appearance and energy.

She sat in the chair across from her son at the small kitchen table. She could see he had something weighing on his mind, but she knew him well enough to know that trying to pry the information from him would never work. If he had anything he wanted to say, she needed only to let him know she would listen.

Nate stirred two packs of Splenda into his coffee but didn't make eye contact with his mother. Lost in thought, or memory, he sighed. After another moment of protracted silence, he stood and walked to the window and looked out over the backyard. He held a single empty yellow sweetener packet between his fingers, folding and unfolding it over and over.

Sherri noticed the packet in her son's hands and cleared her throat. "I heard from Amber last night. She called." She guessed at the train of his thought. She could see her son's shoulders tense, but he didn't turn to face her.

Bingo.

"Oh, yeah, what's she got to say these days?" he asked.

"Her mom's doing much better. She's just finishing everything up. Wanted to make sure everything was in place. You know Amber, ever the faithful daughter."

Nate grunted.

"She asked about you," Sherri said.

At this, Nate did turn and look at his mother. They held each other's gaze, neither wanting to be the first to speak. She watched as his shoulders rose and fell, as if he'd come to a decision. He walked back to the table and sat across from her.

Sherri inhaled and opened her mouth as if to speak, but Nate beat her to it. "I'm thinking about asking Jackie out."

Sherri closed her mouth with a pop. "The brown-haired girl at the coffee shop?"

"Yeah," he said, taking a drink from his cup. "I've been thinking about asking her out for a while now." He lied.

Sherri studied her son's face and forced a smile to her own, a smile that failed to reach her eyes. "That's fine, dear, but what about Amber?"

"Amber. What about her?" Nate asked. "I suppose she'll be fine. I mean, we'll always be friends and all." Nate scooted his chair forward and stirred his coffee.

The door leading from the garage opened and Reverend Richards, Nate's father, and a teenaged girl came into the kitchen, laughing.

Reverend Richards smiled, his white teeth glowing in contrast to his coffee-colored skin. Like his wife, he too maintained his physical appearance and stature; his muscled body belying his sixty-one years.

"Nate," the young lady said and crossed quickly to him.

Nate stood and caught the girl in his embrace. "Gracie, how are you, kid?"

She pushed away from him and slapped his shoulder playfully. "I told you not to call me that. I'm almost eighteen, and as of today, I'm a college student, too. Who would'a thunk, huh? Me, a throw away street kid going to college."

Nate had met Gracie almost eighteen months earlier during an investigation where she had helped Amber escape from a violent street gang known as Abyss. At sixteen years old she had been an orphan, so Nate's parents had taken her in as a foster child.

"I see your grammar hasn't improved." Nate smiled and flicked her raven braid. "And we all 'thunk it'. I knew you could do it." He pulled her to him and kissed her cheek.

Reverend Richards smiled at his son and foster daughter, then crossed the kitchen and kissed his wife who had risen to meet him. "Everything go all right at the orientation?" she asked, her lips brushing his ear.

"Yeah," he said, looking back toward Gracie and Nate across the room. "Our girl's going to do okay. We stopped by financial aid and between grants and scholarships she's looking at a full ride."

"Including room and board!" Gracie called out from the kitchen table where she and Nate had settled.

Nate stared at her, a questioning look on his face.

"What?" Gracie asked. "You think I'm going back to hooking if I have a bad day or something?"

Reverend Richards smiled, but the light in his eye faded as he turned back to face his wife. "Have you told him about her yet?" She caught his eye but didn't respond.

Nate smiled and looked up at his parents who were in quiet conversation and then back at Gracie. "You know what it would do to them if you did."

"Don't worry; I'm not *that* girl anymore. I may not be a Christian yet, but I can still see that the way I was living was nowhere going nowhere fast."

Nate reached across the counter top and squeezed her hand. "I know kid—I mean young lady."

"Besides," she said, getting up from the table, "your girlfriend would have my hide when she gets back here and finds out I had turned stupid." She went to the refrigerator, grabbed a can of soda, and headed up the stairs. "Gotta go study. See ya." She kissed his cheek as she passed him, heading for the stairs.

Nate watched her disappear up the stairs, and then wondered at her words, *"your girlfriend."* Apparently, Gracie still saw him and Amber as a couple. He looked at his mother, who'd been watching the exchange and shook his head.

Nate turned to face his father, who seemingly had been talking and not paying attention to his and Gracie's verbal intercourse.

"...assigned to this one too?" The older Richards had just finished.

"What? Oh yeah," Nate said, trying to track the conversation back in his mind. "Yeah, Mac and I. I guess our success with the Abyss case gave us dibs for the next big one that came up."

Reverend Richards leaned back in his chair and sighed heavily. "Son, you need to get your mind around this whole Amber thing. You're too distracted."

"No, Dad, I'm not. I was just telling Mom that I was going to ask Jackie out." Nate smiled reassuringly at his father.

"Jackie?" he asked, letting the name hang between them.

"What's wrong with Jackie? She's a believer and-"

"Nothing's wrong with Jackie, Son, I just don't think she deserves to be anybody's backup plan."

"I got to go," Nate said and stood abruptly. "I'm not using Jackie. I'm just tired…. No, I'm through waiting on someone who's not here and can't seem to make up her mind. Okay? I need to go." Nate turned and stalked toward the front door, then stopped. Exhaling deeply, he rubbed his face roughly and then wrapped his scarf around his neck with a harrumph. Without turning, he spoke over his shoulder. "Sorry, Dad, I—"

"She's coming home, Son," his mother said, coming over to stand beside her husband. "Amber's coming home."

CHAPTER SIX

THE NEXT MORNING Nate drifted into his cubicle fifteen minutes late for a.m. briefing. He sat forward in his seat and propped his face in his hands.

"Long night?" Mac asked, poking his head around the wall of the cubicle. "I would ask if you enjoyed the date, but I know better."

Nate lifted his eyes and met his partner's gaze. "Don't ask." Nate's mind drifted back to the sleepless night, and the pseudo argument he'd had with his parents about Amber's return.

"Oh, it's not me you need to be concerned about," Mac said. "I think Brown must have had a bad night because he's—well, he's being Brown."

"That's the last thing I need right now."

"Richards!" Brown's voice crashed over the top of the cubicles. "Richards, get in my office!"

Nate rolled his eyes at Mac and hefted himself from the seat. "Coffee?"

Mac smiled. "Here, take mine, I just poured it. Want me to come with?"

Nate shook his head and accepted the mug of coffee. Taking a long drink and frowning against the bitter heat, he headed toward the lieutenant's office at the far end of the workspace. "Sir?" he said, leaning in through the open doorway.

Brown dropped a stack of newspapers on his desk. "Have you read any of these?" he asked. "The Statesman's calling this freak the 'Angel of Death'," he said, pointing to the morning headlines. "The Tribune called it 'Blind Justice'. The Chief is gonna want to know what we're doing about this and be able to make some kind of statement about our being on top of this mess."

Nate picked up the papers and skimmed the story, checking for any quotes attributed to him. He smiled when he found none. "You know the press, sir. If they can't find the story, they simply make one up."

"Well, be that as it may, I don't want to be the one that comes out of this mess smelling like poop. If it comes down on me—"

"I know, sir," Nate interrupting him, "it'll roll down on my head next."

Brown looked up at Nate with cold intensity. "You watch yourself."

Nate nodded, resisting the urge to issue a comeback.

After a moment of tense silence, Brown stood, turning his back on Nate, and walked over to the window overlooking the rear parking lot. Then seemingly to change gears, he turned back and faced Nate. "Where have you been anyway? The lab's been calling here since last shift looking for you—twice already this morning?"

He faced Nate with what Nate had come to regard as a permanent scowl. Brown wore a rather plain looking navy-blue, two-piece suit, white shirt, and the obligatory yellow and blue paisley necktie. Nate figured the man thought it was still the 1980s. He smiled.

"You see something funny, mister?" Brown said.

The new frown that replaced the old scowl was definitely not funny. "Ah, no sir," Nate said, straightening.

"The ballistics report is back on the three rounds. As best they can figure, the rounds were fired from the same weapon."

"Best they can figure?" He asked confused.

Brown sat behind his desk, but didn't invite Nate to sit. "If you'd been in place, you'd already have this information." Brown spoke with the patient condescension that was his trademark. "They think it may be a pneumatic rifle, one of those PVC constructions."

Nate sank into the empty chair ignoring Brown's silent protest. Leaning his elbow on the desk, he reached for the file that lay open in front of Brown. "How do you trace a bullet that came from a homemade gun? That would definitely account for the jagged wound profile."

Brown looked at Nate askance.

Nate rotated his index fingers around each other. "The rounds would have tumbled, tearing its way in instead of spiraling like a modern bullet," Nate said absently.

Brown pulled the file back from Nate. "But wasn't that Johansson lady shot at with a twenty-two?"

Nate scowled. "That's the question. Why did the perp change his M.O.?" He reached for the file again.

"This is my copy. Yours should be on your desk." Brown closed the file and stared at Nate. "There's the other issue of your being late this morning."

Nate didn't bother responding; he knew it wouldn't matter. He simply waited for the verdict.

Brown inhaled and opened his mouth preparing to speak.

"Nate, we've got to roll. CPS just called, they've got a priority three at the elementary school," Mac said, rushing through the open door and tapping Nate on the shoulder.

Brown looked up at the intrusion as Nate stood and hurried out the door. "I'll get back with you as soon as I finish this call, sir," Nate said, as he exited the office.

The two men headed toward the elevator and exchanged smiles as the doors slid apart. "Thanks," Nate said, grabbing a sheaf of papers from Mac.

Mac nodded and pointed at the papers as they walked into the elevator and turned to see Brown watching them from his office door. "No problem," he said, pointing to a random paragraph on the papers. "But seriously, that pneumatic rifle's got me scared."

The elevator doors slid closed between them and the world of CID, shielding them from the watchful eyes of Lieutenant Brown.

"Let's get out of here," Nate said. "I need a cup of real coffee. Priority three? That's non-emergency. You could have at least said priority one and make it seem important."

"Yeah! But I figured Brown wouldn't know the difference, and priority three sounds more important. Besides, Jackie's on shift at the Library and I was in the mood for a good cup of coffee."

"Yeah, Jackie," Nate muttered.

CHAPTER SEVEN

"EXCUSE ME, MR. SANSOME, but are you saying that the Metro City Police Department is somehow complicit in the attacks that have taken place?" the blond-haired news reporter asked.

"Look, ma'am," Thomas Sansome began, "I'm not saying the police ain't doing their job, but everybody knows how you folks feel about people like me. There's not a one of you that feels bad if one of us registered sex offenders gets whacked."

Another reporter, a man this time, called out his question from the rear of the small crowd. "What makes you think that there's any kind of list or that you would even be on it if there was one? Have you been contacted by the police, and if so, what instructions have they given you?"

Clearly afraid and clearly enjoying his fifteen minutes of fame, Thomas Sansome brushed his thinning hair back from his face and smiled at the camera. His gapped-toothed grin filled the screen just as Jackie turned off the power to the TV.

"Thanks," Nate said, receiving two cups of coffee from the clerk behind the counter.

She turned and smiled at him. Her perfect teeth flashed brilliant white in contrast to the tan hue of her skin and lively auburn highlights in her chestnut brown hair. "No problem, Nate," she said and smiled again. She looked back toward the office near the rear of the coffee shop. "Lance thought it would be a good idea to have a TV up here so customers could watch it as they waited for their coffee."

"Well, tell him I said it was a bad idea. We come in here to get away from that *stuff* for a moment." They smiled at each other and, their gazes held for just a moment longer than usual. She looked away.

"Ahem," Mac said, reaching for the coffee Nate still held in his hand. "Think maybe I can get that?"

Startled, Nate turned to face his partner. "Sure, here," he said, handing the cup to Mac.

"Unh-unh, mine's the hazelnut chocolate, this one's yours." He dropped his chin and shook his head from side to side. "Why don't you just ask her out and get it over with?"

Jackie blushed and pretending not to hear, walked away to help another customer calling for her attention.

"What...nahh, I'm not ready for that yet," Nate said, watching her walk away. "It's still too soon."

"Bahhh, you're just scared. Look, man, Amber left you. You didn't leave her. You ask me, it's time to move on."

"Well, I didn't ask you. Can we just look at those files on that pneumatic rifle?"

Laughing to himself, Mac slapped the file on the small round table top, covering the inlaid chessboard as he did. "I've got a short DVD clip of this back at the office, but being that Brown was about to jump your stuff, I figured the stills will have to do for now." He smiled again and began passing 8-by-10-inch digital photos across the table to Nate.

"Wow," Nate whistled through pursed lips. The first photo depicted a twenty-something man holding a white PVC construction to his shoulder in a typical sniper position. The next image showed an air-hose connecting near the rear of the strange looking rifle and the bolt action being held open by the shooter's hand. The third photo showed the bolt being slammed forward and the target, a huge box with the silhouette of a man painted on it, about seventy yards down range.

Nate flipped to the next picture, which showed the rifle being fired. With what looked like little or no kickback, a small cloud of gas expelled from the end of the barrel. The final image was of the rear of the target, where a plastic gallon-sized container of milk hung above the target's chest, exploded as the projectile tore through the jug and ripped out the back of the cardboard.

Small print at the bottom of the photos read: "No kick and relatively no sound make this rifle the perfect choice for the urban assassin."

Nate looked up at Mac, whose sour expression matched his own. "And you can buy these things online?"

"You don't need to." Mac reached over and pulled another set of papers from the file. Trying to read upside down, he finally pointed to an illustrated page and pushed it toward Nate. "You just download the instructions, and after a twenty minute shopping trip to Home Depot or Lowe's, you've got yourself an untraceable sniper rifle." Mac leaned back in his seat and took a long slow drink of his coffee.

Nate leaned forward, resting both his elbows on the file in front of him. He rubbed his temples with the pads of his fingertips and sighed. *Oh, God, how can we catch a sniper that doesn't even use conventional weapons?* He turned his face toward Mac but found his eyes closed.

"Okay," Nate said wearily, "let's do a trace on all the plumbing and hardware stores and see who bought any of these items in the last two—no make that three months."

"Why three months?" Mac said, opening his eyes but remaining reclined.

"I'm figuring whoever did the shooting must have had to build the thing, and then do a whole lot of practicing to shoot a non-rifled round with any degree of accuracy."

"Well, there's something else."

"What?"

Mac leaned forward again and pulled another sheet of paper from the file. "You wouldn't need the air tank if the shooter attached one of these," he said, pointing to a portable air cylinder. "He could make the rifle completely portable. The whole thing would weigh less than…maybe four pounds."

At that moment, Jackie appeared over Nate's shoulder with two new mugs of coffee. "Here you go guys."

Both men sat up, accepting the proffered cups. Nate looked past her and back into the main room of the coffee shop. "What, our teacher friend back again?"

"No," she said and swatted him with a hand towel that had been draped over her shoulder. "This one's my treat, just to say thank you."

Mac kicked Nate beneath the table.

Nate cut his eyes to Mac while trying to act natural.

Jackie looked down at the open file. "This got to do with the killings?"

Nate looked up and into her eyes. "Ahh, yeah, just a new theory we're working on. It's nothing yet."

She stepped closer and the light scent of flowers mixed with fresh roasted coffee beans wafted past Nate's face. He inhaled.

"Can this thing really work?" Jackie asked, while pointing to the picture.

"Oh yeah," Mac said with enthusiasm. "I've heard they're pretty accurate from over fifty yards. It'n that right, Nate?"

"Want to go to a movie Friday?" Nate blurted.

Jackie blushed and smiled. Straightening, she brushed curly bangs back from her face.

"Well, I'd have to check with my wife first, but I think I'm clear," Mac said in a sing-song voice.

Nate kicked him, and Jackie threw the towel into his face.

"I don't get off 'til nine," she said, turning to Nate, "but that would be great. I'd love to."

"Cool, the later the better. That way if something stupid comes up, I can still make it."

"Trust me," Mac said from behind the towel, "something stupid always comes up on Friday afternoons."

Jackie smiled at Nate. "I'll be wearing basically what I have on now. That okay?"

"Long as you don't mind me wearing this," he answered.

"Okay then," she said and turned to leave.

"Jackie," came Mac's semi-muffled voice.

"Yeah?"

"You forgot something," he said, pointing to the towel still covering his face.

"Oh, I don't know," Nate said, "looks like an improvement to me."

Jackie came back and collected her towel, then turned and walked away.

"'Bout time," Mac said. "That leaves me and Sara two days to get you ready."

Nate picked up the pictures again and started going through them. "I can't believe I just did that."

"What? Jackie's a beautiful girl, and she believes like you. So what's your hang up?"

Nate lowered the file. "I never got the chance to tell you this morning, but last night at my mom's…she told me Amber was coming back."

Mac slapped the table and let out a hoot of laughter. "You gotta be kidding me. This is sweet. I can't wait to tell Sara about this." He started laughing again.

Grabbing the file, Nate smacked his partner with it. "Come on; let's get out of here before I do something else to get myself in trouble."

CHAPTER EIGHT

T HE HANDS POURED a cup of coffee and sat back to read the morning paper. As was their custom, the hands turned on the TV and listened to the news as they skimmed over the Friday edition of the Statesman. On the screen appeared the over-styled hair of Butch Jensen, the local star power for Channel Six. "Good morning, Treasure Valley," Butch said. "We are entering into the third week of the RSO-killing spree."

The hands dropped the newspaper and looked up.

"Last night our own James Craftsen spoke with one of Treasure Valley's local registered sex offenders, Thomas Sansome."

The image changed to a recorded segment. The face of a young black man appeared on the screen. His too perfect teeth and closely cropped hair made him look more like a GQ model than the cub reporter he was.

The camera panned back to the narrow-faced Sansome standing next to the athletic-looking reporter. Craftsen turned slightly to face Sansome and leaned forward lowering the microphone toward the smaller man. "Mr. Sansome, thank you for agreeing to speak with me."

"Oh, that's okay, Jimmy," Sansome said and touched the reporter on his shoulder in a gesture of familiarity.

Craftsen looked at the dirt-encrusted fingernails of the hand on his shoulder before looking back at Sansome and taking a small step away from the man. "Well, thank you, Mr. Sansome. As a registered sex offender, can you tell our viewers what it is like to live here in the valley during this crisis?" Craftsen shifted his shoulders and turned his gaze back toward the camera.

"Well, it's terrible, I tell ya. Every day I wake up and wonder if I've already been killed. Nobody should ought to live with this kind of shadow over them. It makes a man just nervous all the time."

***

The hands trembled with rage, crushing the newspaper into a ball. Snatching open the folder on the counter, and with a finger, traced down the list until the hands found the name. Down near the bottom, the name of Thomas Sansome appeared second to last. He wasn't supposed to be next, but he had been chosen…selected to be purged. Now!

Finding the name, the hands relaxed as a wave of peace washed over them. The hands felt—knew that *God* had chosen them to be His arm of wrath against the unjust. They knew the lies that the Sansome man had told were familiar with his particular form of evil. The hands would let loose their fury quickly. Like lightning falling from the sky, the hands would strike, and Sansome would be judged.

***

Nate stopped his green Jeep Cherokee just outside the Library Coffeehouse. It was almost 8 p.m., and Jackie would be getting off soon. He checked his teeth in the rear view mirror. *Just how did you get yourself into this? Oh yeah.* "Mac."

He checked himself and agreed that he looked okay, and then hoped she would cancel. He saw the rear door of the coffee shop open and Jackie came bounding out. He had to admit, she was beautiful. He wondered how he hadn't seen it before.

Nate got out and stood near the passenger side door. Jackie approached him shyly at first, but then seemed to relax as she came to stand near him. "Shall we?" Nate asked and opened her door.

After dinner, Nate and Jackie sat in the relative quiet at the Olive Garden restaurant, talking softly over partially eaten dessert and sipping coffee. "I'm glad we did this," Nate said.

Jackie looked up from beneath long eyelashes and smiled. "Yeah, me too. It was fun."

"Can we do it again sometime?"

"What, you trying to get rid of me already?" she asked.

"No. No, I didn't mean it like that, I was—"

"Relax. I'm teasing and yes, I'd love to go out with you again."

Nate pointed his index finger at her accusingly and smiled broadly. "You...I never knew you were such a kidder."

She sat forward and rested her chin on the backs of her knuckles. Their eyes met and neither spoke for some time. Finally, Jackie laughed softly and looked away.

"You know," Nate began, "you have really beautiful eyes."

She looked up at him all at once growing serious. "Nate," she said softly.

Nate leaned across the small table and touched his lips to the corner of her mouth. "Ahh...sorry," he began.

She turned to face him and returned his kiss, sealing his lips with hers. She rested her fingertips along the curve of his jaw, and then brushed his ear with her knuckle.

Nate sat back heavily into the chair rocking it backwards as he did. "Wow," he whispered.

"Let's get out of here. Let's just walk," Jackie said, standing.

Nate stood to join her and after leaving payment for the dinner and a sizable tip, he helped her put on her coat. Bundled against the cold, they grasped hands and walked out into the brisk night air and under the radiant glow of moonlight, crunched through the partially melted snow.

For some time they walked in silence, just enjoying being together. Then Nate turned to look at her, waiting for her to acknowledge him. "It's been a while since I've been out with anyone. I wasn't sure what to expect."

"And?" She smiled and her face seemed to glow with reflected moonlight.

"Well," Nate said nervously, "I've really enjoyed myself. You—well, you're easy to talk to."

"I hope that's a good thing," she said and squeezed his gloved hand.

"I'm not doing a very good job of this, am I?" Nate asked. They stopped beneath an oak tree, its leaves long gone, its bark white in the moonlight. Nate leaned against the tree and grabbed both her hands, pulling her toward him. "I feel I need to be honest with you."

"Look, Nate," Jackie said, her voice soft and warm, "I know how things ended with you and Amber, and I won't lie to you, I was hoping you'd ask me out. So, what do you say we just give us a chance and just see where this goes? We don't have to plan for forever." She smiled at him, and her eyes seemed to glow from beneath the cream-colored knit cap. She closed the distance between them and rested her head against his chest.

The silence enveloped them. From a short distance away, playing on the restaurant's outside speakers, soft strains of Dean Martin's "That's Amore" floated on the crisp cold air. Ignoring the chill, Nate lifted her chin and looked down into her face. This time when he pulled her to him, they kissed each other with no hesitation, long and deep.

Grasping hands again, they headed back toward Nate's Jeep. As he reached for the door handle, his cell phone rang in his pocket. Seating her first, Nate flipped open his phone. "Richards," he answered.

Closing the door, he raced around the Jeep, suddenly intensely aware of the frigid temperature, and leaped in behind the steering wheel. "What'd-ya got?" he asked, starting the engine. The bun-warmers heated up first warming their seats and taking the edge off the chill in the car. Nate turned up the heater as he looked apologetically at Jackie. He mouthed sorry and then spoke back into the phone, "In about forty minutes, but I can hurry if I need to."

Jackie turned to face him and leaned the side of her face against the headrest. Her eyes beamed with affection, and a smile crawled across her face. She touched his cheek playfully. When he looked up at her, she said, "It goes with the job."

Nate snapped the cell phone shut, then rocked his head back and closed his eyes. "And tonight was going so well," he sighed.

"Well," Jackie said, "I guess there'll just have to be a tomorrow."

Nate turned to look at her without lifting his head from the headrest. A sense of wonder washed over him as he quickly compared her reaction to what he remembered of Amber's and, just as quickly, rebuked himself for doing it. He smiled and reached out and touched her face. "Then...I will look forward to tomorrow." He dropped the shifter into gear.

CHAPTER NINE

JUST BEFORE 6 A.M., Thomas Sansome rubbed his face and strained to see into the early morning darkness. The pre-dawn cold made his warm bed all the more inviting and added just one more argument against starting the day. But today he had a meeting that if it worked out as he planned, would change his life forever. Lighting his first cigarette before getting out of bed, Thomas inhaled deeply, both savoring and hating the nicotine at the same time.

Finishing the cigarette, he threw back his covers with a huff and an involuntary shiver, then hefted himself from the low bed. Scratching himself absentmindedly, Thomas rubbed his arms trying to warm them and shuffled slowly the few feet to the kitchen. Turning on the burners on the stovetop to warm the small room, he held his hands toward the blue and yellow flames and spat in the small sink, still crowded with dirty dishes. Taking a cup out of the pile, he filled it with water, and put it in the microwave to make a cup of instant coffee.

Thomas' graying hair stuck out from his head like grass caught in a wind through a field. His stained tank top tee shirt had long since ceased being white. He scratched a four-day growth of beard and took another long drag on the recovered cigarette, which he had saved from the night before.

"Let me see what the papers got to say about you today, old boy," he said to himself. Opening his front door, he shivered and grabbed the daily paper off the front stoop. "What? Nothing on the front page?" He threw the paper on the table and retrieved his water, now ready for coffee. "Well, Tom my boy, I think it's time we called that fancy reporter back up and get us another fifteen minutes of fame." He laughed at his joke.

The telephone rang. Thomas leaned back from the table and grabbed the receiver from the wall-mounted phone. "Yeah," he answered.

The phone line went dead. "Well of all the stupid…" Thomas didn't finish the sentence. Instead, he picked up the newspaper again and flipped it open to the community section. First grabbing a pair of scissors and a brand new photo album from the cluttered kitchen table, he began flipping through the newspaper searching for articles and images of himself. As he settled into the chair, a knock sounded at his door.

"What's a man gotta do to get some peace and quiet around here?" Thomas said, crinkling the paper and slamming it onto the table. "One minute," he called out and hefted himself from the chair.

Not expecting any guests, and not caring if any dropped by, Thomas didn't bother making an attempt at straightening up the small bachelor apartment. He opened the door.

"Oh, it's you. Come on in," Thomas said. He turned and walked back to the small table.

The visitor stepped into the apartment, and flexed gloved hands, before quietly closing the door against the chill. Looking around the apartment, he noticed that clutter and filth seemed to be the main theme in its décor.

"I was thinking maybe you'd be dropping by here sooner or later, wanting to hear the details, I 'magine." Thomas chuckled. "When you didn't come by yesterday, I began to think you'd forgotten all about it, but I didn't 'spect you so early this morn'n." Thomas reached into the shallow sink and recovered a mug. Dumping the remains of what had been left in it. He rinsed it before making a second cup of coffee for his guest. Starting the faucet, he called over his shoulder. "Take off your coat and stay awhile. This interview gonna take some time. Mine's is one heck of a story. You wanna know about the first kid or all of them?"

The visitor reached inside the full-length coat, and with a steady gloved hand, retrieved a nine inch serrated knife. Taking the two steps that separated them, the visitor grabbed Thomas by his chin jerking his face around, and snatched him backwards. The hands dragged the knife across Thomas' throat, burying the blade deep into the sagging flesh of the man's neck.

Thomas gurgled as if he were gargling with mouthwash, and then collapsed forward into the sink. The gloved hand reached forward, turned off the water, and then cleaned the blade of the knife across the back of the dead man's shirt. The job completed. Judgment passed. The gloved visitor reached with a trembling hand to first turn the thermostat down, and then carefully checked for any sign of having been in the room. Once assured, the visitor turned off the lights, shut the door and locked the apartment.

The visitor walked slowly away. The relief of having been obedient was almost overwhelming. The sense of righteousness having been established, bringing his world nearer to being balanced in the valley. The job was not complete, of course, but it was getting closer.

As the hands settled behind the wheel of the small truck that had been parked a few blocks from the apartment, the sense of heaviness returned. That woman was still alive. She had somehow avoided judgment the first time, but she would not escape the verdict decreed upon her.

A violent shaking overcame the visitor as the burden of failure came rushing in again. Despite the cold, sweat burned the visitor's eyes as stressed muscles ached with the clenching and unclenching of gloved hands on the steering wheel. A tap on the frosted window drew the visitor's attention to the shadowy figure outside the iced-over glass.

"You all right in there?" a uniformed police officer asked.

Rolling the window down just a tad, the visitor managed in a strained but controlled voice, "Yes...yes officer, just thinking about getting my day started. I had a rough night last night." The smile was forced.

"If you're sure you're all right," the officer said sounding cautious.

The visitor started the vehicle's engine and waved off any further concern. As the officer stepped back, the visitor glanced at the dashboard clock and smiled. There was still time to make the call and get to work on time. No questions asked.

***

Nate sat behind his desk staring at his computer monitor and smiling absentmindedly. He didn't hear Mac enter the pod.

"Hey, hey, mister lucky," Mac said with a lilt in his voice, slapping his palms down on the desktop. "Tell me all about it. How was it? Did you kiss her?"

Nate jumped. "What?" He looked up into Mac's knowing smile.

"Come on. Don't 'what' me; you know darn well what I'm talking about. How was the date?" He pulled his chair around the corner of Nate's desk and sat down. Kicking his feet up on the desk, he grabbed his cup of coffee, leaned back, and fluttered his hand toward Nate like an absentminded conductor. "Okay, now, go ahead."

Nate turned to face his partner, his own smile growing. "Well to begin…it's none of your business. I don't ask you how your dates with Sara go, do I?"

"Nahh, but we're married. There's nothing to tell. Come on."

Nate shook his head and swung his chair back around to face his computer. "Actually I got called in—"

"What? No way!"

"Turned out to be much-ado about nothing, but it was probably good I got called."

"What do you mean? How could getting called in be good?"

Nate smiled. "I think I was starting to enjoy our date *too* much. If you know what I mean?"

"No, I don't. But that's besides—"

The desk phone rang and Nate raised his index finger silencing Mac mid-statement. "Richards," he said into the receiver.

Mac frowned.

Nate nodded as if agreeing with something. Then pulled a pen from his shirt pocket and began scribbling notes.

Mac dropped his feet to the floor and looked over Nate's shoulder. "You need to learn how to spell."

Nate waved him off like a troublesome gnat and leaned forward cradling the phone between his neck and shoulder. Securing the notepad with his left hand, he wrote more clearly, and then pushed the paper toward Mac so he could read it.

"Oh," Mac mouthed, but then shook his head from side to side dismissively. "Man, you really need to work on your penmanship."

Nate sighed and raised his eyebrows in exasperation. Mac leaned back as if unconcerned. "Don't shoot the messenger."

Nate finally put the phone back into its cradle. Standing, he grabbed his coat. "Ready?"

"No," Mac said and stood, "but when has that ever made a difference?"

***

It was about nine-thirty by the time Nate and Mac arrived at the shabby apartment on East Third. The light snow had added to the already icy roads bringing traffic to just more than a crawl through the downtown corridor. The windshield wipers on the Jeep thumped back and forth, a slushy serenade, brushing away the wet snow coating the curved glass. "I really hate winter," Nate said, as he turned the vehicle's engine off. He opened the door and thinking better of it, turned the engine back on.

The men got out of the car and waved to the patrol officers who had already roped off the area around a small apartment with yellow barrier tape and were holding the scene waiting for detectives. Nate wrapped his scarf around his neck and tucked his chin deeper into the collar of his coat.

One of the uniformed officers broke away from the group and made his way over to where Nate and Mac approached. "Hey, Richards. Mac." He tilted his chin upward in a quick jerk of his head in greeting to the plain-clothes officers.

"How's it going, Shef?" Nate asked and extended his hand. Shef, short for Ryan Sheffisky, was the scene officer and had taken the dispatch call as an "unknown problem" when he discovered Thomas still draped over the kitchen sink.

"It's messy in there," he said, tilting his head back toward the direction he'd come from. "The body was discovered when one of his buddies came by looking for him when he didn't show up at work this morning. Looks like one smooth pull of a blade across the throat. No sign of a fight and nothing seems to be stolen…. Not that there's anything in there worth stealing."

Nate looked around the small apartment complex, noticing the cracked and broken walkway leading to the small doorway that sat three steps below the street's surface. The roads were narrow on this side of town and the walls of the buildings thin. The structures were set rather far apart, but still near enough that someone could have seen or heard something. "Who did the canvas?" Nate asked.

Shef blew into his hands and pulled his collar up a bit. "Smith and Callins started about twenty minutes ago. Should be back soon. Ready to see the scene?"

Nate exchanged looks with Mac. "Naa, not yet. Not inside anyway."

Mac turned to Shef. "What was the dispatch info?"

Shef pulled out his notepad and reviewed the information with Mac. Nate walked away studying the paths to and from the apartment. As he turned, he overheard Shef tell Mac that co-workers had called when Thomas failed to show up for his shift at the downtown mission, and a buddy had come by. The voices faded.

Closing his eyes against the brightness of the snow, Nate listened, hearing the sounds of the neighborhood. From all around, the faint noises of television shows could be heard along with a mix of radio talk shows and music in the background. Nate reasoned that if he could hear the sounds of life from nearby apartments, then perhaps the neighbors had heard the killer that morning. He exhaled, creating a small cloud of steam that surrounded his face before drifting away.

Nate walked toward the front door, careful to stay off the walk, checking for evidence as he made his approach. "What was it you always said, Sabrina?" he said out loud, thinking of his old partner. *More evidence is missed by cops, buried beneath their feet walking into a scene, than is destroyed by most perps.* He smiled at the memory. Then he stooped and collected what looked like a strand of white hair stuck in a droplet of blood on the wall of the second step. Waving Mac over, he tucked the folded piece of notepaper with the enclosed sample into an evidence bag.

"What ya got?" Mac asked.

Nate looked thoughtful. "Don't know yet, but looks like a hair and blood droplet. Maybe it'll match our killer." He turned, bent over from the waist, and looked in through the open doorway.

"Ready?"

Mac smiled and cupped him on the shoulder. "Naaaa, not really, but when has that ever made a difference?"

Nate smiled at his partner. The small apartment was cold. The body of Thomas Sansome slouched in a semi-standing position over the sink; his hand still holding a coffee mug partially filled with lukewarm water. Bright crimson streaks painted his neck and chest plastering his tank top against his small, but protruding belly. Very little blood had made it all the way to the floor. It pooled between the body and the sink and ran over the sides covering the already soiled dishes.

Nate looked around. The bed lay unmade. Breakfast sat uneaten on the table, and the smell of stale cigarette smoke hung heavy in the air. Two cigarette butts were smashed into the ashtray; a third apparently left to burn itself out. "No fight. No struggle. No theft. No surprise."

"Think it's our same guy?" Mac asked from near the small stove. Using a pen, he pushed a small saucepan to the side, revealing the thick layer of grease and grimy buildup.

"Think so...looks that way," Nate answered somewhat distracted. He rested the back of his hand against the upper portion of the gas range. "The stove is still slightly warm to the touch, must have been on earlier."

"Think our perp turned it off before leaving? That was mighty nice of 'em," Mac said, shaking his head.

They both laughed. "Maybe our killer likes to conserve; maybe he was feeling green," Nate said and turned as a shadow blocked the gray light from the doorway.

Shef stuck his head through the open doorway. "Coroner's here. Want me to have him wait outside?"

Mac looked at Nate and then back to Shef. "Go ahead, send 'em in."

Both Nate and Mac left the apartment just as the deputy coroner was making his way in. It was starting to snow again. Still pensive, Nate tapped Mac on the shoulder to get his attention, "Let's go somewhere we can talk."

As the small apartment emptied, Nate confirmed that the crime scene team was en route before joining Mac at the curb. Nate called Shef off to one side; he cautioned the scene officer to stall the coroner in collecting the body until the crime-scene-tecs released the apartment. Shef nodded his agreement.

Walking away, Nate turned back to the uniformed officer. "By the way, after the coroner has bagged the body, he'll need some assistance loading it in the van." He smiled.

"Library?" Mac asked.

"Not good. You forget last night already? Let's head back to the station. I need a whiteboard anyway. We'll drink the coffee at the station."

Opening the door to the Jeep, Nate found that the CD he'd left playing had been ejected and was now laying face up on the floorboard.

"You didn't get the CD player fixed? You get the whole front end repaired and don't get the CD fixed. Why?" Mac asked, shaking his head as he climbed into the passenger side seat.

***

Twenty minutes later, Nate poured himself and Mac a cup of coffee from the pot in the upstairs meeting room. The snowcapped crown of the Boise Foothills on the eastern horizon glowed white in the early morning sunshine as fresh snow continued to fall. Looking out the window, Nate shook his head, frustration growing.

Upon entering the briefing room, Mac overlaid a rough grid drawing on the enlarged city map showing the locations by reporting districts (RD's) and addresses, where the three murders had occurred. Using a different colored dry erase marker, he drew in the locations where the remaining twelve RSO's on the list lived. He made a special notation indicating where Crystal Johansson lived and beside it wrote, "St. Luke's."

In a third color, he marked their known places of employment, and finally, numbered the names according to their appearance on the list.

Nate set the Styrofoam cup on the table in front of Mac and dropped a couple packets of Splenda into his own cup. Pinching the empty packets between his index and thumb, Nate held them suspended over the trash bin, his mind miles away. For a moment, he saw himself with Amber and her customary stack of empty Splenda packets as she absentmindedly stirred sweetener into her coffee.

Mac was talking. Nate snapped his attention back, and tried to recover what Mac had been saying. "…it just doesn't add up," he was finishing now and looking to Nate expectantly.

The numbers. "You're right. Thomas was number fifteen out of fifteen. Why him? Why now?"

"And why so personal. A knife instead of a gun?"

Nate looked at Mac and then at the board. "I think the miss on Johansson stirred something loose in our killer. Like it messed up his rhythm…his order or something."

"We have to figure it out." Mac said, picking up his cup. "Whoever this guy is, he has a reason for doing what he's doing. And whatever it is, it makes sense to him. Heck, we're not even sure if it is *a him.*"

Nate chuckled. "Now, all we've got to do is figure out what that reason is," he said and took a swallow of coffee.

"Oh joy! We'll be done by dinner if that's all we got to do."

The men laughed, relieving some of the tension.

Just then, the door opened. "You boys got nothing else to do besides sit in here drinking taxpayer's coffee and laugh the day away?" It was Lieutenant Brown. He appeared to be in an uncharacteristically good mood. At least he wasn't screaming at the moment.

"Just trying to make the idiotic make sense, sir," Nate said.

Mac stood. "Cup of coffee?"

Brown came in and let the door swing shut behind him. "Don't mind if I do." He accepted the proffered cup, refused the two packs of creamer, and tasted it before adding a pinch of salt. He studied the board. "What made Sansome so worth killing?"

Nate and Mac looked at each other puzzled, both by the question and the fact that Brown was being civil. "That's just it—" Nate began.

"He was the smallest fish in that particular pond," Mac cut in. "Don't make sense that the killer would go after him next. He's violated his own rule. It doesn't make sense."

Lieutenant Brown stood and walked toward the whiteboard. "That is unless he said something in his news interview that made him a more urgent target. The key is to try and see it from the killer's point of view. What's important and what's not." With that, Brown stopped, drained his cup, and headed for the door. He looked at his watch before dropping the empty cup into the trash. "Thanks for the coffee. Gentlemen, try and see this from our killer's perspective." Then without looking back, he left the room.

Nate and Mac looked at each other and both took a long swallow of coffee. "You know what?" Nate asked.

"Yeah, we need to get that news video," Mac answered.

CHAPTER TEN

THE FIRST BELL RANG starting another day of school. The mixed group of eleventh and twelfth graders filed into their first period class, caught up in various levels of conversation. Soon they sat in stunned silence, not used to having their teacher late for class. This was a new experience for them.

The second bell rang.

The door opened and Mary Higgins walked into the classroom, a little harried and looking a bit out of sorts. She stopped and leaned back against the inside of the doorjamb, exhaling a deep sigh. She turned to face her class. "Good morning, students," she said, pushing her glasses back up the bridge of her nose, her voice sounding crisp but thin.

While she made her way to her seat, muffled whispers floated around the room as students vocalized their guesses as to why Miss Higgins had been late. She sat behind her desk, composed now, and looked around the room again. The whispering stopped.

"I ask you to forgive my tardiness this morning. I had a personal situation that came up at the last moment that demanded my attention. But I assure you it will not deter me from the performance of my duties to you this morning." This time her voice had its usual timbre and her green eyes held a playful sparkle.

Soft chuckles floated forward.

"Please open your textbooks to page 179. We will begin by reading the first four stanzas of Milton's, *Paradise Lost.*" The whir of pages being flipped and the shuffling of students adjusting their bodies into more comfortable positions for reading, broke the shallow silence that attempted to rush in behind Mary's instructions. She sighed ever so softly.

Opening her desk drawer, she pulled out a one and a quarter inch diameter plastic cap and played with it absently before setting it on the corner of her desk. The yellowing PVC cap rested dully against the stark white papers stacked neatly beside her container of pens and paperclips. In contrast to her jumbled emotions, the orderly desk spoke of a mind that fought to keep everything in its proper place and everybody at a safe distance.

Mary looked up as one of the students laughed and blurted, "I'd rather be a 'door keeper in Hell…'." She'd missed the rest of the statement as the resulting laughter rose, again, lost in her private version of Hell.

As the students read the singsong phrases, rising from her desk, Mary Higgins hugged her arms, rubbing her biceps as if chilled and looked out at the freshly falling snow. The gray skies seemed to fold in on themselves, and the barren trees looked forlorn and sad. She leaned her hip against the windowsill and could feel the chill from the stone seep into her body. She looked down at her hands; they trembled slightly. Shifting, she rested her fingertips on the glass and saw her reflection staring back at her.

Cloudy green eyes gazed back through small wire framed glasses. She saw a face she thought could be pretty if not for the faint scar on her right cheek. She pulled her ash blond hair forward, trying again to cover what others barely saw. The plain glass of her lenses, not used to aid her vision, was just one more layer of the mask she hid behind.

The class, oblivious to their teacher's troubles, read on, entertaining each other with deep Shakespearean voices and drawn out proper King James English. In this way the hour passed. When the bell rang the class filed out, leaving Mary alone once again.

***

Nate parked his Jeep in the parking lot at the Channel Six News building. The sloping green metal roof caused the snow to pile up behind the giant red six, illuminating on the station's KIVI logo. Butch Jensen was standing beneath the awning, wearing a full length, double-breasted wool coat buttoned to his throat, waiting for them, waving them forward. "I hate having to ask this guy for anything," Nate said, cutting his eyes over to Mac.

"Well, I hate it more, but this is faster than having to subpoena the file." Mac harrumphed. "At least you like him. I don't even like the guy."

Nate laughed. "Come on." Locking the doors, he left the Jeep's engine running, keeping the heater on low.

Jensen extended a gloved hand first to Nate then to Mac. "Welcome, gentlemen. Come on in! Let's get out of this cold." Jensen stepped aside for the two officers and fought to hold the door open against a sudden gust of wind.

Inside the lobby Nate unwrapped his scarf and draped it across his arm. Beside him, Mac took off his outer coat and stomped snow from his shoes. Jensen was talking as he escorted the men into the back offices. "I was surprised to get the call from the girl at your office, but as always, I'm happy to help you guys out." Jensen sat behind a desk and began toying with a compact disc in his hands.

Mac looked at Nate and rolled his eyes. Nate smiled and turned back to face Jensen who had not seen Mac's antics. "Well Butch, thanks for the help on this. We think it might help us understand why Mr. Sansome was killed."

Jensen, who had been extending the disc toward Nate, folded his wrist pulling the CD back. He eyed Nate then the disc in his hand. "So you think there might be information on here that'll identify the killer?"

"Look, Jensen," Mac said, taking two determined steps toward the desk. "You don't want to be interfering with an active investigation."

Jensen sat back in his large chair behind his desk and smiled. He dropped the disc onto his lap and folded his hands across his stomach. "Look, Detective MacGilvery, I can do whatever I want with my own property. I don't remember you showing me a subpoena when you walked into *my* office."

Nate raised both hands showing his palms to Jensen. "Look, look, gentlemen, this is not a spitting contest." He sighed and looked at Mac, a cautioning glare in his eye. "Now, Butch, we're trying to stop a killer. Let's try and not lose sight of that; all right?"

***

Pulling the Jeep back onto the roadway, Nate eyed Mac. Mac raised a hand cutting off Nate's criticism. "I know, I know…but that guy really gets on my nerves. He's so smug, so blasted arrogant." Mac turned away and stared in silence as the snow covered landscape slipped by.

Nate inhaled, smiled at his younger partner, and shifted his attention back toward the road. "Look, we got the disc…that's all that really matters for now."

They rode not speaking; each man lost in his own thoughts. "Look," Nate said, checking the time on the dashboard clock, "it's getting late. I need to see somebody. Why don't I just drop you off at home, and I can pick you up later if the need arises?"

Mac remained facing the window. "Yeah, that's cool. I need to see Sara and the baby anyway. I haven't seen my baby girl in two days."

Like a heavy blanket, silence settled over them.

***

A half hour later, Nate found himself parked in front of a single level house in a middle income neighborhood. The lights were on inside the modest house. Outside the street lights were just starting to glow, fighting against the growing blue-gray of dusk. Nate switched the engine off but left the stereo playing on low. He rested his head back touching the headrest and closed his eyes against the growing darkness. The music of Andre Crouch played softly, filling the cabin of the Jeep with words of encouragement and hope. Nate relaxed at the declaration that Jesus was the needed answer for the world, and sighed. Old music, but it still filled the void.

A sudden knocking on the window startled him from his reverie. Snapping forward, Nate turned his face toward the window and found himself looking directly into the wide-eyed face of a little black girl.

The girl had her hands cupped around her face and was peering into the deepening dark inside the car. Long black braids spilled out past the white fur trim of the powder blue hood of the little girl's jacket, framing her face around a gapped-toothed smile.

Nate sat forward and lowered the window separating the two of them. He smiled.

Dropping her hands the girl said, "My grand-ma wants to know if you're coming in or if you want her to fix you a plate to take with you?"

Nate opened the Jeep's door and raised the window while sliding his legs out of the car. He smiled again, touched the little girl's cheek with a knuckle, and looked up just in time to see the corner of the curtain drop. "You tell your Grandma Sabrina, I'm coming right in." The girl spun and ran hurriedly back to the front door.

***

A few minutes later, Nate found himself sitting in a well-lit dining room around a modest table filled with foods indicative of their southern roots. Fried chicken, oven-baked macaroni and cheese, creamy potato salad along with both brown and white gravies, covered the table beside trays of cornbread and home-baked dinner rolls. The rich fragrance of the deep fried foods, mingled with the wafting of sweet potato pie, mixed with the sound of laughter, gave the gathering a true family holiday flavor.

"I hope you don't cook like this every night," Nate said, pushing his now empty plate away from him.

"Nah-nah, now, you just leave my wife alone," Karl said, patting his bulging stomach. He leaned to his side and kissed

Sabrina's upturned face. "You go head and cook for your man anytime you want, Baby."

"I ain't studd'n neither one of you. I cooked for my Baby-Girl. It's our birthday week and we're celebrating all week long. Aren't we, Sugar?" Sabrina asked smiling at her granddaughter sitting across the table still eating and smiling, knowing she was the topic of discussion.

After dinner and a few minutes of small talk, Nate got up and helped carry dishes to the kitchen. Putting a serving tray on the counter near the sink, Nate turned and leaned his back against the marble surface. "Look here," Karl said, "I know you two want to talk, so why don't Baby-Girl and I get some coffee ready, and then get started on these dishes while you guys catch up."

"I love a man who knows his way around a kitchen," Sabrina said and, after kissing her husband, headed back toward the family room.

Nate shrugged his shoulders and dropped the dishtowel he'd just picked up over the little girl's outstretched arm. Swatting her on her backside as she scampered by, Nate smiled at Karl and then followed Sabrina through the door.

"So…" Sabrina said, lowering herself into an easy chair. Nate watched her closely as she grimaced slightly, but worked hard to cover the show of weakness.

"So, how ya doing?"

She pointed to the faded scar at her temple. "This old thing?" Sabrina rubbed the pale mark just beneath her hairline where she had been shot just over two years earlier. The bullet, fired from the barrel of a rogue cop's gun, had been intended to kill her because she and Nate were getting too close to uncovering the officer's involvement in a recent cop killing. "Karl says it gives me character, but that's not why you came by here. Now talk."

A few moments of comfortable silence passed before Nate brought himself to speak. "I suppose you know about the recent killings here in the valley?"

"What killings?"

Nate looked up, locking eyes with Sabrina before realizing she was joking. "Yeah, right," he said. "Anyway, as I was saying, these new killings...I can't make heads or tails of them. We know he's killing from a list of RSO's here in the valley, but why now...all of a sudden?"

"Who says it's sudden?" The door separating the family room from the kitchen swung open, and the five-year-old backed through balancing a serving tray before her. As she turned, she took slow tentative steps until she delivered her charge to the small table situated between Nate and Sabrina.

"Look Grand-ma, I didn't even spill." The girl crowed exultantly. Her face lit up even more as Sabrina grabbed her and kissed her cheeks. "Grandpa says he'll bring in the cream and sweet'ner in a minute." The gap in her teeth gave her words an airy quality.

As if on cue, Karl walked through the door. "Somebody call my name?" He placed a smaller tray containing a spouted cup, wet with condensation, and a small glass trough stuffed with several packets of Splenda. "Looks like this ought to do it," he said as he set the thermal carafe next to assembled trays and turned to face his granddaughter. "You ready to go watch a movie, Pumpkin?"

The little girl, clapping her hands, scooted off her grandmother's lap and began to jump up and down. "Veggie Tales—Veggie Tales! Veggie Tales!" she repeated as she dragged her grandfather by the hand toward the TV at the far end of the room.

"What?" Nate asked as they returned to their conversation.

"I said, 'who said it was sudden?' Are those your words or the killer's?" Sabrina poured herself, and then Nate, a cup of coffee.

Nate accepted the proffered cup and then leaned back into the overstuffed chair, Karl's chair. "I don't follow."

"Son, didn't you learn anything working with me? What did I tell you about making assumptions?"

Nate chuckled as he watched Sabrina settle back in her own seat and take her first drink from the cup she held with both hands. For a minute, he was back at the Library Coffeehouse with Sabrina in their favorite booth, and once again, *school* was in session. She was teaching him the finer points of investigation; the kind of stuff you never get sitting in a classroom.

Focusing again on her voice, Nate came out of his daydream and said, "Assumptions make a..." he looked over at the back of the little girl's head and lowered his voice, "...makes everyone look bad."

"Close enough," Sabrina said laughing. "Now, what other assumptions have you made? Did the killer tell you he was a guy or is that more of that famous male chauvinism that says 'women can't be bad people' leaking through?"

Nate put up both hands. "Guilty."

"Sometimes, boy," Sabrina laughed and slapped Nate playfully across the knee. They both looked up when Karl and the granddaughter began laughing as Larry the Cucumber sang one of his many silly songs.

"But seriously," Sabrina continued, "you've got to get your assumptions out of the way and let the facts tell you their own story." She sipped her coffee. "Now, tell me what you do know."

CHAPTER ELEVEN

THE NEXT MORNING Nate stood in the rear of his father's church listening to the end of the sermon. The voice of the elder Richards was still as strong and urgent-sounding as it had been when Nate had listened as a child. The congregation of about two-hundred members all sat and echoed their responses in various shouts of "Amens'" and "Tell it Preacher" or "That's for sure."

As if in a scripted duet, the voice of the Reverend and the organ spoke alternately, one supporting the other.

"...Daniel knew what it was like to be stuck between a rock and a hard place," Reverend Richards proclaimed.

The organ reverberated in three sharp blasts of sound.

"...he was stuck between the King's decree that he should be killed unless he could tell old Nebuchadnezzar what he had dreamed about."

The organ played a series of notes in crescendo, building suspense.

"...But Daniel had a friend..."

Two loud blasts.

"I said Daniel had a friend."

One long.

"Do you have that friend this morning? Do you know Jesus like Daniel knew Jesus?"

The voice of the organ and the voice of the preacher now worked in unison, overlapping and rising in intensity and fervor. The voices from the congregation, not to be outdone, sang back their answers of "Yes" and "I know Him" and "Yes, sir" and "Amen!"

Nate smiled, then frowned and patted his breast pocket as his cell phone began to vibrate. For a moment, he'd forgotten he was on call this weekend. He stepped quickly and quietly out into the foyer, catching his mother's eye just as the door swung shut behind him. She was sitting near the front of the sanctuary. "Richards." Nate clipped into the receiver, regretting his sharp tone almost as soon as he'd spoken.

The voice on the other end, a male voice, sounded apologetic. Corporal Bryant cleared his throat. "Hey, Nate, I can hear you're at church, but we found a baby girl wandering around near Clarene and Linder just north of the canal."

Nate sighed, rubbed his temples as a sudden anger swelled within him. He looked outside at the gray oppressive sky. "How old? How's she dressed?"

"Says she's three. She has on boots, a wet diaper, and a sweater that looks like she's had it on for the last week. Nate, it's thirty-six degrees out here."

Nate sighed again. "Get CPS en route and I'll be there in ten…. Maybe Child Protection has history on the kid. You got uniforms knocking on doors looking for mommy and daddy?"

A quarter hour later as Nate pulled into the sub-division, a uniformed officer waved him over. "Nate, Sarge said to have you come on over. They found the house. Just continue up around the curve and take the tip-out on your left side. The house is on the top of the curve at about the one o'clock position."

Nate raised a brow at the directions.

The officer smiled a wry smile. "Just follow your nose. Trust me, you can't miss this one."

Nate looked back at the officer.

He smiled again. "Why do you think I'm standing out here in the cold?" He waved Nate through and turned his attention back to the lanes of traffic.

Nate drove slowly on the ice-covered road. He wondered again how people could allow their children to walk away unnoticed. He chided himself for his cynical attitude as he remembered how his own nephew had sneaked out through the patio door and left both his sister and her husband busy in the house. *Good people make mistakes, Nate.*

"Sometimes life happens; kids will be kids," he muttered to himself.

Spotting the patrol cars parked at odd angles in the cul-de-sac, Nate took note of the unkempt yard. Broken toys lay strewn on the partially snow covered lawn, or what would have been the lawn had there been grass. A Ford F-150 sat on four flats, a missing hood, and a cracked windshield. The fence surrounding the yard had several missing planks, and the gate hung at a forty-degree angle on its hinges. From what he could see of it, the back yard was in no better condition.

Even after the front door of the house had been left standing open, the odors of marijuana blended with human filth met Nate as he approached the doorway. As he crossed the threshold, the stench of cat urine and unwashed bodies added to the noxious potpourri, while several cats threatened to trip him as they scurried by. Off to his right was the main hallway, which led to the bedrooms. It was cluttered with soiled laundry, leaving a narrow lane clear for walking. The kitchen to his left smelled of rotting food and mold. Just beyond the kitchen, in what should have been the dining area, sat five people in a circle on the floor; a hookah pipe centered between them. The two adults, a male and a female, and three teenagers, two girls and a boy, all appeared to be high, if not completely stoned.

Nate learned that the toddler's name was Christina and that these two adults were her parents. At least this was the baby-mama and the guy was the latest "father" in a long series of fathers. Nate looked down at the couple and could see some resemblance between at least one of them in each of the three teens. He figured it to be a blended family. "Which of you is Christina's parent?" He asked despite his deductions.

"I am," the woman said, her voice slightly slurred. She sat up straighter, attempting to look dignified. She failed. "Why? Why do you want to know?"

Nate tried not to show his depth of disdain for the woman and man who had created the mess he had to wade through. "Because, ma'am, we found her wandering in traffic about four blocks from here, wearing nothing but a wet diaper and a dirty sweater."

"I told that little heifer to go to bed," the woman said in an emotionless tone. "She was supposed to be asleep."

Nate turned his attention to the man of the house. "So what's your claim to fame, sir?"

"Hey, don't hassle me, m-man, I'm just a working stiff who's taking care of his own kids and hers too." He tilted his head toward his lover. "So back off and go find a real crook to mess with." The man's hair stuck out from around his fleshy face in conflicting angles, his eyes and nose were both covered with spider veins, shaded a bruise-purple. He stank of cheap stale alcohol.

Nate turned to the uniformed officers. "You guys do FST's on everybody here?"

"Yeah, they all failed…admitted they been drinking and smoking weed since *last night.*" Then he smiled.

"What?" Nate asked feeling like he was being set up.

"Ask them what last night was," the officer said, turning his shoulder to the couple and lowering his voice so only Nate could hear.

Nate looked from the officer to the group on the floor and back to the officer. He raised a brow in question before turning back around. "So the officer here says you guys have been real honest with him, and I appreciate that. I want you guys to be honest with me for just a little while longer, okay?"

No one answered.

Taking a shallow breath, mostly through his mouth, so the odor wouldn't linger in his nostrils, Nate asked, "So you guys started smoking and drinking…when?"

"Last night," the man said.

"'round seven or seven-thirty after the game was over," the woman added.

"Uh-huh, it was after that because we had just finished watching that movie," the older teen said, pointing to the dust jacket from what looked to be a B rated sci-fi flick.

Nate turned his attention to the teenage girl, whom he judged to be around sixteen. "And you guys have been drinking and smoking since after the game on Friday and then watched the movie together?"

The girl didn't answer, but looked at her mother before dropping her gaze.

The woman spoke up, "Yes, sir, since Friday after the game. Look, I know this looks bad," she said, readjusting her small frame on the floor and pushing greasy hair back from her face, "but at least we got our kids here at home with us. We spent one night partying with our kids. What's the harm in that? At least they ain't out running the streets."

Nate looked at the woman incredulously. "It's Sunday afternoon. Get them out of here," he said to the uniformed officers. Nate turned and walked out the front door filling his lungs with fresh air. Just then, a state car pulled up, and Nate recognized one of the new hires, Casey, from Child Protection Services. He met her at the curb.

After relaying what he'd seen and heard, he released her to do her walk through of the property. Together, she and a police photographer recorded images of the residence, cataloging its appearance and marking drug paraphernalia and the related drugs to be collected by the evidence techs later.

About twenty-minutes later, the father was walked out, hands cuffed behind him and escorted to a marked patrol car. He saw Nate. "Hey, why-why you arresting me for, anyway? I ain't done nothing."

Nate watched as the man was secured in the rear seat, then walked over and leaned down to look him in the face. "Sir, you are being booked for possession of a controlled substance and injury to a child."

"Injury to a child? I ain't hurt nobody."

"Sir," Nate began. He exhaled crisply before allowing himself to finish his answer. "You can't sit around and drink and smoke dope with your teenaged children and allow a toddler to wander around in freezing conditions. It's against the law."

The man looked up, dumbstruck. "Oh."

Nate stepped back and swung the door shut. "Get him out of here."

Behind him, the CPS social worker called, "What do you want to do with the teens? I can try and place them, but to tell you the truth, it's gonna be hard with them still high…having just recently used."

Nate rubbed his face and blew into his hands to try and warm his fingers. He looked over at the toddler, now asleep in a dry diaper and blue pj's in the car seat in the social worker's car. "Place the baby. I'll book the teens in Juvi. They should hold them for the night at least."

Casey frowned. "Yeah, then they'll call me to place them anyway since mom and dad will still be in jail."

Nate shrugged.

She smiled at him. "Well, at least until eight when the court opens." They both laughed at the irony of the situation, and she headed for her car.

Nate watched her go then checked his phone, confirming the time. If he hurried, he could still make lunch at his parents. He waved the corporal over. "You got this?"

"Yeah, we got a car on the way to transport the kids. You want reports on your desk?"

"Nahh, just route them. I'll get them through channels." He checked the time again. "Call if you need me. I'm headed to my parent's for lunch and a little football."

While driving away, Nate realized he hadn't spoken with Mac since they left the TV station on Friday afternoon. *Just one more mess I have to deal with.* He wondered why it was that Mac had such a problem with Butch. Butch got on everybody's nerves—that was well known, but Mac had reacted—no, overreacted to the man. Nate knew he would have to get to the bottom of what was bugging his partner…*but not today.*

CHAPTER TWELVE

MONDAY MORNING BEGAN with a rainstorm, which meant that, although the snow was melting, the roads would be covered in thick sheets of ice. Nate yawned and stretched before getting out of bed, careful to put his feet into his slippers and not on the cold floor as he made his way to the shower. Four boiled egg whites and a cup of oatmeal later, Nate hurried out the door on his way to the station.

Despite his hatred of winter, he had to admit the winter landscape was beautiful dressed in crystal and lace. The trees were capped in glittering ice. The barren rows of a farmer's field, stretching away toward the horizon, glistened in the early morning sunlight as if the ground had been sprinkled with diamonds. But the roads hid long sheets of treacherous black ice. He estimated the number of accidents and slide-offs that would occur during the morning rush hour.

Careful to watch his speed, Nate laughed upon remembering some of his earlier exploits on winter roads in Idaho where all having four-wheel-drive meant was you could have all four tires spinning out of control instead of just two. He eased into the flow of traffic and slowly brought the Jeep up to speed, about ten miles-per-hour below the posted limit.

***

Mac was already at his desk when Nate came in. "Morning," he said from behind the pages of a case file and leaning around the corner of the computer monitor.

"Morning." Nate dropped behind his desk and booted up his PC. Bringing up his calendar, he prepared to check his outside appointments to see if any would conflict with those on his work schedule. Flipping open his notebook, he immediately recognized the flowing script of his mother's handwriting.

"Amber returns in two weeks." His mother had written. *Thanksgiving week.* The message had been circled and underlined. "Didn't want me to miss this one did you, Mom?" He asked of the air.

"What you got?" Mac asked, standing over Nate's shoulder.

Nate looked up into Mac's face. He seemed tired, no, more than tired. He appeared worn out. "You look like…. Well, you know what you look like. Everything okay?" Nate pushed back and spun around to face his partner.

"Yeah," Mac said and sat down in an extra chair near Nate's desk. "Yeah, everything's all right. It's just…my kids. Well, not my kids, but my ex. She's being my ex, if you get my meaning."

"Is that why you blew up at old Butchie-Boy last week, because of that series he's been running…what was it he called it? 'Ex's and Messes'?"

Mac gazed at him, his face suddenly blank. He sighed and stood. "Wanna cup of coffee?"

Nate studied his friend realizing that it was not coffee that he needed. "Yeah, I could use a cup." Together they walked in silence to the coffee pot. Mac stopped, turned, and faced Nate.

"It's not just that. He ran that series on police brutality, remember. I just get so tired of people blaming the police all the time. I did everything I could to save that—to fix that.... And this fool," Mac gestured with his cup, "in one report paints every cop, good and bad, in the same light. He put that woman on TV as if she.... Let's just say it makes me sick to my stomach." He took a long drink of his coffee and grimaced. He stared into the cup and winced as if trying to figure out what it was. Dropping his still full cup into the trash, he turned and rested his palms on the countertop.

A few years before, Mac had been part of a drug raid that had gone bad. Although the Intel had been good, a middle-aged woman who just happened to be in the wrong place at the wrong time had gotten hurt, bad. Both Mac and the other officers had been cleared of any wrongdoing, but they had been crucified in the press and Butch Jenson had been the lead reporter.

Lieutenant Brown looked up from his desk across the small hallway. He raised an eyebrow and shook his head disapprovingly. Walking to the door, Brown looked at the two men again and swung the door slowly closed, effectively closing them out.

"Sometimes I really hate that guy," Mac said and rested his hip against the counter.

Nate smiled. "I'm not going there. I promised Amber I'd be good." *Where'd that come from?*

Mac looked at him askance. "Just how bad *was* your date with Jackie?" Mac crossed his arms over his chest and smiled, some of the heaviness lifting.

"Brain burp, that's all," Nate hedged. He thought about his mom's note and shook his head.

"All right, be that way. Keep your secrets to yourself. Com'on, I'll buy you a cinnamon roll and a cup of decent coffee."

"Library?"

"Where else? Unless you've got a problem with going to our favorite coffeehouse," Mac said teasingly.

The men laughed easily. "Get the elevator and I'll grab my keys." Grabbing his keys off his desk, Nate saw that he'd left his cell phone as well. Picking it up, he prepared to drop it in his breast pocket when it began to ring.

Nate looked at the clock hanging on the far wall: 8:15. Mac pointed to his wristwatch and rolled his eyes as the elevator doors slid open. "You gotta be kidding me." He groaned.

"How come your phone never rings?" Nate asked.

"I don't turn it on," Mac said straight-faced.

Shaking his head in laughter, Nate flipped open his phone. "Richards." Pressing his phone between his ear and shoulder, he wrestled himself into his jacket. He mouthed to Mac, "Sarge."

Mac walked into the elevator and held the door open for Nate.

Nate nodded, "Yes sir." He headed toward the waiting car. "He's right here.... I'll bring him with me.... About twenty-minutes." He smiled. "Well, we were gonna get a cup of coffee. Mac offered to buy me a cinnamon roll.... I'll tell him, sir." Nate ended the phone call and finally dropped it in his pocket.

"Well?" Mac asked.

"Sarge said you needed to get him a cinnamon roll too and bring it with you." Nate leaned against the back wall smiling at his partner as the doors slid close.

"Where? Bring it where? What was that call all about anyway?"

"We got a baby en route to St. Luke's. CPS report says it's got bruising and bite marks. Good thing, though, the case is from out of county."

"No paperwork." They said in unison. The men slapped hands in a high-five.

"So my friend, let's grab a cup and the rolls and go sit around the E.R. until we know if we're needed," Mac said.

"I do have paper on my desk that needs doing," Nate said sounding troubled.

"Like you really want to do it. Let's go."

CHAPTER THIRTEEN

TIM JACKSON PUSHED his cleaning cart into the janitor's closet at the end of the school's longest hall. Before pulling the door closed behind him, he turned and watched Ms. Higgins sigh and sag against the wall outside her classroom. He wondered if he should feel bad about what he was doing to her but reasoned that in every war there would always be casualties. In many ways, he reasoned, she should be happy he had selected her. Now she would be a part of the plan. He shrugged, pulled the door shut, and continued into his office.

Settling himself into the cracked-leather chair behind his small desk, he sat slacked-faced staring at the cluttered surface. Fatigue, like a wet blanket clung to him, making his arms feel heavy and slow. With a sigh and great effort, Tim shoved aside boxes of tools, piles of paperwork, and towers of empty soda cans, clearing a workspace. The smell of machine-oil, dust, and wet mop hung in the stale air, and the yellowed light of a lone fluorescent tube added to the room's depressing atmosphere.

Glancing around with quick nervous jerks of his head, Tim checked to make sure he was alone. Only then did he pull out the list. Folding his hands beneath his chin, his fist trembled. He squeezed his eyes shut. His breaths came in short, rapid bursts. His chest heaved.

"Argh," an anguished cry escaped his lips; spittle flecked his cheek. "I'm sorry, God. I'm so...so sorry I-I've been a poor servant, but I'll do better. I will make them pay." He sprang from his desk, striking the chair with his legs, forcing it into the wall behind him. It landed with a crash.

He paced like a big cat trapped in a too small cage.

Rubbing his unshaven face with a trembling hand, Tim wiped sweat, mingled with tears, onto the thighs of his worn khaki pants. He looked at the creased and stained list in his hand again, his eyes landing on the name, Crystal Johansson. He knew he would have to kill her. It was what the voices demanded. Her kind had to be judged. *This pain,* he rubbed his temples, *is all her fault. The voices seemed to agree.*

"Mr. Jackson? Are you in here?" A timid voice called through the slowly opening door. "Mr. Jackson, Mrs. Carol asked me to come get—"

Tim spun and faced the small-framed girl, his face contorted in pain. He stuffed the list back into his shirt pocket. "What?"

"Mr. Jackson, are you okay? Do you need me to call a doctor?" The girl hurried to the janitor, reaching out her hand to steady him.

Tim stepped back from her touch, looking down at her hand, composing himself. "No, I'm fine...just need a minute to.... Just need a minute to get myself together." He raked his fingers through his thinning hair and stood straight. He looked around the room again before grabbing the handle of his cart. "There's a problem in the kitchen?" he asked.

"Yes, sir. Some kid threw up. Mrs. Carol wants to get it cleaned up before the next class comes in for lunch." The girl turned and walked out of the janitor's closet, chancing one quick look over her shoulder just before closing the door.

***

Crystal Johansson sat up in her hospital bed and touched the bandage covering the corner of her temple. She groaned as she swung her legs off the edge of the bed. A wave of nausea, which started in her stomach, swam through her causing the room to tilt and spin. Behind her, the various motors and gauges beeped and whirred in an unending sonnet. She sat still for a moment waiting for her stomach to catch up to her head.

Stretching her legs tentatively, the usually tight muscles had become flaccid after almost a week in bed. As the light from the open window shade fell across her skin, she noticed her toenails needed painting. *Funny thought.* Resting her head in her hands, she sighed.

After a few minutes, she tried again. She stumbled to the sink and splashed her face with cool water. Finding her robe hanging from a hook in the closet, she put it on. "Maryann," she smiled in gratitude, her voice cracking, thanking her P.O. for bringing her personal items from the house.

Still moving slowly, she finished freshening up, brushing her hair and applying just a bit of blush and foundation, adding color to her face. Again, she thanked Maryann.

She had just returned to her bed when a knock sounded and the door opened. "Crystal?" Maryann said, coming into the room. Crystal could see the uniformed pant leg of an officer sitting right outside the opening. When Maryann cleared the doorway, the officer, a twenty-something muscled type, turned and leered at her through the open doorway. A roguish smile pulled at his lips as he raked her with his eyes.

Following the line of Crystal's eyes, Maryann closed the door. "Men," she said.

"Yeah, it's always the same. Once they find out about my past, they think it's open season...that I'm easy." She turned away from the door and sat on the foot of the bed. "Have a seat," she said, indicating one of the two typical hospital room chairs.

"News flash, they'd still act like that even if they didn't know your history. Wishful thinking."

Tugging on the collar of her robe, Crystal said, "Thanks for bringing my makeup too."

"Well, a girl's gotta look her best, even in here." A silence descended between the women. After the protracted pause, Maryann spoke. "There's been another killing."

Crystal inhaled audibly, pulling her robe closed across her chest as if for protection.

Maryann was still talking. With a flick of her head, she tossed her long auburn hair out of her face, securing it behind her head with a black scrunches. "This time the killer went to the victim's house..."

Crystal jumped from the bed and walked over to the window.

"...which leads the cops to think that the killer knew the victim," she finished.

Crystal turned to look at Maryann. "Was it-"

"Yeah," she said, cutting her off, "the killer made a call to the police informing them of details of the murder. The message also stated that he would finish what was started...that it was 'God's will' for him to rid the city of the RSO's."

Crystal staggered back to the bed and sat heavily on its end. "I can't handle—I've got to get out of here."

"Whoa, slow down, lady. I feel sorrow for you, but you're still on parole, kiddo. You do anything stupid and the only place you're going to go is back into lock up. Be careful or you're gonna lose everything you've worked so hard for. Don't let this guy force you into doing something dumb." Maryann was standing now, every bit the parole officer.

Crystal looked up at Maryann and her shoulders slumped. "Okay. What now? What do you want me to do?" She laid her hands on her thighs, palms up.

A knock sounded at the door interrupting whatever it was Maryann was about to say. The door swung open. "Excuse us," Nate said, leading Mac into the room.

Crystal adjusted her robe and sat up straight on the bed. "Detectives." She lifted her chin as she spoke.

Mac closed the door behind him, again, interrupting the uniformed officer's visual inspection. "I guess you heard by now the murderer has killed again?" Mac said without preamble.

Nate cut his eyes at his partner and smiled at the blond woman. "May I?" he asked pointing at the empty seat. Crystal nodded.

"I spoke to the charge nurse. Looks like they're gonna be releasing you today." He rubbed his chin with his index finger. "Now, we can't make you do this, but we'd like you to work with us to help catch this madman."

"You want to use me as bait?" She stared at them, shaking her head. "Maryann, you knew this? You knew they were coming here to ask me this? You're going along with this…this madness?" Crystal, her heaviness forgotten, paced to the window snagging the IV stand behind her and gazed out over the parking lot with the snow covered mountains off in the distance.

"It's not like you've got much of a choice, lady," Mac said, perhaps a little harder than he intended. He softened his tone. "Either way, the killer's out there."

Nate joined Crystal at the window and tentatively placed a hand on her shoulder. "Crystal, look, I know this stinks, but the best chance we have in stopping this madman is to keep a watch on you." He walked around her, forcing her to look at him. "My partner just said it: Either way, the killer is out there, and he's not going to stop killing until either we catch him or he finishes his mission."

She began to cry. "But why is he after me?" It was not a question she wanted answered, but rather a release of the anguish in her heart. She slid down the wall until she sat crouched on the floor beneath the windowsill. Crying, she hugged her knees.

Nate looked from Crystal to Maryann who was still sitting on the edge of the bed. Finally, he spoke. "We'll have guards on you twenty-four hours a day until this is over. We won't leave you, okay?"

She lifted tear-filled eyes to his face, and he could see her fear. He could feel her silent pleas for an assurance he couldn't give. Assurances, nonetheless, that his job demanded that he promise. "I promise you, I won't let anything happen to you," he swallowed as he said the words.

***

As the last bell rang ending the school day, Tim Jackson pushed his cart just past the open doorway to Ms. Higgins's classroom. She sat behind her desk talking with a few students who had been kept after. Clearing his throat, he made his presence known. "Ahem, excuse me, but I'd like to get a start on the classroom if you don't mind."

She turned to him and smiled, her eyes warm and inviting. "No. Mr. Jackson, come on in. We'll just be a few more minutes, and then we'll be out of your way."

He waved a hand acknowledging her. He knew as soon as she turned around she would forget he was there. They all did. He began to sweep the floor and straighten the desks, all the time listening.

This was the same girl he'd seen in the hall the day the detectives had visited. He knew her type. He'd seen her type too many times. The boy though, he was the kind that needed to be stopped. Tim knew his kind preyed on the weak, took advantage of those even a little more needy than he was himself.

The boy looked up, and Tim averted his eyes.

Ms. Higgins was speaking. "Josh, since last week I've noticed that your behavior has improved. That's good, but I've been around long enough to know that what goes on here in front of me may be entirely different from what happens in the streets." To his credit, the boy met her gaze, refusing to look away. Ms. Higgins took a breath and paused.

The girl bounced uneasily from foot to foot while twirling a finger through her short-cropped hair. "Ms. Higgins, I told you Josh is not a bad kid. He didn't mean nothing by that—by what you saw. He was funning." In a furtive glance, the girl cut her eyes to look at the unobtrusive janitor.

"Karrie, how many times do I have to tell you, if you don't stand up for yourself, guys like Josh here will walk all over you." Even though she had addressed Karrie, her eyes had been locked on to Josh. "The reason I had the two of you stay after was so I could invite you to my sexual abuse survivor group. It's for victims of abuse and those who could be abusers, as well."

"I don't need no stupid group. I ain't abused nobody." It was the first words Tim had heard the boy say.

"Well, Josh, let's just say it won't hurt you to attend." She turned her attention to Karrie. "Look, sweetheart, I was once where you are now, alone, confused, and wanting someone to make me feel like I was loved. There's always a Josh, a cousin, or an uncle in the crowd to take advantage of your pain, sweetie—"

"Hey," Josh said, interrupting her, "it ain't like I'm not sitting right here. You talking about me like I'm invisible or something."

She stopped and looked at Josh. "It's not that you're invisible Josh, but I want Karrie to know that we don't have to be afraid of the 'Josh's' in our lives. Karrie has her 'Josh' to overcome as I had mine." She stood up and looked down at the seated boy. "I'm going to do everything in my power to make sure she understands that." Then turning, she looked up and saw Tim in the rear of the room, bending down as if scraping gum or candy off the floor. She looked back to Karrie. "We meet every Thursday here in the main office conference room at 8 p.m. I'd love to have you come."

Signaling that the meeting was over, Ms. Higgins began collecting her papers and, in a very precise manner, began placing them into her briefcase. After checking her desk again, she walked toward the door. "Goodnight, Mr. Jackson." She turned and walked out without waiting for an answer.

Tim looked up from the floor waving his hand in a lazy circle and smiled as the door closed behind them. He was finally alone. Quickly pulling a shortened pencil from his pocket, he made notes of some of the comments he'd overheard. He wrote down the time and location of the next meeting and thanked the *voice* again for having sent him the perfect person to make it possible for him to achieve his goal. Pulling the gloves out of his pocket, he slipped them on. With reverent slowness, he held up his hands and examined the gloves. He knew that soon he would be able to complete his task; the weight would be lifted from him. He rubbed his hands together, and with deliberate caution, he went to the desk. Bending over, he held his face level with its polished surface. He smiled. He'd found what he was looking for.

CHAPTER FOURTEEN

AFTER LEAVING THE HOSPITAL, Nate drove to his parents' place for dinner. Nate had the two-story Victorian-style home built for him and his fiancée, but the relationship had failed when they both realized that neither of them was ready for marriage. Nate had been too unsettled, and she a bit too much so. Amber had helped him come to understand that as well. Nate shook his head at the memory. Rather than simply lose the house, he sold it to his parents instead.

He parked his Jeep at the curb and waited for a second before turning the engine off. Michael W. Smith's remixed version of "Friends" was just ending. Nate marveled as the song recounted that a *lifetime was not too long to live as friends*, and smiled. As the music faded, he killed the engine. "I liked the old version better anyway," he mumbled.

Suddenly feeling angry, Nate slammed the car door behind him. It was the song, it always reminded him of Amber, and thinking of Amber always made him mad. At least lately it did.

Amber-Jackie-Amber-Jackie! The two faces played in his mind. The one he wanted wasn't here and the other, well, that was the question. What exactly was the other? He reached for the doorbell and the front door swung open.

"Hey, you," Gracie, greeted him. Flinging her arms around his neck in an excited embrace, she almost caused them both to go sliding down the thin coat of ice that had built up on the low porch. "I missed you."

Freeing himself, Nate laughed. "I've missed you too. Mom didn't tell me you'd be here for dinner. I thought you'd be out with your friends." Nate still marveled at the difference he saw in Gracie. A little less than two years ago she had been just another "Honey" a gang-girl, used for everything from running drugs to sexual comfort and prostitution.

But since being rescued by Amber during her own escape from the gang, Gracie had been living here with Nate's parents and making the best of her second chance at life.

Nate grabbed her hand. "Come on, let's get inside before Mom comes out here after us." Giggling, they both hurried inside, slapping their arms against the chill.

Sherri met them at the door. Her honey-blond hair, just starting to show a little silver around the ends, was tied back from her face and held in place with a floral patterned scarf. After kissing his mother's cheek, he looked at her headdress. "Flowers, Mom? It's not even Thanksgiving yet, and you've got spring wrapped around your head."

"You like?" She said and turned like a model allowing him to see the full effect. She had on a pair of pink capri pants, beige flats, and a sleeveless gray-green top. The greens, yellows, and muted reds in the scarf were a perfect complement. "I just didn't feel like winter this evening, so I decided to go spring instead."

"Mom's a hoot. I love that she doesn't care much what folks think about her. She's just fun," Gracie said and ran past Sherri and sat on the sofa curling her legs beneath her.

Nate raised an eyebrow at his mother, noting Gracie's use of the word "Mom." He didn't say anything, and she smiled at him in return.

"Well, you might think it's spring, but that doesn't mean I'm gonna pay to heat all of outdoors just so the neighborhood can play along with you." Reverend Richards came out of the kitchen carrying a serving tray.

"Hey, Pop," Nate said, kicking the front door closed. He met his dad in the center of the room and kissed his cheek. Taking the tray from him, he set it on the coffee table.

***

After dinner was finished and Sherri and Gracie excused themselves to the kitchen, Nate and Reverend Richards sat alone in the living room. Nate spoke first. "I can't believe how well Gracie's doing. Every time I see her, she's like a brand new person. She's growing."

Reverend Richards smiled and sat back in his easy chair and picked up his cup of coffee. "Yeah, your mother's a wonder. It always amazes me what love and a little bit of patience can accomplish; that and a whole lot of prayer and trusting Jesus." He smiled again.

A comfortable silence settled between the two men. Nate leaned back onto the sofa and stretched his legs toward the fireplace. The sound of wood crackling in the fire and the slight scent of fruit filled the air as the apple-wood logs burned slowly. Outside, the wind gusted and a sheet of icy rain, which had just begun, splashed against the window. Nate took another sip of hot coffee and closed his eyes, enjoying the comfortable silence.

"Your mom says," Reverend Richards began, breaking the silence, "that Amber will be home in a week or so."

Nate kept his eyes closed, enjoying the radiant heat against his face. "Yeah?"

"You going to be okay with that? Mom invited her to stay here since she hasn't found an apartment yet."

Nate swallowed. After a moment, he opened his eyes and sat up slowly. He looked at the door leading to the kitchen before he spoke. "I don't know, Dad. I just don't know." He stood and walked to the mantel, setting his cup on the edge. Without looking back at his father, Nate spoke as if confessing to the fire. "I don't know what to think about Amber. First, she says she loves me. Then once I figure out I love her too, she takes off. Then she doesn't write. Won't call. She doesn't even answer my calls. Then to top it off, she calls Mom all the time like they're best friends." He turned and faced his father. "No, Dad, I don't know what to think."

The elder Richards played with the cup in his hands breathing in the moist warmth. He inhaled as if to speak but said nothing. Nate looked at his father expectantly. "What, no advice? No sage words of wisdom?"

"What can I say, Son? I've been preaching and teaching this Bible for almost forty years now," he said, as he patted the back of the King James Version of the Bible on the small table near his chair. "And in all those years I still haven't found anything that can explain the mind of a woman."

Nate laughed despite himself. He was still laughing when his mother came back into the room. "What's so funny?" she asked.

"Oh, just thinking about the blessings of womanhood," Reverend Richards said with a smirk.

"Emm-hmm, I bet you were," she said and sat in her chair opposite the small table where the Bible rested.

"So, Mom, where's Gracie?" Nate asked feeling the beginning of a set up.

"Oh, she went up to bed. School tomorrow," Sherri said and picked up a paperback and opened it with a casual flip of her wrist.

Nate looked at his mother and smiled. "Since when did Gracie start going to bed at eight O'clock?"

"Well…" his mother began.

Reverend Richards picked up the Bible and opening it, began to read silently, ignoring the both of them.

"What are you up to, Mom?"

"Me? Nothing, what do you mean?"

Nate cut his eyes toward his father who was avoiding looking at him. "Come on, Mom, what you got cooking?"

"I don't know what you're talking about." She made a point of opening her novel and beginning to read.

Nate smiled and cleared his throat. "I was telling Dad earlier…"

At this, his father lifted a brow and looked toward him.

"…I was telling Dad earlier that since I had Thanksgiving and the day after off, I thought I would just stay here with you guys and not bother with all the driving back and forth. You know, with the roads being so icy and all."

Sherri slapped the book closed. "James Richards, you told him, didn't you?"

"Told him what, dear?" he answered, his voice dripping with sincerity and genuine curiosity.

"Told me what, Mother?" Nate chimed in, his tone matching his father's.

"Oh, don't you Mother me. You know darn well what I'm talking about. You know you can't stay here. Gracie has her bedroom and Amber will be in the guestroom, so it just won't work. You'll just have to stay at your apartment and drive over."

Both Nate and his father began laughing, and after a moment, Sherri joined them. "You know, Mom, I know how you feel about Amber, but I can't promise that anything will ever happen between us. You know, she has something to say about this too, and besides there's Jackie to consider."

"She's coming back, that's got to mean something. Look, Son, just give it some time, see where the Lord leads. If there's a chance for you and Amber, you owe it to yourselves to find out."

Nate didn't answer his mother, but lost his thoughts in the flickering dance of the flames. "I don't know," he finally muttered. "We'll see, okay?" Okay!?"

Reverend Richards closed his Bible. "So, how's this new case going? Any closer to stopping this killer?"

"I hope so," Nate answered. "I stopped by and ran over the details with Sabrina. She seems to think that the killer may be a woman." He chuckled. "She's supposed to be retired, but by the time I got around to seeing her, she had already worked up a profile."

"She also thinks the killer's a white-female, mid to late thirties, relatively new to the area and just released from prison or some other institution. Sabrina also thinks these are vendetta killings, personal, that our *girl* has been sexually abused and sees this as a type of cleansing."

His parents looked at Nate with astonished gazes. "You think she's right?" his mom asked, after batting her eyes and opening and closing her mouth several times.

"Sabrina's been pretty right on in the past," Reverend Richards answered her. "But where are you on all this, Son? Are you asking the Lord for help?"

"Yeah, but it's not as easy as all that, Dad." He held up his hands palms facing outwards. "I know, the Bible says we have not because we ask not, but I still have to make it all make sense in court. And telling the judge that the Holy Spirit told me who dunnit, won't work. I've got to have all the facts." Nate tried to keep the exasperation out of his voice, but he knew he was failing.

"This is where Amber came in so well," his mother said. "She always had a way of getting you back on track." Before Nate could respond, she lifted her book and began reading again, cutting off his response.

Sighing, Nate looked from his mother to his father. They'd had this same "conversation" time and time again, but he could never make them understand that he did trust God to help him. It was just that he had his own way of doing things.

"What about that other woman, Son? What was her name, Johnson? Jennison? Something like that. I read about her in the paper. Says she had a close call," Nate's father said from behind the leather bound Bible.

"Johansson," Nate said, pulled from his thoughts.

Shaking his hand and pointing, Reverend Richards snapped his fingers. At the sound, Sherri looked up. "That's it!" Reverend Richards said, "Crystal Johansson. That's her name. How long you guys gonna keep her locked up in that hospital?"

"She's not locked up. We can't keep her locked up."

"Seems like the safest place to be if you ask me," his mother said, not bothering to look up from her book.

"I like the idea too," Nate added under his breath.

"I remember what it was like when Sabrina was in there. Police officers up and down the hallway all the time…. Day and night. It was the safest place in the city," Sherri finished.

Nate stared into the fire again.

Reverend Richards closed his Bible softly and looked up at his son. "He's going after her again, isn't he?"

CHAPTER FIFTEEN

CRYSTAL CLOSED THE DOOR against the cold and watched as the last uniformed officer left her home. Walking toward the kitchen, she felt a growing sense of dread. Poking her head into the kitchen, she expected to see shattered glass and destroyed cabinetry, reminders of the killer's assault. Holding her breath, she saw that the kitchen had been cleaned, and the shattered windows covered by sheets of plywood screwed into the frames.

Her pulse quickened as she stepped into the room. She ran her fingers over the holes in the wall where the crime scene technicians had dug out the recovered projectiles, and sighed. Overcome with a sudden sense of fear and vulnerability, she slid down into a crouched position in a corner, and rested her forearms on her knees and began crying.

A shadow moved across the window, and the silhouette of a man fell across the floor. The silhouette crept slowly, moving from right to left, stopping just shy of the partially boarded sliding-glass patio door. Crystal gripped her mouth in an attempt to stifle the scream and pushed her small frame deeper into the darkened corner. Her throat constricted.

As the shadow moved nearer to the edge of the door, the man pressed his face against the glass peering into the darkness.

Crystal forced herself against the floor hardly daring to breathe. She slid along the base of the cabinets trying to meld into nothingness—to disappear.

Across the kitchen, she could see the light on the phone's digital recording device begin to flash, although the phone remained silent because the ringer had been turned off. The shadow stopped just outside the door and turned toward the phone, his attention drawn to the flashing light. Crystal could only watch as the door jerked, then glided soundlessly along its track.

Summoning her courage, Crystal lunged for the phone as the door slammed open. A man grabbed her by her shoulders and threw her back against the cabinet. She screamed as she hit her back against the wall. Scrambling to her feet, she reached for the knife drawer. The overhead light came on. She screamed. Turning, she found herself staring into the barrel of a Glock Model 27, semi-automatic, .40 caliber handgun. "Freeze!"

The uniformed officer held the service duty weapon level at her head. "Don't move."

Two more uniformed officers broke into the back door, weapons drawn. The first officer held up his left hand, four fingers extended. "Code four! It's code four." He focused his eyes on the woman with her hand still extended into the drawer. "Miss Johansson, it's all right. We're the police. You're okay. You're safe. We're here to protect you."

Crystal raised feral, unfocused eyes, scanning the room, torn between one of two unconscious actions. Part of her mind screamed with the need to escape, locked in the struggle between fight or flight. Snatching the cutlery drawer open, she dug through it sending multiple pieces of silverware clanging against the porcelain-tiled floors. Abandoning the search, she screamed and attacked the nearest officer.

Deflecting the claw-like fingers and capturing the outstretched arms, the police officer spun Crystal around and trapped her against his chest, locking her arms against her side.

"Miss Johansson, settle down. I don't want to hurt you. Now stop it!"

A second officer came around in front of her, careful not to expose his centerline to a possible kick or knee lift. He grabbed the screaming woman's face, as a knee slammed into his thigh. "Crystal...Crystal, settle down. You're safe. You're safe!"

Her eyes locked on to the young officer's face in front of her and she collapsed. The officer standing behind her caught her full weight and lowered her to the floor. He looked at his partner, an unspoken question on his face. Visibly uncomfortable, he mouthed, "Call the VWC," as Crystal turned and cried against his chest.

Crystal wrapped her fingers into the loose material around the officer's sides. Putting her face against the man, Crystal hugged him and cried, her shoulders heaving. The officer eyed his partner and repeated his request. "Call the Victim Witness Coordinator!" He peered at the woman crying in his arms. "She needs help, now!"

Thirty minutes later, Renae Gonzaga, one of five Metro Police Victim Witness Coordinators, arrived at Crystal's home. Shaking snow from her shoulder length honey blond hair and stomping ice and granulated snowmelt from her boots, Renae smiled. The apple of her cheeks glowed from a combination of the frigid night air and her natural cheery disposition. "Hi, I'm Renae Gonzaga," she said extending her hand to Crystal.

Calmed now, Crystal felt embarrassed as she sipped her tea and sat hunched on the sofa in her living room. "I'm sorry you had to come out on a night like this." She raised her head and faced Renae. "You really don't need to be here. I'm all right now," Crystal said, her voice softer than she intended.

"Nonsense, this is what I do. Have these guys explained what I do in these cases?" she asked. Before Crystal could answer, she said, "Of course they haven't. Well, anyway, what I do is…." She explained the function of the VWC as she escorted Crystal back to the kitchen and began to make them each a fresh cup of tea.

***

The officers watched as the two women walked away, Renae chatting briskly as if they were old friends and Crystal relaxing into the older woman's one-armed embrace. The officers sighed in relief, happy that Renae had arrived.

The larger of the two officers, Tennedy, the one who'd caught Crystal, smiled at the smaller and lower ranked officer as he pointed toward the front door. "Play ya to see who goes out for first watch."

"Two out of three or winner takes all?" Todd asked.

"One and done…winner takes all," Tennedy said, pulling his gloves off and flexing his fingers.

"On three," Todd said, stretching his own fingers like an old west gun fighter. "One-two-three."

On three, the men began to pound the fleshy sides of their fists into the palms of their opposite hands. With a slap, Tennedy laid his hand flat against his palm, while Todd maintained his hand in a fist.

"A-ha, a-ha. Paper covers rock, you lose," Tennedy yelled like an eight-year-old playing with matchbox cars. "You lose, you're outside buddy. I'll be watching the ladies."

Todd picked up his gloves and began to zip up his jacket. "Don't get cocky. You know what they say about payback." He smiled and headed for the door. "See you in two hours."

Tennedy smiled back and saluted, touching his forehead with the tips of his index and middle fingers. "See you in two."

Todd pulled the door open and a gust of snow-laced windswept in around his boots. "Hey you, wait up," Renae called and rushed to him with a mug of hot tea. "Take this with you. It'll warm your insides."

"Thanks, Renae, this will go a long way into making a cold night better."

She giggled before turning back toward the kitchen. "Be safe out there, and I'll see you in the morning." She spun on her heels and disappeared into the kitchen.

Todd lifted his mug toward Renae's retreating back and stepped out into the cold, dark of night.

Backlit from the house, Todd stood in contrast against the dark. The cloud of steam encircled his face as he drank the hot tea.

From across the lake hunkered down in the brush, Tim Jackson watched him. The voice, incessant in his mind, commanded him to carry out his orders. The Johansson woman must die. His hands began to tremble. Despite the cold, sweat ran in rivulets down his face. He had no desire to hurt the officers; after all, they were on the same side. They served *God* as well. Didn't scripture say that God had given them the sword to protect the innocent?

At first, only one voice whispered and then many all at once. The voices grew in intensity. Demanding. *Kill her!*

Tim hugged the high-powered rifle against his shoulder sighting down the barrel.

Breathing slowly, trying to stop his trembling, he focused through the scope on Officer Todd walking the perimeter of the property, his form glowing like reflective tape through the night vision scope.

Kill her! Kill her! Dropping the rifle, Jackson grabbed the sides of his face and cringed as if in pain. "I can't hurt the officers. They are servants of God! They are servants of God!" He repeated the five words as a mantra. Soon the voice softened and then ceased. Jackson allowed his weight to settle onto the snow-dusted ground.

Across the lake, the back door opened and Officer Tennedy walked out and slapped his upper arms against the cold. Jackson could see that the men were talking, but he was much too far away to hear their conversation. He guessed they were talking about the Johansson woman.

Looking down at his watch, he realized that two hours had passed. Somehow, he had lost two whole hours. The last thing he remembered was the first officer drinking a cup of coffee or some other hot drink. Then the voice had started again. The voice wanted him to finish the job, to do the duty laid on him by God, but he couldn't hurt the officers. Could he? But that would have to wait; too much time had passed. The neighborhood would be waking up soon, and he couldn't afford to be discovered near her house. He had to leave.

Scooting backwards, Jackson slid down the small rise until the crest of the hill hid him from view of the house on the far side of the lake. Breaking the weapon down, he stowed it in the canvas bag he carried over his shoulder. Covering the disassembled parts with rolled newspapers, he sauntered to his car, confident that even if seen, he would disappear into the early morning backdrop.

***

The Monday before Thanksgiving dawned clear and cold. Nate Richards sat at his small table eating oatmeal and boiled eggs. Like eyes poking out of the bowl of hot cereal, raisins peppered the creamed-colored dish. On the screen of the small TV sitting across the counter, reporter Butch Jensen's smiling face greeted him.

Nate wasn't really watching the program; he had turned on the set for background noise more than for any other reason. Then something Jensen said caught his attention.

"Up next," Jensen began, "segment two of my investigative series on police brutality here in the valley. I have a special guest who will give us an insider's view of what it was like for her to be caught in the middle of gangland violence and the police violence that can go along with it. She'll tell us what this experience has come to mean to her as we go into the holiday season. We'll be right back after these messages."

Jensen flashed his high voltage smile as the picture faded, and a series of commercials began.

After a short break, Jensen's voice floated across the small kitchen again. Jensen looked directly into the camera and, dropping his chin, began in a serious voice. "This is Butch Jensen.... And this morning we're talking to Miss Sandra Blightwood. Good morning, Sandra. It is okay that I call you Sandra, isn't it?"

Across from him, a thin woman with distinctive Native-American features nervously smiled back at Jensen. "No, that's fine Butch, you go right ahead. I watch your show all the time."

Jensen reached out and touched her knee. "Now, Sandra, you live in the middle of Old Town. That's a pretty hard area. Go back with me to the events of just over a year ago, just after your son turned two. Can you tell our viewers what impact those events have had on you, and what difficulties you've had in raising your son alone?"

Sandra reached for a tissue and dabbed at her eyes, taking a deep breath before answering. She made a show of collecting her thoughts. "Well, Butch, I never wanted my marriage to end...." She began to sob. "We'd plan to move to the south side of the city. We wanted to grow old together. We'd made plans. Then one day everything went wrong."

Butch turned his face toward the camera, positioning his chiseled features to capture the studio's best light. "What was the hardest adjustment you had to face, Sandra?" He crossed his legs at the knees and leaned back in his chair.

"When the police started shooting and the bullets...when the bullets came through the wall." She lowered her face into her tissue and began to cry, her shoulders heaving with the effort. "Butch," she said, looking up, "I just wasn't prepared to be responsible for everything."

The cell phone rang, drawing Nate's attention from the television. Nate looked at the number and wasn't surprised to see that it was Mac. "Hey, partner, I see she's working this, getting her fifteen minutes of fame."

Mac launched into several minutes of venting. Nate let him spew. After a while, Mac quieted enough for Nate to get a word in. "Hey, Bro, better let that tongue cool off before kissing the missus." He chuckled.

"I know, I know. I'm not so much angry with her. I know that Sandra is...a lying, manipulative, petty—have you seen her rap sheet? It's almost as long as the gangsters' we took down. Her husband was no saint either. She didn't say that her dear sweet husband was the one who was selling the rocks on that side of the city or that he shot and hit two cops before he was taken out himself. I get so tired of one sided reporting."

Nate nodded as he listened to his partner and waved a hand in the air; Mac began another tirade. "Hold on there sailor, virgin ears," Nate said, pulling on his earlobe even though Mac couldn't see him. "What do you say I meet you at the Library for a cup of coffee?"

"I don't—"

"I'll buy. I need to see Jackie anyway." Nate hung up and turned back to the TV as Jensen was beginning his closing monologue. He turned the TV off and prepared to leave the apartment. As the screen faded, Nate shook his head from side to side. "Jensen, you're a jerk," he muttered and pulled the door closed behind him.

***

When Nate arrived at the Library, Mac was sitting at their usual table near the rear of the large back room. He had two cups of coffee and a couple of cinnamon rolls on small plates in front of him, one hot and one at room temperature. He looked up when Nate entered. Nate smiled. "I told you I was buying."

"Don't worry, I told Jackie to put it all on your tab."

Nate sat across from his partner and grabbed the mug holding it against his face. "Ahhh," he said, absorbing the heat into his wind chilled nose. When he opened his eyes, Jackie was looking down at him. "Hey beautiful," he said and reached out to take her hand. He kissed the curl of her knuckles.

"Hadn't seen you in a couple of days. I was beginning to wonder," she said.

Nate looked at her again and smiled disarmingly. "No excuses, just been busy. This time of year, you know."

Mac cleared his throat. "You guys need me to leave for a while? I could go for a walk or something."

She slapped playfully at him with her towel.

"I'm just saying," Mac teased.

She reached out and touched Nate's cheek. "Some of us actually have work to do," she said. She focused on Nate. "See you later?"

Nate grabbed her hand pulling it from his face and kissed her palm this time. "You'd better. I've been looking forward to it."

She smiled flirtatiously and turned to walk away. Both men watched her as she left the room.

"You okay," Nate asked, turning back to Mac.

"No. I'm mad, but I'll get over it. I figure Butch just isn't worth the energy. I still don't like him though, and I really do want to slap him up side his head."

Nate laughed.

"Nah, I'm just kidding, I really want to punch him in his smug face." This time Mac laughed too.

"Time to get back to the real world.... Serial killers and baby rapers," Nate sighed and sagged into his chair.

"Yeah," Mac said, raising his cup in a toast. "Happy Thanksgiving to us, huh?"

"Yeah, happy Thanksgiving to us."

CHAPTER SIXTEEN

AMBER COLES SAT UP with a start. The wheels of Southwest Airline's Boeing 737 touched down at the Boise Airport; the ice and snow piled along the sides of the runway making shallow valleys along the otherwise wide open space. She pressed the heels of her hands against her face and rubbed tired, dry eyes. Exhaling, she looked out the small window and, for the first time in almost two years, saw the place she's always known as home.

All around her, excited voices filled the cabin as passengers gathered their bags from overhead bins and impatiently crowded the narrow aisle. Suddenly feeling heavy, Amber leaned back in her seat and allowed the other travelers to pass her by. She sagged, hoping she'd made the right decision in coming back. Hoping there was something worth coming back for.

Amber jumped when a petit flight attendant tapped her and said, "Excuse me, miss, this is a non-continuing flight, you'll have to disembark. I can help you find your next gate if—"

Amber inhaled slowly and tried to slow her racing pulse. "No, that'll be okay. This is home for me. Besides, the terminal's not that big." To her surprise, she realized the other passengers had deboarded. Giggling nervously, she stood to collect her bag from the overhead compartment. Starting down the boarding ramp, she wondered who would be there to meet her.

All around her, people hurried to meet their loved ones and friends as they poured through the tube-like opening. Amber silently watched the crowd thin and soon found herself alone. Clutching her bag, she began the short walk through the concourse and into the doubled glass door foyer. Riding down the escalator, Amber spotted the inlaid map of the state of Idaho with the four corners of the compass sharply indicated, highlighting some of the state's bragging rights. She smiled as she walked toward it. Pausing for a moment, she stood in the center of the huge circle focusing on the sounds as they faded into silence, owing to the fantastic acoustical arrangement of the foyer.

Heaving a sigh, she shifted the slight weight of her bag and started toward the baggage carousel.

"Amber! Amber!" Gracie screamed as she ran and leaped into Amber's arms.

"Gracie," she squealed in response, "how did you get here? You're driving in this weather?"

"Now, what kind of gentleman would I be if I let that little lady out on these roads all by herself?" Reverend Richards said, walking up behind her. "The Missus and I went to park the car, but Gracie insisted on jumping out along the curb so she could be here when you got your bags."

Sherri beamed at her husband before gathering Amber into her embrace. "Come here, girl. Welcome home," she said. She kissed the younger woman on both cheeks before pushing her back to arm's length looking at her again.

Amber's eyes lifted from Sherri's face and swept the cavernous room, searching. "He's not here," Sherri whispered into Amber's ear pulling her back into her embrace.

Amber smiled and fixed a 'who's not here' look on her face before turning to check for the rest of her luggage. Sherri exchanged knowing glances with her husband then sighed and joined Amber and Gracie as they grabbed bags from the conveyer.

***

Nate hung up the phone and pushed back from his desk. He looked at the digital clock in the lower right corner of his monitor and sighed. "I don't need this. Not now."

"CPS again?" Mac called from the other side of the partition. He stuck his head around the edge. "What now?" His voice had a deflated quality.

Nate looked at his partner. "Nah, it's my mom…."

"Everything okay?"

Nate leaned back and closed his eyes. "Well, Amber just got in."

"Wow," Mac said, rolling his chair around the edge and into Nate's cubicle. "What you gonna do?" What're you going to tell Jackie? Remember the, 'I'm looking forward to seeing you again'?"

"I remember, I remember…. Don't remind me. I don't know." Kicking his feet forward, Nate dangled his arms at his side, his head rolled back in resignation. "All I know is Amber's been gone for almost two years, and as far as I know, she didn't even come back here to see me."

"So every time this Coles woman shows up, you gonna go stupid on me, Richards?" Lieutenant Brown stood behind Mac, his arms folded over the curving arch of his stomach. "Sorry to mess up your pity party, but the girls in the lab have been calling

135

for you." He rocked up on his toes and then back down on his heels.

Mac jumped, turning his face toward Brown, startled by the voice suddenly over his shoulder. Nate snapped forward, adjusting into a seated position. They answered simultaneously.

"Sir?"

"No, sir."

Brown chuckled and walked away. "You guys make it too easy." He chuckled again, shaking his head as he did. "You better hurry down to the lab; they've been expecting you for a half hour already."

They could hear him still laughing as he closed the door to his office. Nate looked at Mac and shook his head. "We'd better see what Rosie has for us."

"Already walking," Mac said, standing up. The two men headed to the basement.

As the elevator doors slid shut, Nate turned and looked at Mac. "I really don't like that guy."

"Well...good thing Amber's back; she can help you with that little issue." He grinned at Nate as the doors closed.

"Rosie Boats, what ya got, girlfriend," Nate said as he pushed through the door. He sat on the corner of her desk while Mac leaned his shoulder against the doorjamb, his arms crossed.

The older woman looked up from her computer and scowled. Rosie pushed her glasses up the bridge of her nose before finally taking them off. "What? You think I got nothing to do but sit around here waiting for you to come down here?"

"Sorry, I got tied up on—"

"Sorry my—"

"Hey...wait, somebody's supposed to be a lady here," Mac said coming forward and hugging Rosie around her shoulders.

Rosie looked up. "Big dumb boys."

They both leaned forward, kissing her on her cheeks. Rosie scrunched up her face, pretending not to enjoy the affection. Slapping at the men's hands and shooing them away like gnats, she crossed her arms across her ample chest.

"Come on, Rosie," Nate intoned.

"Please," Mac added in his singsong voice.

"Oh, stop it," Rosie said, breaking into a smile. "Big dumb boys." She got up and headed to the evidence vault. "I ought to make you come back later." Her voice sounded hollow coming from the cavernous room beyond the heavy metal door. Mac and Nate waited, curiosity building, still not knowing exactly why they had been summoned.

Rosie came back carrying a single large envelope and a sheaf of papers. She dropped them on the desk in front of Nate. He leaned forward reaching his hand to grab the package. "Ouch," Nate said, rubbing the back of his hand. Mac burst into laughter.

"Not until you chain it to yourself," Rosie said.

"All right," Nate said, pulling a pen from his breast pocket. Lifting the envelope, he signed and dated the package in the chaining history, indicating that he had taken possession of the evidence.

Nate sat at an empty desk across the small office from Rosie's desk. Mac stood over his shoulder scanning the papers as Nate flipped through them.

Mac reached down and picked up the discarded envelope. "Who collected these?" He looked at Rosie.

She smiled. "I'm good, huh?"

"You're golden, girlfriend," Nate said, looking at the papers.

"You found these in Thomas' apartment? That's a miracle in itself," Mac said, recalling the little man's disheveled and dirty residence.

Nate shook his head and smiled. "Looks like Sabrina might be right after all."

Rosie looked up at him. "Sabrina…what's that old heifer up to?"

They all chuckled. "I'll tell her you called her that," Nate said.

"Don't bother, I'll tell her myself when I see her for lunch next week." Rosie winked and poked her tongue at Nate.

"Next week?"

Rosie leaned back in her chair, her feet dangling an easy four inches above the floor and smiled. "Boys. It's Thanksgiving, duh."

Nate looked over at Mac before dropping his gaze back to the papers, his face darkening slightly. He couldn't help but think about what this Thanksgiving would be like. Shaking his head, he looked up and forced a smile.

"Well?" Mac asked.

"I told you," Nate began. "I reviewed the case with Sabrina. Turns out she had already been following it and doing her own profile based on what she gleaned from the press and some of her contacts." He made quotation gestures with his fingers. "She determined that our killer would be female and white." He dropped the DNA lab report on the desk.

Mac gave Rosie a high-five. "How did you find those hairs in all that mess?"

Rosie smiled. "The hair was not the problem; the place was covered with hairs. The real boon was finding a hair with the follicle and a live dermal papilla."

"A what?"

"A viable root. That's where the DNA is found." Rosie stood, stretched, bent forward, and rubbed her lower back. "Boys, and just think, they let you guys carry guns." She leaned forward again, twisting from the waist, further stretching her back. "I've got a doctor's appointment guys. So you can either take the stuff with you or chain it back to the lab." She pointed at the evidence package as she headed for the door grabbing her coat.

Nate replaced the report and the hair sample into the evidence packaging, sealing it with red tape and signed the log. He stood and followed her toward the hall. "Thanks Rosie."

She sighed, turning serious. "I know it's not a lot, but it's the only break we got. So catch this...er girl."

Nate and Mac followed Rosie out of the lab as she pulled the door closed behind them, setting the alarm. "You got it," Nate said.

***

Mary Higgins sat at her desk and sighed as the last of her students left the classroom for Thanksgiving break. Again, she looked out at the gray sky lost in thought as wet snow clumped against her window before melting and running down the frosted panes. She looked up at the clock at the rear of the classroom and thought about the meeting she would attend later that evening. Opening her middle desk drawer, she pulled out a yellowed, creased envelope. Opening it, she pulled out the letter and read it again then sat staring at the grainy photo.

Mary stood abruptly. Grabbing her jacket and purse from the back of her seat, she opened it and removed the Beretta 3032 Tomcat. Holding the small .32 caliber handgun up to her face, she pressed the cold steel against her closed eyelids and sighed.

She thought again about her meeting later that night, and a tight smile barely lifted the corners of her mouth. Dropping the gun back into her purse, she closed her bag and spun slowly, taking in the sights and smells of the classroom, committing them to memory.

"Miss Higgins," said Mr. Jackson, "you ready? It's time to go."

Mary smiled at the familiar face. Clutching her purse to her chest, she walked confidently toward the door. She looked at the wall clock, again, seeing it was only one-thirty, school having been let out early for the holiday break. "Yes, Mr. Jackson it is about time."

As she left, Mr. Jackson switched off the lights and pulled the door shut on an empty classroom.

CHAPTER SEVENTEEN

A MBER POKED HER HEAD into the room and spotted Sherri Richards in her overstuffed chair with her eyes closed and her Bible lying open across her chest. The black leather book rose and fell in a steady rhythm with her respiration. Amber came into the room and smiled at the matronly figure. She tipped-toed softly and lifted the Bible from Sherri's chest, noting that she had been reading in the Gospel of John. Closing the book, she laid it on the table between the two chairs. She smiled and, curling her feet beneath her, sat in Reverend Richards's La-Z-Boy recliner.

"No greater love hath any man," Sherri said from behind closed eyelids.

Amber jolted, then chuckled more from being startled than from what Sherri had said. "Ooo, I thought you were asleep. John chapter fifteen, right?"

Sherri sat up. "'This is my commandment, that you love one another, as I have loved you. Greater love hath no man than this, that a man lay down his life for his friends. You are my friends, if you do whatsoever I command you.'" Sherri finished and stretched. "Mmmm...that was a good stretch."

"Wow. That was word for word, if you're into that old translation. Good nap?"

Sherri rocked forward then stood. "It's almost one o'clock, I'd better start lunch. Gracie will be home soon."

"Gracie?" Amber said, standing as well. "She'll be in school for another two hours or so."

"Early out today, tomorrow's Thanksgiving, my dear." She headed into the kitchen and began preparing the noon meal.

Amber followed her. She touched fingertips to her face, "Oh, I forgot." She smiled coyly. After a pregnant pause, Amber sighed and said, "Mrs. Richards—"

"I thought I told you—"

She raised her hand to halt the protest. "I'm sorry. I forgot...I mean, Mom. I need to ask you a question—to talk to you about something." Glancing down, she wrung her fingers together in unconscious action.

Sherri set the bag of corn chips she was opening on the snack bar. "What is it, sweetheart?" Amber sighed deeply as Sherri stopped what she was doing and made her way to her. Sherri touched Amber on the shoulder and guided her to one of the nearby stools.

Sherri studied Amber. Amber took a deep breath and then looked up. A single tear pooled and then spilled over her lashes. Sherri knew before Amber spoke what was on the young woman's heart.

Amber sighed as she brushed the tear away. "I've been here since Monday and he hasn't even called. Do you think I waited too long to come back? Do you think he's given up on me, on what we could have been?" Her eyes pleaded for an explanation.

Sherri inhaled and whispered a silent prayer before answering. *Lord, help me help this child.* "Amber, I don't know. You know I love you and always wanted the two of you to get together, but-Nate is...well he was hurt when you didn't stay in touch with him. He had such hopes for the two of you. It took him so long before he would even admit to himself that he loved...that he was in love with you."

Amber focused on the older woman's face. She had a feeling that although she needed to hear what Sherri had to say, she might not find it at all pleasant. "What is it? What aren't you telling me?"

Sherri's smile never reached her eyes. "Am I that transparent?"

Amber nodded and smiled, "Only to me and the good Reverend." They laughed comfortably and then Amber returned to the topic at hand. "You were about to say...."

Sherri stood and walked over to the pantry before answering. "Nate's started seeing someone." She had spoken over her shoulder, not wanting to see Amber's face as she gave her the news of Nate's dating.

When she turned, she saw Amber slumping on the stool. She appeared crestfallen. Sherri walked over to her.

Amber looked up. "So I'm too late."

"Shame on you," Sherri reprimanded her and placed her index finger beneath the girl's chin lifting her face. "I don't remember there being a ring on Nate's finger the last time I saw him."

"What?"

Sherri smiled mischievously. "Now, you screwed up once already by staying gone too long and being indecisive."

Amber looked at her feigning shock.

"And...your being indecisive has caused my boy to go stupid. Now it's time for you to be the woman he fell in love with and remind him why he did in the first place." Both women burst into laughter. They were both brushing tears from their eyes when Gracie walked in through the back door stomping snow from her boots.

Gracie looked at the two women and smiled. "What's going on here, somebody inherit a million dollars and forget to tell me?"

The laughter started again. This time Gracie joined them.

CHAPTER EIGHTEEN

CRYSTAL SAT AT HER DESK regretting deciding to work here instead of at home. Every time the door chime jangled, she jumped, afraid it was the killer. The female undercover officer, Julie Pratt, did little to assuage Crystal's fears. Crystal had always thought of herself as being a progressive woman, but she felt safer with one of the two male officers who had been assigned to guard her at her home. Both were huge and looked as if they could have been headliners in the WWF, lean faced and square chinned.

The patrol sergeant had gone out of his way to assure Crystal that Julie, Officer Pratt, was more than capable. Crystal hoped his belief in Julie's ability would not be tested.

Julie sat at the receptionist's desk facing the front door. She wore her hair short, but not boyish. She was fit and moved with the athletic grace of someone in tune with her body. Although she wore plain clothes and looked like the secretary she was pretending to be, Crystal knew the woman carried two handguns and at least one knife that she was aware of. When she'd spoken, it had been brief and to the point.

The phone rang and Julie extended an olive toned hand, accented by glossy red fingernails, and lifted the receiver.

"Treasure Valley Computer Center, may I help you?" Julie said smoothly.

The door opened and a lone man entered the foyer. "You Crystal Johansson?" His faded jean jacket lay open despite the cold, exposing his bare chest.

Julie shook her head. "One minute, please," she said into the receiver and extending a finger, pressed the hold button, a single elegant nail reflecting the fluorescent light. She rolled her chair to the corner of her desk, inserting herself between the man and the rear office, while keeping an eye on the strange visitor.

Snow covered the man's shoulders and his pants were wet from the knees down. Scratching and picking at his face, the man raised his voice. "Crystal Johansson. Crystal!"

"I'm Crystal Johansson," Crystal said nervously, stepping out of her office. "May I help you?"

"Yeah, you can help me. You the one that likes young boys, right?" Without warning, the man lunged at Crystal, his arms extended, his fingers clawed. Screaming incoherently as spittle flecked his lips and his eyes bulged wide, he raged.

Crystal drew back and screamed. Frozen, she watched as the man descended upon her. She observed the action distantly like a DVD playing at slow speed. The telephone receiver crashed into the man's temple, then snapped back, as Julie jerked the coiled line wrapped around her wrist. The man reeled backwards from the shock of the blow from the phone receiver against his temple.

Seizing the opportunity, Julie executed a low-level semi-kick, catching the man in his groin. The man bowed forward grabbing his crotch. But before he could respond further, Julie delivered a left cross to his jaw followed by an elbow strike across the bridge of his nose. The man's head recoiled with a quick jerk, and he dropped to the floor unconscious.

By the time Crystal finished screaming, Julie had rolled the assailant onto his stomach and handcuffed him. She was already retrieving his I.D. from his wallet.

With her knee in the man's back, Julie looked up at Crystal. "You all right?"

Crystal nodded and swallowed hard but said nothing.

"Are you hurt?"

She finally found her voice. "No…. I mean, wow! That was amazing."

Julie harrumphed and rolled the man to his side. Pulling out her cell phone, she called for a black-and-white to transport the suspect for questioning.

Twenty minutes later, Nate walked into the small storefront office and slipped on the puddle of melted snow from the battered bad guy's jacket. "Hey…a fellow could get hurt in here," he said in a lighthearted tone.

Crystal approached him as soon as she saw him enter. With a familiarity that belied their relationship, she leaned against his chest and sighed. Nate reluctantly wrapped his left arm around her shoulders and held her for a brief moment before gently pushing her away. Looking around the office, he noticed a number of uniformed officers and a Hispanic female he assumed to be the secretary. The woman looked up and locked eyes with Nate, and his breath caught in his throat.

"Can you, ah, get Miss Johansson a cup of water, please," he stammered. Turning his attention back to Crystal, he listened as she relayed the details of the attack, and the heroic actions of Officer Pratt.

Nate noticed that the woman moved with surprising grace as she returned with a small plastic cup of water for Crystal. As he reached to accept the cup, Nate looked up and spotted a large, muscular officer coming in from the back room. Nate turned toward the man and extended his hand. "Officer Pratt..."

The officer looked at Nate with furrowed brows then tapped his nametag, which read "Jenkins." Then he pointed over Nate's shoulder, arched a brow, and, shaking his head, dragged a finger across his throat. Grabbing Nate's shoulder, he gave it a squeeze and shook his head, smirking as he walked away.

Nate turned and saw the small yellow cup still extended. The hand remained graceful despite the abraded knuckles and chipped nails. Covering his face with his hand, Nate sighed and smiled between splayed fingers. "Oops."

"Yeah, oops," Julie said. "I hope you're a lot better at spotting bad guys than you are at spotting cops." She turned and sat back behind the desk.

"It was an honest mistake," Nate began, but stopped when he caught Julie's gaze.

Crystal walked over and sat opposite the two officers holding her forehead in her hands, her elbows propped against her knees. The cream-colored pants suit and matching heels still looked dry cleaner fresh. Even though she had been attacked, her hair and makeup weathered the storm untouched. She rocked back and forth, contemplative.

Nate approached Julie and put out his hand. "Truce?"

She grabbed his hand in a firm handshake and stood, not quite matching his six-foot frame, but she communicated that she could hold her own. "Truce." She smiled. "So this is how you guys in CID do it, huh?"

Nate smiled in return and sat at an angle on the edge of the desk, so he could keep an eye on Crystal while they spoke. He held up both hands, arms bent at the elbow, palms upward and his fingers spread in a "what, who me," gesture.

This time Julie giggled, and the smile touched her eyes. "So you get to go play while we in SART get to cover your…." She started to say a more industry common word, but looked over at Crystal and reconsidered. "Cover for you," she finished.

"SART, so that's where I know the name from," Nate began. "I didn't know they had accepted any females into the unit, thus my earlier confusion."

"Riiiiight."

Just then, Renae, the VWC, walked in. Going directly to Crystal, she draped a mothering arm around the woman's slender shoulders. "Come on. Let's get you out of here and get us a cup of coffee. They'll be here awhile going through stuff, so let's go somewhere quiet."

Crystal looked up with a jerk, fear in her eyes. "Julie…I mean Officer Pratt, you are coming?"

Julie nodded. "Wouldn't miss it. You coming, cowboy?"

He stood. "Like you said, wouldn't miss it."

***

A half hour later, the four of them sat in a booth in a Moxie Java coffeehouse watching the traffic flow by on Fairview heading into and out of the city. Nate and Julie sat with their backs against the wall keeping a wary eye on the people coming in and out of the coffee shop. Crystal put her cup down after taking a sip of chai tea. "You know, this is good," she began, her voice trembling as she tried to steady her cup. "But the tea at the Library is much better." She exhaled, staring into her cup, her shoulders slumped.

"Isn't that the place you guys usually go over on Carlton?" Renae asked.

Nate sat his cup down with his thump, spilling coffee on the tabletop. "Yeah, but we were so close to this one already. It seemed a shame to drive all the way across town." He looked up, and, for a moment, his eyes met Julie's then he looked away, an awkward smile on his face. "Besides, after putting my foot so deep into my mouth, I needed to redeem myself quickly." Julie met his gaze and smiled.

Setting her cup down again, Crystal leaned forward, placing her forearms on the table. She sighed. "Is it over now? That was him, right?"

Nate and Julie exchanged glances. "I'm afraid not," Nate said. That's not our guy. "

"But how can you be sure? He came in. He asked for me….Those things he said. He was trying to kill me!"

Renae draped a comforting hand over Crystal's arm, giving it a soft squeeze. Nate rocked forward in his seat and cleared his throat. "Crystal, that guy…that guy, was just a copycat. Our guy is too organized to just barge in that way."

"But-but…"

"But we'll stay with you, and we will catch this guy. We will," Nate finished and sat back. He locked eyes with Julie, and the two of them nodded ever so slightly at each other.

***

Across the street parked in a rusted tan 1989 Ford Ranger, Tim Jackson sat and watched as the foursome drank coffee and talked. Arriving at the computer networking company just as Crystal and that same black detective he'd met at the school were leaving, Tim wondered why so many patrol cars had been in the parking lot. The windshield wipers on the truck swished, struck with heavy thumps back and forth throwing clumps of wet snow off to the sides of the windshield.

His hands trembling, Tim wiped sweat from his face before opening the vinyl box on the seat beside him. Taking a deep breath and leaning his head against the steering wheel, he pulled out a Carl Zeiss T-3 riflescope and tried to focus on Crystal. Sweat stung his eyes.

Carry out your duty. The voice echoed inside the truck cab pressing in on him like a physical force.

The thump, thump, thump of the windshield wipers seemed to keep time with the hammering rhythm of Tim's heart. Sweat pooled then streaked down his head and face, running down his neck and back. The swoosh of the wet snow echoed in his ears, sounding like blood being forced through his constricted veins. Tim lowered the scope and dropped his head into his hands. Filling his lungs with a deep cleansing breath, he tried to steady himself. When he looked up, the group was gone.

Turning his face from side to side and looking up and down the street, Tim dropped the scope back into the box and jumped out of his truck. Shielding his face against the snow, he looked around trying to see which direction they had gone. They were nowhere in sight.

"Hey, it's you again. Seems like I always run into you at the oddest moments," a uniformed officer said.

Tim spun so fast he slipped, falling against the still open door of the truck. The truck creaked and moaned as it swayed with his weight. "Hold on there mister, don't be killing yourself," the uniformed officer said, stepping forward with hands outstretched offering assistance.

Tim righted himself. "No, no, I'm okay. You just startled me." Tim looked at the officer trying to remember where he'd seen the man before. "You work at one of the schools," he ventured.

"Use to, but when I met you a week or so ago you had problems with your truck—"

"Oh yes," Tim hurried to say, not wanting the officer to tie him to being near the apartment where Thomas Sansome had finally been judged. It wasn't that he feared being caught or even going to prison; what he feared was not completing his mission. The mission only he could do. "So ready for Thanksgiving tomorrow?"

"As ready as I get," the officer said. "I'm single and I'm working tomorrow. So double-time plus holiday pay. I'd say I got something to be thankful for. How 'bout you? You got family in the area?"

Tim shoved the door to the truck closed and stepped in front of the window, blocking the officer's view of the scope and disassembled rifle on the floorboard of the truck. "Me? Nahh, I'm on my own. Just moved here about six months ago. Probably get together with some folks from my church. Well, I'd better be going. Looks like my bowling buddy stood me up," Tim said. Swallowing despite a dry throat, he hoped his nervousness didn't show.

The officer had begun to pull his notepad from his breast pocket, pen in hand, when he stopped, tilting his head to one side. The officer smiled and started to turn away. "Got a call," he said, pointing to the clear plastic earpiece. A dangling curly cable connected the small speaker to the police radio on the officer's duty belt.

Tim sighed as he watched the officer turn and drive away. "Thank you, *God*," he began praying. "Thank you for shielding me from the eyes of that officer. Now I will do what you called me to do. Crystal Johansson will die."

As the officer pulled out into the flow of traffic, he made a mental note of the truck's license plate number. Pulling a F.I., field interrogation card, from his clipboard, he held it up and contemplated it, thinking about whether it was worth the effort to fill out the descriptive information on the interesting man that had a way of just showing up. He jotted down the license plate number, but then clipped the small form to the patrol vehicle's visor to remind himself to finish it later.

CHAPTER NINETEEN

MARY HIGGINS CLUTCHED HER PURSE to her breast and sighed as she sat in the back of the medium-sized auditorium. The community meeting started early, forcing her to take a seat near the rear of the lecture hall and from there scan the audience for her target. As she looked around the room, her hand found its way to the three-inch scar on her cheek, unconsciously fingering its raised surface. With her left hand, she reached inside her purse rubbing the cool surface of the handgun.

"Miss Higgins?" Mac said, sitting in an empty chair next to her.

Mary turned with a start, snatching her hands from both her face and the barrel of the gun. She looked at the plainclothes officer, both fear and relief on her face.

Mac touched her shoulder. "Sorry. I didn't mean to startle you. You were looking right at me. I thought you saw me coming."

She smiled weakly. "I guess you caught me daydreaming." With that she turned her shoulder to him and resumed taking in the room. "Looks like the program is about to start," she said, turning her face toward the front of the room.

Mac had the distinct impression he had been dismissed. He opened his mouth to speak, but seeing she had turned and was staring forward, he closed his lips with a slight popping sound. Folding his arms across his chest, Mac sighed, leaned back against the curve of the metal folding chair and pretended to be interested.

"I hate these meetings," Mac said, leaning his head toward Mary.

She didn't respond.

Unfazed, he continued. "I know why I'm here. I was ordered to show up, but what about you?"

With a stiff spine, Mary shifted in a slow deliberate motion to face him. "It is part of my continuing education. I have to attend at least three of these per school year." She turned back toward the podium.

Mac kicked his legs out in front of him and tilted his head back, his mouth lulling open. "I just have to take pictures with the guy speaking…you know, the community policing thing, and after that, I'm off for four days." He held up the fingers of his left hand to emphasize his point.

"Mr.?" Mary said, twisting in her chair to look at him again.

"MacGilvery. Detective MacGilvery," Mac said, sitting up and extending his hand to her.

"Detective MacGilvery, while I appreciate the job you do and am overjoyed that you have the weekend off, I am trying to listen to the speaker and do not have the desire nor inclination to chit-chat."

"Oh, sorry," Mac said and retracted his hand. "I'll just be over there by the door. Have a nice evening." She had turned away before Mac finished speaking. He stood and walked to the near wall and rested his shoulder against it.

Professor Geoffrey R. Coulter, the main speaker for the evening, approached the podium. Standing tall and regal in his smoke-gray double-breasted suit, Geoffrey Coulter's muscular frame filled out the suit as toned muscle moved easily beneath the surface of the pastel-green silk shirt. His almost white hair glimmered halo-like under the lights as he raised his hands to halt the applause. He cleared his throat. "Thank you, Madam Chairman," he said, looking back to the dais.

"On this most special of evenings, we find ourselves assembled here to discuss the problem of violence and sexual assaults in our community. Perhaps, it being Thanksgiving is prophetic in its timing."

Mary's breath became shallow and tense. Sitting forward and bracing herself with straight arms locked against the seats to her left and right, Mary's vision began to darken. She felt as if a vice had been wrapped around her chest, and someone was rapidly tightening the screws. Pinpricks of light danced at the corners of her vision, and the sound in the room seemed to fade away with a soft echo as if from a distance.

She staggered to her feet, lost and unaware of her surroundings. All she knew was that she had to escape. She fled from the auditorium.

***

As Mary brushed past Mac, his first thought was to ignore her, but one look at the woman's face, and he knew she was in trouble. Looking after her and then back to where she had been sitting, he saw that she'd left her purse. He retrieved it before following her out into the hall.

Holding the bag by its medium length strap, the purse banged with solid force against Mac's knee as he raced out after the woman. He found her on the floor with her knees pulled up to her chest. Her face was wet, apparently having been splashed with water from the nearby fountain.

Mary heaved a deep sigh dropping her forehead to her folded arms levered on her knees. She lifted her face and looked at Mac before looking away and dropping her face again.

Mac stood above her and said nothing. As the awkward silence grew, he put his fist to his mouth and cleared his throat. "Miss. Higgins, you all right?" His voice was soft. He knelt down in front of her, forcing her face up with a finger beneath her chin. "Miss Higgins, what happened? Do you need me to call someone?"

Taking a deep breath, Mary focused on his face and sighed. "No," she said in a hoarse voice, "it was just anxiety, an attack, but I'm better now."

Mac stood and offered her his hand. Taking it, she accepted his help and stood. She put her hand to her face, covering the pale scar. "Have you seen my—"

"Glasses," Mac said, interrupting her frantic search.

With greedy hands, she grabbed the glasses and shoved them on, pulling loose strands of hair with nervous fingers covering the scar.

"What'd'ya got in here, a gun?" Mac said, bending forward and rubbing his knee cap where the purse had banged against him.

She didn't answer, but looked at the purse with wide eyes. She snatched it from him. "You didn't look in my purse, did you?"

"Hey lady, you got a strange way of saying thanks. You left it inside, remember?" Mac stood and crossed his arms over his chest. "What's your problem, anyway?"

Even disheveled, Mary held herself in aloof dignity. She raised her chin slightly and brushed hair to the side of her face. "Detective MacGilvery, I do not owe you an explanation. You're beginning to make me regret the cup of coffee I bought you and your partner."

Mac shook his head from side to side. "Lady, you're something, you know that. You have to be the only person I know who can find a way to make a person feel bad for trying to help you. You know, the next time you go running out of an auditorium all dazed, and leave your purse behind on the seat, I hope you do it in front of someone else. Good evening, Miss Higgins." Mac headed toward the sound of laughter and applause coming from inside the large room. With only one quick look back, he disappeared through the large double doors.

Mary watched him go and released a breath she didn't realize she'd been holding. She opened her purse and grabbed a hold of the cold steel handgun. She fingered the weapon and, with soft fingers, touched the scar on the left side of her face.

***

Nate parked his Jeep Cherokee at the curb in front of his parent's home. He watched as silhouettes of people walked back and forth inside. The music of Andre Crouch played softly, the gentle bass in sharp contrast with the soft entreating tenor sang, asking not so much for a new beginning as much as to be taken back to an earlier state of mind, to a place of clarity and understanding. "Yeah," Nate said into the air, "take me back.

Here we go, Lord, I could really use some help in there." He switched off the engine and got out of the car. Stepping gingerly in the snow, Nate walked in a slide step over the ice, which lay hidden beneath the surface of the snow. Before he could ring the bell, the door swung open.

Almond shaped brown eyes greeted him. "Hi, Nate," Amber said, her voice tentative and soft.

Nate didn't move, but stood with his hand poised over the doorbell. He had wondered how he would react when he saw her, but now all his plans and practiced phrases failed him.

"You planning on heating the whole neighborhood, Son?" Reverend Richards called from inside the house. "Get on in here and close that door."

"Oh, leave him be. You keep it too hot in here anyway," Sherri said, reaching past Amber. She pulled her son into the house and kissed his cheek.

Outside, the wind picked up and brought with it new wet snow and the promise of an icy morning drive. Nate stamped his feet clean on the mat by the door and then gathered Amber into an awkward embrace. "Hi, it's good to see you again." He pushed her back to arms' length. "You look real good. You grew your hair out."

She smiled up at him, and rubbed her cheek where his face had touched hers and brushed back loose strains of hair tucking it behind her ear. "You too," she squeaked before clearing her throat, and then saying it loudly enough for him to hear.

"Oh, stop it already, the mush factor is going off the chart," Gracie said as she hugged Nate around the waist. "You'd think you didn't know each other."

The tension of the moment broke. They laughed and moved as one into the living room.

Nate sat on the sofa nearest the fire while his parents sat in their usual seats near the reading light. The fragrance of pies and cookies hung heavy in the house. Gracie came in from the kitchen carrying a tray of fresh baked cookies, and Amber followed with a coffee pot and service; she smiled at Nate. Their eyes met.

"How long you going to be in town?" Nate asked.

"Oh, I don't know. I was thinking about trying to get my old job back, but I think I'd like a new place to live. Too many bad memories," Amber answered, as she poured coffee for the reverend and his wife. Setting the coffee on the table, she sat across from Nate and held her hands toward the fire.

"You children planning on being at the service tomorrow morning, aren't you?" Reverend Richards asked.

They all looked at him. "What you preaching 'bout?" asked Gracie.

"The gift and the value of life," he answered.

"Why don't you just tell us all about it now and then we can sleep in," she said and began laughing.

Sherri shoo-shooed the girl. "You know, service won't even start until ten, so you can sleep well past your normal time."

Gracie laughed even more as she took a peanut butter cookie from the table. "I know, Momma Richards, but I love giving the Rev a hard time." She walked over and kissed the older woman's cheek and squeezed Reverend Richards' shoulder.

"Say, Nate," Gracie said as she headed toward the stairs, "speaking of sleeping, you staying here tonight? Amber's already in your old room." Her voice held a singsong quality, obviously teasing.

Nate was pouring himself a cup of coffee but stopped and looked at the teen as she ascended the stairs out of sight. Cutting his eyes first to Amber, he said to Gracie's retreating back,

"Nahh, I was just thinking about crawling in with you, Little Sister."

"Nate," Sherri said looking up.

Reverend Richards harrumphed.

Gracie giggled and ran the last few feet up the stairs. "You'd better not. You wouldn't want to make Amber jealous." They heard a door close and knew she was in her room.

Nate turned and purposely avoided looking at Amber. "So, Dad, you were saying about tomorrow's sermon."

Sherri exchanged glances with Amber, and they smiled knowingly at each other.

"What? You planning on skipping church and getting the Reader's Digest version tonight?" Reverend Richards said with a chuckle in his voice.

Nate fumbled for words, and this time he did look at Amber. He could feel himself losing himself in her gaze. With one penetrating look into her eyes, all his long buried feelings came back on him in a rush. He placed his half-filled cup on the table and stood. "I…ah, I'd better check in with Mac. He had to…ah, cover a meeting for me so I could stop by here. Excuse me." He walked with quick steps into the kitchen and leaned his forehead against the cool surface of the stainless steel refrigerator.

Reverend Richards lowered the newspaper he'd begun to read and looked askance at his son while Amber and Sherri shared another knowing look. Reverend Richards peered at his wife then at Amber and shook his head. "Poor boy," he muttered as he lifted the paper hiding his face.

162

CHAPTER TWENTY

THANKSGIVING MORNING ARRIVED covered in wet snow. Outside, tree limbs and power lines wore a fine dress of silver gossamer. The wind swept through the valley in mournful wails and inside his small bedroom Tim Jackson paced, his face and body covered with a fine patina of sweat.

"I know, I know," he said into the empty room. "I've tried. I will stop her." He jerked his face to the side as if his attention had been suddenly drawn that way. He turned to face his unseen guest. "I'm sorry. I'm so sorry, but that cop…he came just as I was fix'n to do it."

He snapped around facing the opposite direction. "No, *sir*, I'm not making excuses."

He whipped back the other direction and taking two quick steps, dropped to his knees. "No, please don't…. I will do it! I will do it! Just give me one more chance. I won't let you down. This time she will pay for her sins. Like Gideon, I will be your sword of vengeance."

Tim bowed his head to the floor, a beatific smile on his face. "Thank you, my *Lord*. Thank you."

"Tim," the gravelly voice of an older woman called from downstairs. "Tim," she called again.

Hurriedly, Tim rose, opened his bedroom door, and stuck his head out. "Yes, Mother."

"You come on down here. Breakfast is on the table and it's time to eat," his mother said.

Tim knew his mother, Clara, thought the world of him. Of all her children, he had been the one to return to her, to care for her. After all, he had suffered as a child in this house; this finally proved that he was the good son.

As Tim came down the stairs into the kitchen, the odor of homemade pancakes, fresh scrambled eggs, and fried pork sausage attacked his senses. A cup of hot black coffee sat beside the overfilled plate and beside that stood Clara, squeezing the remains of an orange into a glass.

Upon seeing him, she straightened her aged frame and shuffle-stepped across the worn linoleum floor, her feet snug in a pair of faded fuzzy slippers. Making her way with careful arthritic steps, she brought her son the glass of fresh squeezed juice. "Happy Thanksgiving, Son," she said as he leaned forward accepting her kiss on his cheek.

"Happy Thanksgiving, Mother, but you didn't have to do all this. Toast and coffee would have been just fine." He walked over and sat at the head of the small table. Despite his comments, Tim attacked the plate with a fury. His mother stood behind, watching him as he emptied the plate and drained several cups of coffee. He looked up from eating and saw his mother's smile, full of pride as if he had been a three-year-old finishing his plate of veggies.

Finished, Tim pushed back from the table and stood. His mother quickly, as quickly as she could in her shuffling gait, cleared the table and began to wash the dishes at the sink. He watched her work and took pride in her feeling encouraged by her example of faithfulness to duty. If she could do her job—

fulfill her *duty,* in spite of her age-weakened body, he knew he could do what it was his *Lord* had demanded of him. He would do his job today. Today, judgment would find Crystal Johansson.

***

Nate awoke to the beeping of his cell phone. The phone hadn't rang, but sent the caller directly to voicemail. Rubbing sleep from his eyes, he swung his legs over the edge of his bed and felt the shock of the cold floor against bare feet. He hoped he hadn't missed a callout.

He stretched and looked at the digital clock on the nightstand next to his bed, 6:30 a.m.; his Bible still lay open to the passage he read the night before. *My one day to sleep in.* Nate grunted and stood.

He reached for the cell phone, but gazed back at the Bible before dragging it toward him. "Proverbs 16: 1-9," he mumbled the text under his breath. Opening the cover on the cell phone, he read the number and his breath caught in his throat.

"Jackie. I forgot all about her." He rubbed his face again, sighed, and hefted himself out of bed.

Grabbing his Bible, Nate walked to the kitchen and started a pot of coffee. He thought of the women in his life, Jackie, and now again Amber and even the possibility of Julie. Closing his eyes, he allowed the wall to support him, the heaviness of sleep still pulling at him.

The smell of fresh brewed coffee quickly filled the small space and drew his attention back to the kitchen. After a few minutes of contemplation, he filled a cup for himself. Sitting at the small table, he opened the worn leather cover of the Bible again to the passage in Proverbs and placed it on the table before him. He traced the lines of text as he read silently, moving his lips as did; the onionskin paper moved like a wake along with his finger. Stopping at verse nine and tilting his head back, Nate closed his eyes and spoke into the silence of the apartment, "'In his heart a man plans his course, but the LORD determines his steps.'"

He wandered over to the window and, using the palm of his hand, wiped the film of condensation from the pane, feeling cool dampness against his skin. "If ever I needed direction, Lord, it's now," he whispered against the glass.

The phone rang again and Nate started at the sound. With leaden legs, he walked back into the bedroom and sat on the edge of the bed. He looked at the caller I.D. and this time his heart tightened. He took a breath and composed himself. "Amber, good morning," he forced cheer into his voice.

"Nate." She sounded hesitant.

Nate swallowed and adjusted the phone against his face. He looked back at his Bible and reiterated his prayer for direction.

"Hey girl, happy Thanksgiving."

"Ah...happy Thanksgiving. You're going to the worship service, right?" She didn't give him a chance to answer. "Can we meet first...I mean before we go to church? We need to talk."

He smiled at her directness; it was one of the things he loved most about her. He looked at the clock again, 6:39 a.m. "How about the Denny's on Fairview in about twenty. We can make a breakfast of it." He could hear the smile in her voice.

"Okay, see you there."

She hung up.

Nate looked at the cell phone in his hand then flipped it closed and again rubbed his face. *Should've known she'd be dressed and ready before she placed that call.* He couldn't help the thrill that coursed through him; he was going to see Amber, alone.

***

They sat in the same booth they had been in almost two years ago when Nate received the call of the Franks' shooting. He looked across the table, and though she looked the same, she somehow seemed older, more mature. He wondered if he looked different to her. With deliberate action, she stirred her fourth packet of Splenda into her coffee before stacking the empty packets in a neat pile beside her cup.

Finally, she looked up. Nate's breath caught in his throat. He attempted to cover it by pretending to cough, putting his fist to his mouth and taking a quick sip of coffee. *Man, she's beautiful.*

Placing the spoon on the saucer beside the cup, Amber stared at him. "Nate, I missed you."

His eyes narrowed slightly. "You got a funny way of showing it." That had not come out the way he'd wanted, but nonetheless, there it was. He'd said it.

She dropped her gaze for a moment and then looked back up at him. "I guess I had that coming."

The silence hung heavy between them for a long moment.

Amber took a shallow sip from her cup, sat it down, then picked it up, and drank again. "Nate," she said finally.

He locked eyes with her and all the anger, frustration, and confusion he'd carried for the last few months simmered just beneath the surface of his control. "Can you at least tell me why?"

"Well…"

He leaned forward in the booth. "You let me go on and on about how much I loved you and how I wanted to spend my life with you. You could have stopped me at any time before I made such a fool out of myself."

"But—"

"And then…" he continued, "and then like a cross-eyed junior high kid, I write and write, pouring out my feelings, and you didn't even have the decency to tell me to stop."

He leaned back, his hands thrust forward on the table. "You're no different than—"

She slammed both palms onto the table causing the silverware to bounce and dance across the laminate surface.

Nate had begun to compare Amber with his ex-fiancée, Patricia, before she stopped him. After a year's engagement, Patricia had left Nate a letter breaking the engagement and informing him that she no longer loved him, that she'd fallen in love with another man. Afterwards, Nate had allowed himself to sink into a deep depression, one from which he almost hadn't recovered, saved by the grace of God and Amber's friendship.

He leaned forward resting both elbows on the table and cradling his face in his hands. "I'm sorry." His voice was just above a whisper. "That…that was uncalled for, and unfair." He leaned back and sighed.

After a short while, he braved a smile.

Amber was leaning forward and reaching out to touch one of his elbows with her fingertips. "Come on, we used to be friends. Can we at least start there?"

He looked up and saw something in her expression he couldn't describe. *What was the look in her eyes?* He couldn't define it. Shaking his head, he raised his cup in salute. "To being friends."

"To friends," she echoed unenthusiastically. Nate watched her reaction and knew her well enough to know she hated herself for being the cause of his pain. "I hear you're seeing someone," she said.

Nate dropped his cup spilling hot coffee across the surface of the table.

Grabbing handfuls of napkins, Amber began stacking them along the edge of the table, blocking the heated stream from pouring into her lap. Laughing, she looked up. "You gonna help or what?"

Jarred from inaction, Nate grabbed napkins as well, and began laying them around the table sopping up the coffee, but too late to save his pants. A steady stream, having first pooled, now poured over the edge and onto his legs.

Amber giggled. "Try explaining that one to Old Lady Jennifer when you walk into the sanctuary this morning. She won't be able to wait until after church so she can 'share' it with the rest of the ladies in her prayer circle."

Nate heard Amber's jesting, but he was still stuck on what she'd said "seeing someone" and found it hard to follow the flow of her conversation after that. "Wha-what did you say?" His voice sounded feeble, even to him.

Stacking the coffee sodden paper wads onto her emptied plate, Amber smiled at him, the corner of her brow arching mischievously. "Was it supposed to be a secret?"

"Ummm, no," Nate stammered. "Of course not. I mean, I went on one date…to the Olive Garden."

"Oh, my favorite restaurant. What did you have?"

"Well, I had the…. Wait I'm not doing this. Who told you, anyway, and what about you? You were gone a long time; did you go out with anyone?"

"A couple different guys, but nothing special," she said matter-of-factly.

Nate was taken aback by her bluntness. He suspected she had dated, but hearing her say it so plainly felt weird at best.

She drank from her coffee. "How many different girls have you taken out," she asked, looking at him through the wafting veil of steam.

Nate looked into her eyes making sure he had her attention before answering. "One. Last week."

"Oh."

***

From the far corner of the dining room, Tim Jackson watched as Nate and Amber talked. He refilled his coffee cup from the bronze and black decanter left on his table and smiled. "With that detective off today with his girlfriend, Lord, that Johansson woman should be unwatched." He smiled as he swallowed, his lips moving in quiet whispers in concert with his prayers.

Jackson rubbed his hand across his chin and smiled again, holding his head to one side as if listening intently. "Yes, yes, I can do that," he said softly.

When the waitress happened back by his table, Tim pretended to be reading the newspaper lying open on the table. He giggled when the woman walked by, exchanging his almost empty coffee decanter for a fresh one.

Tim looked up. "Just like your Bible says, Lord, even before I could pray, you done already answered me. First, you let me see that detective so I know where he is, letting me know that today is your chosen day; and then you made that woman bring me more coffee. I can see that I have your favor, Lord. I won't disappoint you. Judgment will fall today and we will all have one more thing to be thankful for." His eyes danced around the restaurant in furtive bounces watching everyone's comings and goings.

"What about that other one, Lord, the partner? Should I still do it today or is he watching her?" Jackson's brows knitted together as he lowered his gaze, resting his mouth against his knuckle. Biting and pulling at his knuckle with coffee stained front teeth, Jackson's voice took on a pleading sound. "Please God, give me a sign. What should I do?"

Across the room, the lady sitting with the detective slapped the tabletop. Her spoon jumped in the air and careened around her plate. "Nathaniel Richards!" she'd almost screamed at him.

"Yes," Jackson said in the same whispered voice, "that was what he said his name was, Richards, and his partner was Mac something or other."

Jackson picked up the paper, deciding that the Lord had spoken to him through that couple. He watched, listened, and continued to pray. "Is this the day your judgment gets poured out, Lord, or should I wait for another?" He spoke the same words like a mantra, over and over, his lips moving in nervous repetition. Occasionally, he flipped a page of the paper to keep up the appearance of reading.

Jackson swallowed, his throat feeling dry. He looked around the interior of the restaurant before shutting his eyes tightly against the distractions. He concentrated listening for the voice. Beginning to worry that the voice of his God had abandoned him, he redoubled his efforts, praying faster and faster. "Is this the day? Is this the day? Is this the day your wrath gets poured out? Is this the—"

A commotion from the table drew his attention again. Looking up, Jackson watched as hot coffee poured off the edge of the table and into the lap of the police detective. The officer managed to stifle a small yelp, but Jackson knew the man had felt the heat of the coffee on his sensitive skin, and he also had his answer.

Jackson waved the waitress back to his table, and smiling broadly, he ordered the giant cinnamon roll.

The forty-something woman pulled a pen from her apron pocket marking his order on a small pad. "You want that heated, sweetie?"

"Yes, as matter of fact I do…and add some extra icing on that, and I'll make it worth your effort."

"You got it, sweetie." The woman turned and headed toward the kitchen. "One roll heated extra icing." She slammed her hand against a small chrome colored bell and clipped the paper to a wheel mounted from the ceiling of the small pass-through window separating the dining room from the kitchen. She gave the wheel a soft spin sending the order through the window where the cook pulled it from the clip.

"Yes, indeed," Jackson said, "some things are better when served hot."

CHAPTER TWENTY-ONE

MARY HIGGINS ROLLED OVER in bed and stared at the alarm clock. Next to it laid the still loaded handgun. Without lifting her head from the flattened pillow, she reached out and stroked the cold metal. She wrapped her fingers around the barrel and then cradled it against her breast.

She hadn't slept well and could feel the pull of fatigue heavy upon her like a leaded coat. She sighed and poked absentmindedly at her scar. Without warning, the memories crashed in on her like wave after incessant wave. She gasped and tried to sit up but felt weak. She struggled. She couldn't breathe.

Mary could feel *his* hands again, searching, seizing, pulling, possessive hands. The shadow loomed over her. She refused to see his face; she couldn't bear to look at it. She had begged, but her cries had gone unheeded, discarded. She had jumped, had attempted to scoot away. The light reflected from the blade; it seemed to sparkle in the shaft of moonlight that streamed through her window. Out of the corner of her eye, situated around the room, she had seen pictures of happier times, smiles and laughter. She had known joy then.

Mary fell from the bed, striking her face against the floor, breaking her free from the memory. Tangling herself in the twist of sweat-soaked bedding, she buried her face in her hands. Heavy sobs shook her shoulders, and her silent wails filled her chest. When she could contain them no longer, they escaped in an anguished cry.

The gun slid from the bed and hit the floor with a dull clunk. Mary turned her head in a precise movement until all she could see was the dark, hollow tunnel of the upturned barrel. With trembling hands, she picked up the gun and held it against her face. Hot tears brushed against cold steel before falling against her arms, chest, and thighs.

She fingered the scar tracing it with the pad of her index finger. From just above her ear near the temple to just below the curve of her cheekbone, the dull welt rose above the smooth skin.

Taking a deep cleansing breath, Mary sat up. She combed tear-wetted strands back from her face with her fingers. With determination, she looked at the gun in the curve of her hand…and smiled.

Lifting it to her cheek, she looked down the length of the barrel and saw the chambered hollow-point round; it sat ready in the tube stacked atop others waiting their turn to be discharged. She rubbed the scar one last time and took another cleansing breath. She strolled into the bathroom and closed the door behind her.

***

Crystal Johansson walked from her shower into the kitchen, the plush chenille shawl robe wrapped loosely around her lithe muscular body. Steeping a cup of tea, she stared out the back window overlooking the lake and the golf course beyond. The sun was beginning its trek across the crisp autumn morning. It was Thanksgiving and she was still alive. She decided to do something she hadn't done since before her big mistake—go to church. She strode back to her bedroom.

CHAPTER TWENTY-TWO

CRYSTAL NOTICED JULIE PACING. Already dressed, Julie wore a soft green pants suit, the causal jacket covering a slight bulge at her hip. Pulling the soft collar of her robe close around her neck, Crystal slipped her feet into silk slippers of the same muted gold as her robe and sat before the vanity mirror. She dried and brushed her hair.

Taking time to paint her nails and repair the coat on her toenails, she pondered how to bring up the topic of church with Julie. Standing in front of the floor to ceiling mirrored door of her closet, she thought about what to wear. *Considering your face has been all over TV as the woman who had sex with a 15 year-old boy, you had better wear something conservative.*

"Having trouble deciding what to wear?" Julie stood just inside the doorway.

Startled, Crystal whipped around and then giggled releasing nervous energy. "I guess I'm a little stuck."

Julie looked at her but didn't answer.

"I, ahh…was thinking about…well I thought I'd go to church, this being Thanksgiving and all."

Julie dipped her chin and turned to leave the room. Stopping, she looked back. "I'd go with something conservative.... The situation being what it is."

"Thanks." Crystal swung back to her closet and pulled out a navy-blue skirt outfit. Next, she selected a cream-colored blouse and gold accented earrings and necklace. She held the ensemble up to her chin. Liking what she saw, she choose a pair of cream-color shoes with a similar gold toe-trim and buckles to finish the look. She laid the items across the foot of her bed and left the bedroom to get a cup of tea.

She came into the kitchen just as Julie slammed the magazine into the handle of the Glock 27 .40 caliber handgun. Racking the slide, she seated the first round into the chamber.

Crystal froze, her eyes focused on the pistol. After several seconds, her mouth dropped open but no words came out.

"Strange people go to church," Julie said, answering the unasked question she read in Crystal's face and then slid the gun into the holster now at the small of her back.

Crystal smiled and nodded her head. She found her voice. "Coffee?"

"Sure." Julie sat at the counter with her back to the hall leading to the bedrooms and hallway bathroom.

"The table's more comfortable. I got those stools to accent the decor. I never use them." Crystal buzzed around the well-appointed kitchen. She placed a fine porcelain cup and saucer trimmed in hand painted silver edging at the small table. Lifting the matching coffee carafe, she poured the coffee then folded silverware into a cloth napkin and placed it and the creamer at the seat. "You take sugar?"

"I'll sit here if you don't mind," Julie said not unkind.

Crystal felt her face turning red as the old feelings she'd worked so hard to be free of returned. "Don't want it said you shared breakfast with a child molester, huh?"

Having collected the cup and perched on the bar stool, Julie froze in mid drink, her arm bent at the elbow. She looked over the rim of the cup at Crystal.

Crystal's back was to Julie. She leaned on the granite countertop for support. "No one ever asks me what happened. You just assume that I seduced some kid and had my way with him. I'm tired of it. I get so tired of being judged all the time. Assumed on." She turned and looked at Julie who was now finishing her coffee, her face a neutral mask.

Crystal sighed and sank into one of the chairs situating her back toward the kitchen interior. She began talking as if to herself. "I'd been married for five years. I married my high school sweetheart, Ric. It wasn't long after we were married that he started beating me. It wasn't bad at first, just a slap or a push, but soon it grew worse." She looked up at Julie who was still drinking her coffee.

Crystal released a cheerless chuckle and continued talking. "He beat me. One day after a beating, he began to choke me, and I knew this time he was going to kill me. I lay there no longer fighting just waiting to pass out, expecting to die. The next thing I knew, I woke up in a hospital E.R. with a sore throat and a police officer asking me if I wanted to file charges.

The next few weeks were a blur. He eventually went to prison for domestic violence, strangulation, and a number of other charges I knew nothing about." She shifted in her seat and took a drink from her own cup, hardly tasting it, before glancing at Julie who had put her mug down and sat listening.

Crystal ran a hand through her almost white, blond hair and then propped her forehead against her open palm. The fawn-colored tips of the French manicured nails rested against her forehead. "I was depressed for a long time after that and on meds. I rarely left my house. I didn't know who I was anymore. My Ex, Ric…actually Richard, had defined me ever since I was sixteen. He had become my world. All of a sudden, I was alone in a new city with no family. No friends. No nothing. He had made sure I never met anybody.

"There was this one kid he had hired to do the yard work and other small jobs around the trailer where we lived. He was the first, the only person I'd met out here. We began to talk, and one day the talking led to listening and the listening to holding hands. Then one day I kissed him."

Crystal sighed and then lowered her voice. She stared into her cup as she spoke. "The kissing…well, the kissing went too far. Afterwards, I knew what I'd done was terrible, and I told him he could never come back. That made him mad. He was confused. I was too, I guess. He must have felt like I had used him. Maybe he was right…." She stood and walked to the sink dumping her tea down the drain. "I don't know. Well…he told his mom and that's how I got my name on the killer's list." She sighed and ran a hand through her hair.

She turned and gazed at Julie. "It was one time. One stupid mistake, and now my life is all screwed up because of it. So I would appreciate it if you would cut me a little slack, please." She felt drained. She slumped against the counter with her hands on its edge holding her.

Silence hung between them. And in that silence, awareness dawned. Crystal began to feel just the smallest portion of the burden lift. In that moment, she realized that it had felt good to confess what she'd done even if it was only to this strange and silent confessor.

With her eyes fixed on Crystal, Julie lifted her cup to her lips and finding it empty stood up and retrieved the coffeepot from the counter for a refill. After taking her seat again and enjoying the first swallow, she looked at Crystal. "I'm glad you got that off your chest, but I already knew that. It's covered in the case brief. But you need to know I'm sitting here," she indicated the stool, "because I don't want my back to the windows. Can't watch out for you like that. Can't see what's going on outside."

Julie looked at the clock on the wall and then compared the information against her wristwatch. Finishing her coffee, she rose quickly to put the cup in the sink. "I'm going to get the car ready." She paused in the doorway and looked back at the other woman. "Did you have a particular church in mind?"

"No. Not really...I just felt like going to church, it being Thanksgiving. Do you know a good one?"

Julie smiled. "Yeah, I got one that I think you'll like. You'd better finish getting dressed or this town will have a heck of a lot more to talk about than what you did ten years ago." She smiled and walked out of the room, going out the newly replaced sliding glass door.

Crystal dropped her forehead onto her crossed arms on the countertop with a dull thud. She groaned into the cavern formed by her arms. "Great. That was just great. I go and make a complete fool of myself in front of the only person who hasn't either tried to shoot me or take me to bed in the last two weeks. I think from now on I'll leave the confessing up to the church people. They're better at it."

***

Twenty minutes after going into the shower, Mary came out of the bathroom, all traces of the morning's horror gone. She stood before the mirror brushing her hair and checking her makeup. She smiled at her reflection. "If this is going to be the day of confrontation then you'll want to look your best."

Dressed, she headed to the kitchen determined to have a simple breakfast. She wouldn't need much; indeed her stomach wouldn't tolerate it. She splayed her hand across her stomach and, reaching out with her other hand, caught herself as a wave of nausea swept through her. Taking a breath she steadied herself, determined to go through with her plan.

She sat at the small table in the simple kitchen-dining room area and opened the phonebook to the yellow pages. She flipped until she came to the section separated by the capital C resting above a black bar. She slid her left index finger down the column of names as she chewed the nail of her right index finger. As if noticing for the first time, she pulled her hand from her mouth and inspected her nails. The cuticles were dry and cracked and had bled during the night. She rubbed dry hands together and vowed to do something about them if she still had the opportunity once this was all over. But for now, a simple coat of polish would have to do. She headed back into the bathroom.

***

Mary started her car and hurried back inside to finish getting dressed. Quietness overcame her; a peace she hadn't known in years. She watched through the large front window as frost and ice melted from the windshield. Mary sensed a newness in her spirit; she had reached a point of resolve. For the first time since she'd moved back into this valley, it felt as if she'd made the right decision.

She smiled to herself and picked up her purse feeling the now familiar weight in it. She pressed its heaviness against her stomach as she rolled away from the window and leaned back against the front door. The cold penetrated the wood and leached the warmth from her, sending a slight shiver down her spine. Looking up, her eyes settled on the framed copy of the school's faculty and teaching staff. Smiling at the image of her new friends and the memories of the students she'd met this year, she sighed. She smiled and brushed away bitter tears.

***

Jackie sat on the edge of her bed and looked at the cell phone in her hand. It had been over two hours, and Nate still hadn't returned her call. Laying the phone on the small table beside her bed, she pressed it away from her and with deliberate motion, stood. Looking over her shoulder at the phone, she meandered to the bedroom window and gazed unseeing at the frost-covered landscape. Silvers, crystalline whites, and pale morning blues sparkled in the early morning sunlight contrasting against the grays and muted browns of the winter backdrop. With a finger, she drew lazy circles in the windowpane before sighing deeply and heading for the shower.

Standing in the hot water, the stream cascading over her shoulders, Jackie ran her fingers through long brown tresses combing out the tangles. Kneading the bath sponge between her hands, she stood lost in thought as the soap lathered, foamed and spilled to the shower floor. "Well girl," she said into the water, "you knew the man came with issues and now that Amber's back in town...." She let the sentence hang as she began to wash with absentminded strokes.

Lifting and soaping her arm, Jackie continued her monologue, "Well, she's the one who's been gone for almost two years, and you're the one that's been here. That's got to count for something. Doesn't it?" She rinsed.

Raising the other arm she continued, "And you haven't been pushy...you gave him room to think; time to consider what it was he really wanted." She turned and dropped the sponge. Grabbing her face, she cringed. "What if I gave him too much space? What if he thinks I'm not really interested?" She leaned against the wall, the cool tile goose-pimpling the flesh of her back, and let the water wash over her. Then remembering the kiss, she touched her lips with gentle pressure. Heaving herself off the wall, she slammed the faucet closed, shutting off the water. "Well, I'm not giving up that easy. I'm going to church."

Drying off as she went, Jackie walked with determined purpose to the closet in her bedroom. Pushing aside one outfit after another, she settled on a rust colored dress that fell just below her knees and snuggled in at her waist showing off her curves. She chose a waist cut black jacket with coordinating purse and heels as well. With the decision of what to wear made, she began the process of taming wild brown curls and putting on her make-up.

Finished, she stood in front of her mirror and smiled. *Today is Thanksgiving after all.*

***

Nate grabbed the check from the gray-haired waitress as she approached the table. "It's the least I can do after the mess I made," he said to the older woman.

"Makes no never mind to me, honey. But if you want to give me something to be thankful for, do it with the tip." She laughed making the comment fit in the air of cordial banter.

"You got it," Nate said, leaning back into the cushion of the cloth-covered booth.

"Hey, I invited you to breakfast," Amber said, reaching for the ticket.

"Don't fight over me, sweetheart, you can both leave me a tip," the older woman said, as she turned to leave having collected the last of the dishes from the table.

They both looked at her retreating back as she sashayed down the aisle toward the kitchen. "She's so proud of herself," Nate said.

"She thinks she's cute."

"Well, she is, in a sassy grandmother kind of way."

They both laughed. "Still though," Amber said, reaching for the check again.

Nate stood and placed a ten-dollar bill on the table. "Not gonna happen. If you want to pay for something, leave the sassy grandma a worthy tip."

Amber laughed and pulled a ten-spot out of her wallet and covered Nate's. "I can't let you outdo me." She smiled and slid toward the edge of the booth accepting his hand as he offered it. She held his hand a moment before continuing her slide. She paused, enjoying the warmth and the strength she felt in his grasp.

"You know, Nathaniel Richards, you can be quite charming when you want to be."

Their gazes held, then Nate looked away. "You're not going to make this easy are you?"

She smiled and bore into his gaze. "Not a bit."

***

As Amber drove out of the parking lot, Nate watched opened mouthed and then dropped his forehead against the steering wheel. "Lord, what am I going to do...? Oh no, I forgot about Jackie!" Grabbing his cell phone from his breast pocket, Nate dialed the number from memory.

The phone began to ring as Nate maneuvered his Jeep one handed out of the parking lot and into the westbound traffic on Fairview Road. Nate pressed the gas pedal and the rear wheels spun in place, melting a hole in the thin sheet of ice that had formed at the roadside. The tires caught, and with a lurch, the Jeep leapt forward causing the rear end to swing around, sending the vehicle into a tailspin.

Dropping the phone, Nate spun the steering wheel, turning the wheels into the direction of the spin and brought the nose of the car back into the lane. Just as he crossed the lane dividing line, a mid-sized UPS delivery truck sped past, almost hitting the Jeep head-on. Instead, it sprayed the driver's side window with a wave of dirty slush and sand. Although Nate couldn't hear the other driver's words, when he saw the man's lips moving, he reasoned that the man wasn't wishing him a happy Thanksgiving.

"Hello?" A voice said from somewhere down near his feet.

Nate looked out at the lines of traffic making sure the lanes were clear, then with careful motion, reached down, raked the dropped cell phone toward him with his fingers, and with effort, finally picked it up. "Hey there," he said, steering his car away from the center-lane and back into his own.

"What are you doing? It sounds like you're wrestling or something." It was Jackie. Her voice sounded pleased and somewhat confused.

***

From inside the restaurant, Tim watched as Nate pulled from the parking lot while talking on his phone. He took notice as the woman Nate had met with drove off in the opposite direction, and shook his head. He smiled. Thanksgiving was taking on a whole new meaning for him.

***

The music began to fade, and Reverend Richards stood up from his seat behind the podium. In his 35th year as a pastor, Reverend Richards had seen and experienced almost every kind of church service imaginable. From the wild and enthusiastic, to the quiet and cerebral, to the "I'm so excited. I don't know whether I'm coming or going" type of services. He'd seen them all. But so far this morning's service was having a totally different kind of feel to it.

Standing behind the lectern, he looked again at his notes and then back up to the congregation. He whispered a prayer careful not to speak into the lapel microphone. He had chosen for his text that morning, Colossians 3:17…. "And whatsoever ye do in word or deed, do all in the name of the Lord Jesus, giving thanks to God and the Father by Him." He inhaled slowly, but he couldn't find the peace to proceed.

He lifted his face toward the congregation again and this time spoke with a clear voice. "Happy Thanksgiving."

The congregation responded sending a warm wave of greeting to him, and then at the pastor's prompting stood and began to greet one another. Reverend Richards sunk back into his seat, partially hidden from the view of the milling people, and put his face into his hands and prayed.

As was the custom, the worship band began to play signaling to the congregation that it was time for them to take their seats. The music swelled, and the choir sang. In a soft mellow voice, it sounded as if only one person sang, instead of the near eighty voices paneled behind the pulpit. The choir sang, "Be Grateful". The first word, "be" was stretched and pulled like a wave rolling lazily onto shore. In short, staccato bursts, the choir sang the word grateful with breathy intensity.

***

Nate came in through the rear doors and sat in an empty seat near the end of the row of folding chairs. He was surprised to see the sanctuary so full. The choir continued to sing, and he sang along, the words familiar to him. He saw his mother glance back at him from her seat near the front of the church and smile. Both Amber and Gracie sat beside her; neither of them turned to look his direction.

Just then, the doors opened again, and Nate watched Jackie walk into the church and, at a careful pace, proceed up the center aisle. She stopped and sat on the opposite side of the church from Nate, about six rows ahead of him. He noticed that both

Amber and Gracie turned, and for the briefest of moments, the three women seemed to focus on each other. The music stopped.

Reverend Richards stood again, his arms spread out to his sides, the sleeves of his robe hanging loosely from his wrists. His baritone voice filled the auditorium. "Let us pray."

At the end of the prayer, Reverend Richards held up a small sheaf of papers and shook them. "Do you know what this is?" he asked the congregation.

From the congregation came a small chorus of "No sirs," and "No's" and "Tell us preacher."

Nate looked around, smiled, and settled back. He could feel that his father was moving into the zone, the place where he felt that he could speak with absolute authority from heaven. His father had told him that although anytime he taught from the Bible, it was indeed the Word of God, but there were special moments when he felt that he had received a unique message for a particular group of people at a particular time and place. Nate sensed that this was one of those times.

"Okay," Reverend Richards said, "I will tell you." He placed the papers onto the podium with dramatic flourish. "These papers represent the best of man's—" he lowered his face, took a breath, then looked back up, "...of my efforts."

The organist played a minor chord, and the congregation almost sighed with disappointment.

"But this morning my best just wasn't good enough. The Lord has something special for us this morning. The Lord has changed my plans for His plans. He took my feeble efforts and traded them for His excellence. Is that all right with you this morning?"

The voice of the Hammond B3 organ crescendoed and leapt with excitement as the congregation intoned back, and the preacher warmed to his topic.

"Open your Bibles this morning to John's Gospel, the eighth chapter; the third through eleventh verses." As the congregation turned the pages in their Bibles, Reverend Richards spoke to them about the woman who had been taken in adultery. He explained how the Pharisees, the religious leaders of their day, had caught her in the act. After pausing, he looked up at the congregation and said, "Yes…that means exactly what you think it does." He was rewarded with a spattering of knowing laughter.

He continued. "This morning I want to turn your attention to the seventh verse in particular. Do you see what the Lord said to the crowd? He said, 'let the one of you that is without sin be the first one to condemn this woman'." He held up the sheaf of papers again, his prepared sermon. "I studied…I prepared to teach you about being thankful; seemed like a good idea it being Thanksgiving and all. But, the Lord interrupted my plans. Looks like the Lord wants us to think about forgiveness instead."

"Amen."

"Say it, Preacher."

"All right now, Preacher."

The door at the rear of the church opened again, and Crystal Johansson walked in escorted by Julie. Nate smiled when he spotted the women, then dipped his chin as they walked toward him, Julie doing a quick scan of the room. They sat a couple of rows ahead of him, keeping their faces forward deliberately not looking around the auditorium.

Many in the congregation turned as the two women entered. Around the church, the comfortable laughter changed in segments, like lapping waves into subdued whispers as recognition settled and word passed from lip to ear.

Reverend Richards, not ignorant to the change nor of the tendency of some of his parishioners, raised the tone of his voice as he drew their attention away from their guest and back to the scripture text. "Now, there were many people in that crowd that morning that felt that they had a leg up on this poor soul," he said, allowing his voice to hang over their heads.

"They thought that they were nowhere near as bad—as evil as that poor woman who had been caught in bed with another woman's husband."

The congregation began to settle and, for that moment, forgot about the woman sitting just shy of center in the church. Through the windows set high in the walls to allow natural light, the muted haze of sun could be seen rising toward its zenith; but did little to break the hold that early winter had on the land. A lone bird soared overhead, circled once, and disappeared over the tops of the surrounding buildings.

Reverend Richards' voice rang out in singsong fashion pulling at the minds and emotions of the church members. "Now, that crowd knew they were in the right. They knew that this woman was evil, that she had done the unspeakable. They knew she was without value and deserved to die for her sins; after all, the Law said so."

"Amen."

"Say it, Preacher."

"You said the truth of it, Pastor." The congregation responded in rhythm with their pastor's words. Accentuating each phrase with their own hardy agreements and encouragements, the congregation's voices rose and fell in unison as the organist provided a background of rising and falling chords.

"But what they missed was the most important fact. This was the fact that Jesus brought to their attention." The congregation stirred, feeling that they were being set up for something. The organist played a quick loud burst that reverberated through the church and faded like an echo. Reverend Richards leaned an elbow on the podium and whispered into his lapel-mic. "You see, while they were sitting back on their blessed assurance, Jesus had stooped down and was writing on the ground with his finger.

"Yes, sir. Jesus just stooped down and scribbled in the dirt with His holy finger. Do you know what it was He wrote?"

The congregation was quiet now. Nate felt the tension. He saw that everyone sat a little forward in their seats, their eyes locked onto the preacher's face. But, in the middle of the congregation, he spied Crystal lowering her face. He guessed that she was afraid to look around, afraid that everyone saw her as the defrocked woman in the preacher's illustration. She half hid her face in her hand while shaking her head from side to side.

Nate imagined the thoughts going through the woman's mind, thoughts that she shouldn't have come, that *half these people probably wanted the killer to find her so he could finish what he started.* Spreading her fingers, she peeked up at the preacher.

Reverend Richards scanned the congregation, and grabbing hold of both sides of the podium, he leaned back as if preparing to launch himself into the audience. "Yes, sir," he said in a loud clear voice. He stopped, allowing the phrase to hang.

The silence built.

Crystal prepared for assault.

The congregation held its breath.

"Right there on His knees kneeling down in the dusty streets of Galilee, Jesus began to write in the dirt. He began to write down the sins of all the *good* people who were standing around getting ready to stone the adulterous woman. He began to list all their sins and the Bible tells us that one by one they all began to leave, starting from the oldest to the youngest." Reverend Richards halted again and took a breath.

He searched the faces of the crowd. "Who of you this morning could survive Jesus writing your sins on the ground for all the world to see?" he asked.

Nate looked around the congregation taking notice of the crestfallen faces. He saw many heads swing from side to side in involuntary agreement to the question. He thought about his own sins of pride and arrogance and his continual battle with lustful thoughts, and he too shook his head from side to side as well.

From the pulpit, Reverend Richards continued his sermon. "When all was said and done, Jesus looked up and he was alone with the woman; just Jesus and the woman who'd been caught in bed with another woman's husband. And now...like that woman, it's just you and Jesus in the acknowledgement of your sin. That's where God wants you this Thanksgiving morning. Are you ready to confront Jesus and the issue of your sin?"

***

Around her, the crowd seemed to have disappeared. Crystal looked up and the eyes of the preacher seemed to burn into hers. She swallowed, closed her eyes, and when she looked up again, everything had returned to normal. She stood and stepped out into the aisle, her legs felt unstable. The next moment, Julie was at her side. "You okay?" she asked in a whisper.

Crystal didn't respond, but instead, glanced back at Nate a few rows behind her. Looking back to the preacher, she steadied herself, determined to make a stand.

"You all right?" Julie whispered again, too low for anyone else to hear.

She turned and looked at her. "No. No, I'm not all right. Not at all." Down near the front of the auditorium, Sherri, along with Amber and Gracie, also turned and looked back at her, their faces concerned and full of consternation.

CHAPTER TWENTY-THREE

TIM JACKSON SAT in his darkened bedroom fighting vertigo. The floor swam beneath him, and the walls tilted toward him before falling violently away. His stomach churned and sweat ran into his eyes, forcing him to shut them. Stretching out his hands to the wall, he attempted to steady himself but fell to his knees despite his efforts.

Collapsing to the floor and curling into a fetal position, Tim fought against the voices' mocking laughter. The slurred words of the drunken men accented their equally vile actions. His mother's pleas for them to stop served only as encouragement, ricocheted invasively through his mind despite the years. He could feel rough hands pulling at him, covering his mouth, forcing him to watch. The burning pain seared him yet again. The sickening sweet odors of sweat and alcohol assailed his nostrils as if it was happening again. He screamed.

Time passed.

Moments later, a cool wet cloth pressed against his forehead compelled the memory to retreat. The present returned. His mother sat on the floor beside him, cooing as she did when he was a small child. "It's all right, honey. Mommy's here. It's all right." With his head in her lap, she rocked back and forth. The wrinkled skin of her eyelids folded softly as she closed them. Opening cloudy gray eyes, she focused on the warm moist face of her son.

His mind cleared and the memories faded. Tim sat up with renewed determination. His shirt clung to his chest, arms, and back. His muscles ached as if he'd been in a fight. He focused on his mother's kind face, and for a moment, he saw the bruises and swelling that had once been the norm. Like the face of a plastic doll melting, but in reverse, the many welts and contusions faded into age spots and wrinkles.

"It's okay," she said again. She rubbed his face and ran her fingers through his thinning hair. "Momma's here and he's gone. Him and your uncles, they're all gone. You got rid of them. They can't hurt us anymore."

"Wha-what time is it?" He stammered; his throat dry.

"It's almost dinnertime."

He got to his feet and then lifted his mother, helping her to stand. "The whole day is almost gone. I've wasted the day...." He rubbed his hands over his face, massaging and tugging at his lips with nervous fingers.

"It's okay, baby. Come on, let me fix you a plate and then you can think better. You know those fits always leave you tired." She took his arm, pulling his hands from his face. "Com'on."

He allowed her to lead him downstairs to the small dining room table. The fragrance of roasted turkey, pumpkin pie, and fresh cooked veggies filled the room. A dish of peas, a platter of herb potatoes, and a tray of kernelled corn, a saucer of cranberry sauce, and basket of hot rolls garnished the table.

"Now, sit down and eat something, sweetie, you'll feel better afterwards."

"But, Mom, I still have to finish my work. The Lord—"

She seemed not to hear him. "It's Thanksgiving, baby, and you deserve a day off too. Nobody takes as good of care of that school as my baby…and they know that. So you don't have to worry. They'll hold your job, even if you do take today off. Seems they ought to give you Thanksgiving Day off anyway." She set an empty plate in front of him and began spooning homemade cornbread stuffing onto it.

Tim sighed and studied the vacant expression on his mother's face. He was sure she didn't know what year it was. If not for Thanksgiving, he doubted she would notice the passage of time at all. He caressed her wrinkled face and smiled at her. "I'm going to stop them, Mom."

"Yes, dear," she said.

"I won't let them hurt you anymore. Not ever again." He pushed up from his seat and kissed her cheek. She covered his kiss with her gnarled fingers before continuing to load his plate. He watched as she walked away, as always, refusing to sit at the table with him.

He watched her shuffle back to her small stool beside the stove, and the anger raced through him again. With a rage-stiffened arm, he stabbed with his fork and sawed with his knife the thick slice of turkey breast on his plate. "This is all your fault," he muttered through gritted teeth. "I hate you! I hate you!" He pressed both hands over his ears, his face locked in a pain-induced grimace, as if assaulted by a very loud noise.

The voices returned.

Tim rose from the table and stumbled toward the small window, his hands still pressed against the sides of his head.

You're just like your no good mother. The first voice said and began to curse and swear. The voices attacked him, pressing in on him like a weight.

Nah, he's worse.

At least she has some value.

The *voices* merged into a cacophony of angry laughter, hateful, mocking, chilling, scornful. Their hot breath seared his face and neck. Rough hands jerked him, tearing his skin, forcing him to watch. Tears from the past welled in his eyes, leaking onto the windowpane and adhering to the frigid glass.

Then *the voice* spoke. Like a tower rising out of the fog, it rose above its companions until the rest faded almost to silence. *You have failed me.*

He dropped to the floor. "No," Tim grunted. "I have not failed you." He rolled to his back, scooted to the corner, and pressed his shoulder blades against the wall. "I just need a little more time."

You have failed me. You have failed her. You are a failure! You are nothing to me!

"Please, don't leave me. Don't reject me. Please. I got the other two...the brothers. They've been judged. That has to count. They have to count." Desperate, he could feel the *voice* retreating.

A heavy silence gripped his mind then the *voice* spoke again. *I will give you one more chance. But, if you fail me...I will release them!*

Tim forced his eyes open, but could still see them all standing, like shadows ready to reclaim him as they had always been. Cold, distant, condemning, they skulked, scrutinizing him. Lust and hate radiating from their eyes. Tim knew that *he*, The Voice, was the only reason the rest didn't attack and destroy him now. Without speaking, the delusion of his father walked away.

Like a fog fading in the sun, the *voices* and *images* receded into the shadows. With great effort, Tim's breathing slowed to normal. He rubbed his eyes with the heels of his palms. When he opened them, he spotted the table. His plate remained untouched except for the knife piercing the slice of meat. Weary, he shuffled back, and dropped with a thud into his chair.

His hands, palms up, on either side of his plate, Tim sighed in resignation. Rounding his slumped shoulders, he looked toward the arched doorway. He knew his mother sat waiting for him to finish eating, still obedient to the years of training at the hands of her now deceased husband.

It had been at his father's hands that the abuse had come. First from his dad, and then from the men he had been told to call uncles. When they'd tired of abusing his mother, their appetites had turned to him. At first he had welcomed the attention, thinking that his father had finally noticed him, had begun to love him. But he soon came to know better. This type of attention had very little to do with him and everything to do with his father's and uncle's fiendish tastes.

His mother had fought them until she'd been beaten into submission, and in turn, he fought for her. But in the end, the men always won. Always. They were too strong. He was too small. But he had promised his mother, and himself, that one day they would pay. And they had. But now he had to stop the rest, the rest of the people like them. He had become the hands of God. He was the tool of God's wrath.

With renewed strength, he began to eat, savoring each bite, knowing his mother's hands had prepared it just for him. He smiled; soon they would be free from the past, the *voices* silenced, and his mother able to rest.

RAY ELLIS

CHAPTER TWENTY-FOUR

MARY DROVE with the loaded pistol in her purse as she worked up the resolve to enter the huge cathedral-like building. With its old world spires piercing the gray sky, Shepherd of The Valley Catholic Church extended across its nine-acre plot. The grounds with its quarried stone buildings resembled a castle dominating an English village or gothic shopping plaza rather than the urban religious site it was. With its varied structures set in eye pleasing geometric patterns around the manicured lawn, the property held its own against any of the valley's many golf courses.

Exhaling and resting her chin against the backs of her hands as they clung to the steering wheel, Mary looked over her knuckles at the gigantic engraved wooden doors that led to the main sanctuary. Even from the parking lot, she could hear the music and knew that the priest would soon be performing the Concluding Rite. She opened the car door and crossed the full parking lot dodging the piles of dirty snow.

Mary laughed and gazed at the graying sky. "One thing 'bout us Catholics…no matter what the weather, we do show up for the Eucharist." A gust of chilled wind swept across the open space and stung her cheeks. Folding her arms across her chest,

Mary massaged her upper arms against the cold. The purse hanging from her shoulder swung heavy at her side; the added weight of the gun created a solid thud against her ribs.

Mary sobered as she grabbed the closest ornate wrought iron handle and tugged the huge door, leaning back as she did, marveling at the ease of its movement.

The cavernous room glowed softly from the many candles set about around the room. Deeply carved stone pillars rose like stately oaks, their decorated arms spreading like branches against the arched ceiling above. The priest, a young man, stood with his arms lifted, palms facing the congregation, as if in blessing. "Bow your heads and pray for God's blessings. May the Lord bless you and keep you." The priest said in soft but solemn voice. The congregation answered in one voice, "Amen."

"May His face shine upon you, and be gracious to you."

"Amen."

"May he look upon you with kindness, and give you his peace."

"Amen."

"May almighty God bless you, the Father and the Son and the Holy Spirit."

"Amen."

With mass concluding, the priest smiled at his congregation with fatherly warmth that conflicted with his youthful appearance. "The Mass is ended, go now in peace to love and serve the Lord."

The congregation began to rise as the response echoed in the vaulted space. "Thanks be to God." The murmur of voices rose as the service ended, and the people moved en masse to the aisles. Ducking in an alcove, Mary scanned the crowd looking for the one face that had haunted her dreams and plagued her for over a decade. Subconsciously she fingered the scar.

"Can I help you, my daughter?"

Mary jumped, her breath catching in her throat. She spun and stared into the wizened face of an elderly priest. The crisp white collar of his robe formed a pedestal for the deeply creviced face and his thinning snow-colored hair creating shallow halo.

"Oh my," the man chuckled, his gray eyes sparkling in the flickering candlelight. "My, my…oh dear me." He reached out a wrinkled hand, resting it on her shoulder, giving it a soft pat and squeeze.

Mary clutched her purse to her chest and pressed against the wall behind her. She exhaled, rubbing her face with her left hand and then allowed herself to sag against the wall's cool stone. "Father…" she said, her voice sounding weak.

"Child," he said lingering over the word softening it into a breath. "I didn't mean to startle you. I saw you come in. You looked troubled to my old eyes. Now, how can I help you?"

The man's voice was kind, like an endearing grandfather. It invoked trust, inviting Mary to relax.

The congregation sauntered past them only a few feet away. Families laughing and talking as their children excitedly skipped ahead in anticipation of the feasts awaiting them at home.

"No, ahh, no thank you, Father. I'm all right."

He swept his arm across his body indicating a small bench near the wall where they were standing. "Sit with me, my old knees can't take standing like they did in my youth." And with a creaking moan like a compressor leaking air, he sat without waiting for her response. "Ahh, that's better." He rocked back before settling then reached forward massaging his knees. He peered up at her and smiled.

Mary scanned the thinning crowd with nervous eyes. She still had issues to deal with. She searched for the face of her ex-husband and patted the gun unconsciously through the sides of her purse. She sighed, thinking it ironic that it was Thanksgiving morning before giving in and smiling down at the aged priest.

CHAPTER TWENTY-FIVE

NATE WATCHED, perplexed as Crystal shuffled with slow deliberate motion and began to move forward. Dragging her feet as if pulled over the short knap of the carpeted aisle, her eyes locked onto those of his father. All around him, the parishioners swung in the direction of the blond woman as she approached their pastor, trudging as if against her will. A collective gasp rose. Their mouths stood agape.

Several things happened at once. Nate snapped to his feet and, moving forward to intercept Crystal, ran into a shadowy figure. He saw Julie grab Crystal's elbow yanking her back while whispering into her ear. Without taking her eyes off the pastor, Crystal, in a comforting gesture, laid her hand over Julie's elbow. The elder Richards stood at the altar waiting, his arms extended.

The knot of tension that had begun as a small tug at the base of Nate's skull began to grow. Not knowing what was going on, caused the tension to twist the muscles into several writhing serpents of pain. Gripping the back of the chair in front of him, Nate pushed out into the aisle and focused on the person with whom he had collided.

Nate shifted his eyes from the front of the auditorium to the confused and slightly embarrassed expression on Jackie's face. It took him a moment before realization settled.

Noting his hesitation, she withdrew the hand she had extended toward him. "I—"

"Jackie. I didn't know—what are you doing?"

"I thought I would surprise you." She brushed reddish-brown curls from her face.

"Oh yeah, umm, happy Thanksgiving." He looked into her eyes and recalled their kiss. His stomach tightened and his face and neck heated.

She smiled. "So, you're happy to see me then?" She looked around as some of the church members nearest to them began staring. She cleared her throat.

"Let's move back here," he said, indicating the foyer with a tilt of his head. With a quick glance around, Nate started toward the rear of the church towing Jackie by her hand. He reached the doors and caught a furtive movement out of the corner of his eye.

Amber changed from the simple jeans and sweater she'd worn at breakfast and wore an elegant royal blue skirt cinched at the waist with a wide black cloth belt and a muted flora patterned top consisting of several soft shades. She reached out to Jackie. "Jackie, it's so good to see you," she said, grasping her hand and pulling her into a brief hug.

Nate stared at Amber and blinked in disbelief as she smiled at him over Jackie's shoulder. He mouthed. "I don't believe you."

"You're not leaving already, are you?" She whispered near Jackie's ear. "Please, why don't you come sit with us?"

Jackie smiled pleasantly, if a bit uncomfortably, and turned to Nate who quickly turned his eyes to the floor. "Well, I really hadn't planned to—"

"Oh good," Amber said, slipping her arm through the bend of Jackie's elbow. The two ladies started toward the side aisle.

"Nate," the ladies spoke in unison.

Nate looked up with a start.

"You coming?" Amber asked with a smile that made her glow.

Sighing, Nate shrugged in resignation. He lifted his arms at the elbows, smiled sardonically, and started after them. He jerked when he felt a tap on his shoulder. He turned to see Chris MacGilvery, his partner, looking anxious. "Sorry, partner, but we need to go."

Nate knew something bad had happened even before sighting the uniformed officer standing uneasily by the double doors at the rear of the church.

He made eye contact with Julie, who still stood in stoic silence near Crystal, who was speaking in whispered tones to his father down front. He turned to face the two ladies waiting for him near the wall, and smiled.

He touched the corner of his forehead with two fingers in salute before spinning to follow Mac out the door. Just as the door was closing behind him, Nate chanced one glance back at Crystal and Julie as they stood with his father. It appeared that Crystal was crying, but he could not be sure since she was hiding her face in a cream-colored handkerchief.

Mac nudged Nate then nodded his head toward the double pairs of women. "What's up with that?" he asked with a smirk.

"I'm not quite sure yet," Nate said as he pushed past the young officer holding the door open for them. He swallowed. "Thankfully you grabbed my arm and pulled me away before I had to find out, I think." He grinned.

"Oh yeah." Mac laughed and slapped him on the shoulder. "Man your love life is way too interesting. I can't wait to hear the details."

Nate scowled then looked past Mac down the aisles as the door swung shut. His father had raised his arms, his hands toward the congregation. Nate wondered what he was saying.

Beside him, Mac zipped his quilted jacket and tugged the collar tight against the chill. He blew into his cupped hands then turned serious. "We have another body."

Nate stopped and stared into Mac's face. Of all the things Mac could have said, this had been the last thing he'd expected. "Connected?" He pulled his overcoat closed and stuffed his hands into the pockets.

"Yeah, looks like it might be."

Nate's mood darkened as he walked away from the sounds of celebration growing behind him. The voice of the organ cried out even as the thumping of the bass kept time. The drums carried the rhythm, as the strings sang the melody even as the people's voices rose in a harmonious swell. "Come on. Let's go," Nate said and turned back into a sudden gust of wind.

***

Nate stepped out of his Jeep and watched his foot sink into six inches of wet snow. Above the horizon, the muted yellow disc of the sun cast hazy light in a dull blue sky. From down the hill, he heard the subdued murmur of the gray waters of Robbie Creek as it flowed toward the Mores Creek Crossing, a tributary of the Boise River. Nate observed a line of tracks where the snow had been crushed by emergency personnel making their way in and out of a small roadside campsite beside the river. *The crime scene was already contaminated.*

Bright yellow crime-scene tape fluttered in the slight breeze in stark contrast to the dull bark of the trees in the frozen landscape. The only other color was the green of the occasional evergreen standing in defiance of winter's barrage.

Nate headed down the ice slickened trail, the compacted snow frozen into thin sheets causing him to slide as he stepped. Reaching level ground, he studied the surrounding area, watching for anything that may have been overlooked by the crime scene techs. As he came around the last turn and entered into the campsite, he saw the legs of a man, the pants stiff with cold and covered with a dusting of snow. Above him, interlocking pine boughs platted together with oaks, cottonwoods, and ash. Years of undisturbed growth provided a canopy, shielding the campsite from being buried beneath several inches of snow.

Mac cleared his throat as Nate walked into the matted circle of earth where the body rested on its back. The man's head lolled to one side where blood had spilled from a gash along his temple; then froze. The gore-colored stalactite attached the corpse to the ground like a column of earthen dripstone. The face was locked in a look of surprise, as if whoever had killed him had suddenly appeared and struck with only the slightest warning. He died instantly. D.R.T.

"Who is he?" Nate asked.

Mac turned and accepted a sheet of paper from the scene-officer. "Charles Jackson, 33. State ID number IDOC 1562372A."

"IDOC…let me guess, our boy was in prison for a sex crime?" Nate asked rhetorically. He knelt to take a closer look at the entry point of the wound.

Mac cleared his throat and blew into his cupped hands. "Child rape and manufacturing child porn, as a matter of fact," he said, still reading from the info sheet. "He has a probation violation warrant for his arrest…50k bond. But I guess we won't need to serve that now, huh?"

Nate looked up at Mac and then at the crime scene. "Who found him? Too cold for hikers."

"A couple…hiking." He laughed. "Not everyone hates winter, you know."

Nate rolled his eyes and stuffed his hands deeper into his pockets.

Mac smirked before continuing. "The *hikers* were going through campsites looking for abandoned gear, you know, scavenging. I guess they found more than they were looking for, huh."

Pulling a cotton swab out of an evidence collection kit, Nate prodded the edge of the wound gauging the shape of the injury and guessing at the weapon used. "You see this?"

"Whadaya got," Mac asked, facing Nate before kneeling beside him.

"Look at the shape of the wound. It's slightly triangular." He brushed his chin with the back of his gloved hand.

"Wow, I've seen this before. I'd bet it was a camp axe or a pickaxe. Something like that."

"If you and Dr. Quincy MD are finished with your medical examination…." A gruff female voice interrupted them.

Both Nate and Mac twisted around to see the deputy coroner standing with her hands akimbo, and her glasses perched on the tip of her button-like nose. She wore a dark blue quilted jacket with a light blue lab coat poking from beneath its hem. A silver chain dangled from each arm of the horn-rimmed glasses and disappeared beneath the utilitarian cut of her graying red hair. She smiled and shrugged. "Well you're not cute enough to be Crossing Jordan."

Nate and Mac exchanged glances.

"Don't you guys watch TV? Let's play Jeopardy...TV Medical Examiners for $200.00" When neither man laughed, she giggled at her own joke and stepped past them. "Kids these days."

Nate laughed and moved back allowing the coroner to get closer to the body. He removed the latex glove and extended his hand. "Nate Richards and this is my partner, Chris MacGilvery."

She shook his hand with a grip that refuted her age. "Harriet Morrison, Deputy M.E. This guy one of those registered sex offenders on that list?"

Nate and Mac exchanged glances. "Yeah," Mac said, "number six out of—"

She grunted, grabbed the body by its shoulder, and rolled it onto its side. "Serves the booger right. I don't know how you guys do it. Seems to me that this guy, whoever he is, is doing us a favor."

"Well—"

"But it's your call. You know your job best, I suppose. I just have to collect 'em and cut 'em up." She giggled to herself as she continued inspecting the body.

Nate stood and looked over the woman's back and smiled at Mac. "I like this woman," he whispered to Mac.

"That's good, cause I like you guys too," the older woman said without looking up.

Mac started laughing out loud and Nate tried to hide his outburst behind his hand.

"You guys got what you need off of this one, 'cause once I bag him, he's all mine?"

Stifling his laughter, Nate turned back to the road and spied, rising above the crest of the hill, a news van hoisting an antenna. "No, we're not quite done with him yet. But either way we'll want to see whatever you find before any of it gets released to family or destroyed."

Pushing against her knees, the woman stood with a prolonged grunt. "Okay...I'm going to get my stuff. Be right back."

"Harriet," Nate called after her. She looked back at him. "Don't talk to those guys," he said, pointing to the antenna array.

She waved a hand dismissively. "Don't worry, honey, this ain't my first rodeo." She turned back and continued up the slippery path.

Nate smiled and peered at Mac whose face had turned hard. Nate followed Mac's gaze and watched as a man adjusted his necktie and brushed his hair back from his face with the palm of his hand. *Butch.*

"Don't worry, partner, I'll handle Butchie the newsboy. You don't even have to talk to him," Nate said.

"Yeah," Mac said.

Nate stared up at the top of the hill where Butch was standing. The newsman was adjusting his tie again, making sure his suit-jacket, tie and shirt were camera-ready. He didn't bother adjusting his jeans because he would only be in frame from the waist up.

Turning his back to the news crew, Mac hissed through clenched teeth. "Just looking at that guy irks me." For the next several minutes, he recounted to Nate, again, the many reasons why he hated the newsman. As always, his first complaint was the story showcasing the drug raid gone bad.

"Let's get to work," Nate said and knelt back down by the body. He raised his head, using his hand to shield his eyes against a sudden glare from the sun. "You coming?" He yanked Mac's pants leg like a toddler getting his mother's attention, then snapped on a pair of latex gloves. Mac, chancing a final look toward the hill, grunted, and joined Nate.

Nate sighed and began to inventory the pockets of the dead man. In spite of the cold, the odor from the corpse wafted past his nose. He winced. Pulling out a dark-colored plastic thumb-drive, he held it up for Mac to examine. "This looks like the one we pulled off Bobby Monarch?"

Mac accepted the rectangular drive and studied it. "Looks like...yeah. Maybe we can trace this one and see where and when it was purchased. That might tell us something. Think you can get your friends at the Feds to run the manufacturer's ID number for us?"

Nate took the drive and dropped it into an evidence bag. "I'll check my contacts. Phil in the lab there still owes me a favor or two."

Emptying the remaining pockets, Nate found several sheets of folded paper. Unfolding the pages, which appeared to be computer printouts, he saw that they contained several images of prepubescent children posed in sexually explicit positions. Handing the pages to Mac, Nate shook his head and stared at the dead man. *Lord, maybe this guy is doing us a favor.*

CHAPTER TWENTY-SIX

HARRIET STEPPED BACK down into the circle of the camp. "Okay, gents, let's do our homework." She pulled back the collar exposing the neck and upper chest of the dead man. "First thing first, what don't we see?"

No rookie to crime scenes, Nate knelt beside her and took a closer look at the body. "The skin looks dry."

"Okay...what else?"

Nate looked over his shoulder at Mac. "Well, he's been out here at least three weeks, maybe four."

Harriet looked at Nate. "That would be my guess as well, but what makes you think that?"

Nate smirked. "Well this ain't my first rodeo, partner."

"So, I guess it ain't got nothing to do with the dates printed on these papers we pulled out of his pockets just a few minutes ago," Mac said.

"What papers," Harriet said.

"Traitor," Nate said, looking at Mac who was wearing a "who me" expression.

"Harriet, since it's agreed that he's been out here for about a month," Mac said, pointing at the body. "How do we account for the lack of molestation?"

"Well mister cheater, you want to take a shot at this one?" Harriet looked at Nate, a playful smile tugging at the corners of her lips.

Nate cleared his throat and smiled. "Okay, Doc, I accept your challenge. No bugs or other insects.... Too cold. Critters are asleep or frozen. As for animals not taking advantage of the body, I have no idea."

"Not bad," she began. "You had me scared there for a moment. I thought I was going to have to congratulate you." She smiled.

"First of all, you're right," she said, getting up again. "Flies and critters like that, which would be so useful to determine the time of death in...let's say in May or August are useless to us now. Like you said, all asleep.

"But the million dollar question is why didn't a bear or maybe a wolf or even a skunk not trundle by and take part in the Thanksgiving feast?"

"Foot traffic?" Mac ventured a guess.

"Too close to the water?" Nate added hopefully.

Harriet laughed. "What didn't you guys catch as soon as you came over that hilltop? Odor?" she added, answering her own question. "The cold suppresses the rate of decay, but it also keeps the odor down. Simple. No odor, no carnivores...that is unless one just happens across the body. To be honest, I'm surprised none did; winter naturally being for slim pickings in these parts." Her hands danced through the air with sharp strokes, accenting each word as she spoke.

The men looked at each other and shook their heads, making mental notes for future use. "Hey," Nate said, raising a hand to halt her. "I caught a whiff of old boy stewing when I was going through his pockets," he said in objection.

"Sure. You stirred the pot so to speak. You moved the body around lifting pocket flaps and causing the molecules to rise." She stood, satisfied, and rubbed her upper arms.

Observing her reaction, Nate said, "We're done with the body, although we'll be out here for a while yet. We've still got to go through the campsite."

"Checking for trace," Mac added, "you never know what you'll find."

"Well, I guess it sucks to be you then, don't it? It's too cold out here for my liking. I've tagged him, so if you gentlemen would be willing to help a poor old lady out, we can bag 'em."

Laughing, both Mac and Nate tipped imaginary hats. "Let it not be said that the moment arose where we could have helped a lady in distress and didn't," Mac said.

"Here, here," Nate added.

A few minutes later, the body was zipped closed in a dark blue waterproof bag, a yellow tag hanging from the zipper near the toe, and then loaded in the back of the coroner's wagon. The vehicle's dark tinted windows prevented the news cameras from catching a close up of the tag's inscription. Butch hurried toward the two detectives intending to intercept them before they ducked beneath the yellow barrier tape.

A uniformed officer glowered and moved to block the newsman's path. The large man's face darkened, and his chest seemed to swell, raising a hand, he pushed the newsman in his chest. "Sir," he said in a tone that didn't brook any challenge, "stay behind the tape." He stepped toward the news crew.

Butch Jenson stretched himself to his full six feet and glared at the officer's chin. "Do you know who I am," he asked, straightening his suit jacket.

The officer took another step forward. "The question, sir, is do I care? Now, stay away from the tape, or I'll have to place you under arrest." He smiled as he spoke, aware of the glowing red record button on the camera, bright in the gloaming shadow of the trees.

From just inside the security tape, Mac slapped Nate on the shoulder and laughed. He pointed toward Butch and the officer still staring at each other, paused, and then he disappeared down the trail that led back to the crime scene.

Nate turned and took in the view and shook his head. *That's all I need, one more reason for Brown to ride my butt.* "Hey, I got this one; you go on down and help comb the area. I really don't want to be out here after we lose the sun."

Mac shook his head and scowled at the reporter.

"You know we've got to do it," Nate said, reading his partner's expression. "If we don't, it'll be our butt, and besides, he does slip us a tidbit now and again."

Mac grunted. "You talk to him. I might hit him...by accident." He chuckled, turned, and continued down the trail to the campsite.

Nate watched his partner retreat. "Whew." he forced a breath through pursed lips. He faced toward the officer and reporter, noted their body language, and realized their emotions could cause the situation to escalate. With a deep breath and a forced neutral expression, he stepped back under the tape, calling out as he rose, "What's going on?"

"Richards, will you tell this..." Butch jerked his thumb toward the other man, "officer, who I am?"

"Well, Butch, that depends on whether you insist on being disrespectful to Officer..." Nate glanced at the nametag, "Kiffin."

Butch stepped back inhaling slowly then allowed the air to flow out in one long continuous stream. "Richards, throw me a bone here. You owe me."

"I got him, Kiffin. Let him through. But have him sign the entry log just in case I want to subpoena his records." Nate smiled.

Escorting Butch to the designated area set aside for press interviews, Nate allowed him to set up his camera and get a long range shot of the crime scene. Looking up, he noticed the other four valley news agencies arriving. "So, Butch, what do you want to know?"

"Who was the dead guy?"

"Can't tell you."

"Was he on the serial killer's list?"

"No comment."

"Okay, how did you find the body?"

"Couple of hikers."

"Names?"

"Can't tell you."

Butch swore. "Come on, Nate, give me something here."

"Tell me something first, Butch."

"What?!"

Nate shifted his eyes to the cameraman and then back to Butch. Turning to face his assistant, Butch slashed his hand across his throat, and the red light went out.

"Okay, Richards, what's burning your butt this time?"

Nate smiled. He loved playing with Butch's mind. "My partner. What was up with that story you ran? Did you even bother to check Sandra Blightwood's record or if any of what she was saying was true?"

"Is that what this is all about? Look Richards, I don't tell you how to do your job and—"

"Yeah, but I don't broadcast lies and half truths about your partners, leaving it out there for everyone to see." Nate's voice had risen. From the corner of his eye, he saw Mac look up from the crime scene. Nate held up four fingers indicating a code-four, situation satisfactory.

Nate turned back to Butch. "You can't just lay people out like that and then expect them to help you. That's not the way *this* is going to work." Nate pointed his finger back and forth between Butch's chest and his own. "Now, we have to give you certain pieces of information. You've got it. We need to let you at least see the perimeter of the crime scene. You've got that too. You're done."

"Hey, I was hoping to at least get a close up of the campsite," Butch complained.

Nate called out to Officer Kiffin. "I'm done with our guest. See to it that he stays in the designated area, will you?"

Kiffin smiled and walked toward Butch. "No problem. Love to." His voice had a slight snarl.

Nate watched as Butch, red faced, turned back to his cameraman and began to set up before the other crews got unloaded and crowded his frame. Officer Kiffin stood beside him, the perfect gentleman. Nate made his way down the sloping path watching his footing. As the sun sank and the temperature dropped, the runoff began to freeze making the path more treacherous. It began to snow.

"You about done here," Nate asked as he entered the circle of the camp. He scanned the area checking for obvious signs of anything missed.

Mac looked up catching snowflakes in the palm of his hand. "No, I don't know about you, but I'm done. I am not looking forward to driving off this mountain in the dark on black-ice."

Nate dipped his chin in a quick bird-like action. "Let's get out of here. We'll let Butch and his gang pick over what's left."

Mac stamped his feet trying to generate some heat. "Let's go."

Nate looked around and then nodded again. The two detectives collected the evidence bags, locking them in the plastic tubs used for transport. They trudged up the trail, careful to avoid the ice hidden below the fresh blanket of snow. Cresting the hill, Nate waved a gloved hand at Kiffin. "We're done. Unless you want to spend Thanksgiving evening out here, you can break it down and take off." He chuckled as he watched the delighted smile crawl across the man's muscular face.

As Nate and Mac loaded the evidence containers in the back of his Jeep, he watched the news crews shoot film of the crime scene from different angles, showing the road leading to the turnoff and the path down the hill. The curly haired cameraman assisting Butch headed for the trail leading down the hill, hurrying to be the first to film the scene. Nate stopped. Turning to face the news crew, he cupped his hands around his mouth. "Watch out for—"

A loud crash pierced the twilight, and the man's head disappeared below the lip of the hill. His scream coupled with the sound of the camera and light-unit colliding on the frozen path danced beneath the trees. The shrill noise continued, punctuated by breaking plastic and twisting metal.

"Darn," Nate exclaimed.

"What was that?" Mac said, climbing out of the Jeep where he had been stowing equipment.

The three officers headed to the trailhead unsure of what they would find. "Get five-one en route," Nate called to Kiffin.

The big man raised his left hand, thumb extended, while he compressed the transmit key with his right hand and spoke into the microphone clipped to his left shoulder. Then he ran back to his car.

Mac was the first to the hillcrest. He leaped down, staying to the side of the trail and using the trees to slow his decent. Nate ran behind him staying at his heels. He saw the cameraman crumpled in a heap at the bottom of the path, his leg protruding at an odd angle just below the knee. Vapors of steam rose in ethereal tendrils from a fast spreading pool of blood, black in the low light.

Nate stopped near the man's head checking his pulse. Mac straightened the man's leg and applied pressure to the wound. Removing the man's belt, he fashioned a tourniquet above the knee staunching the flow of blood.

"He's not breathing," Nate called.

Kiffin arrived and passed Nate the plastic pocket mask, which he quickly fitted over the man's face like an oxygen mask in the E.R. The man's eyes were open, but unfocused, looking off into space.

Nate locked eyes with Mac, communicating. The man beneath their ministering hands was in shock, and the snow and dropping temperature added to the difficulty in saving his life.

Dipping his finger in the man's blood, Nate wrote the time on the unconscious man's forehead, indicating when the tourniquet had been secured. Somewhere in an unused portion of his brain, he registered that his family should be home from church and sitting down for dinner. Leaning forward, he breathed into the intake valve, watching as the man's chest rose and fell.

"What do you need me to do?" Kiffin asked.

Nate looked up. "He's gone into shock. We need to get him off the ground."

Kiffin raced toward the hill. "I've got thermal blankets in the trunk. Back in a minute."

From atop the hill, the news crews began filming the scene. Aware that it was one of their own, the atmosphere was somber...personal.

"Get those lights down here. We need to keep him warm," Nate yelled up the slope.

"Walk to the side of the path. We don't need another one of you falling on your—," Mac left the sentence unfinished.

Kiffin came to a sliding stop next to the two officers and threw the blankets at them. "Here, take these. I'm going back up to mark the road with flares so EMS won't pass us in the dark."

"Copy that," Nate said absently."

"His pulse is getting weaker," Mac said. "We've got to get him off the ground and get his legs elevated."

Several members of the four camera crew finally arrived. The heat from their lights raised the temperature notably, as they focused the beams on their comrade. Nate eyed them, assessing their ability to help. "Butch, help Mac stabilize that leg. The rest of you spread out. We need to lift him onto the blanket."

Two of the men positioned themselves near the cameraman's shoulders, grabbing him under his arms while Nate stabilized his neck and head. One man grabbed the uninjured leg while the fourth man unfolded one of the thermal blankets on the wooden picnic table.

In the distance, Nate heard sirens riding the chilled wind as it rose up the mountain. He kept the man's neck straight as they lowered him onto the table. "Quick! Get those lights closer. Point them right at him!" Nate barked.

"I've got the leg. Find some stones or something we can use to prop up this end of the table." Mac looked into Butch's face.

Butch hesitated.

"Now!" Mac ordered.

A moment later, Butch returned, lugging a stone the size of a man's head and dropped it near the end of the table. "This big enough?" he grunted, sweat beading on his face.

"Here's another one," a voice called out. Soon the table's end was raised creating an incline with the cameraman's feet above his head.

"Wrap those blankets tighter," Nate said, his own arms starting to tremble due to prolonged immobility.

Butch walked toward the head of the table, stopped, then stared at the unconscious man's face. "Is he going to be all right?" His voice sounded pinched.

"We've done all we can do for now. Paramedics will be here soon. You can hear the sirens already," Nate said, assessing the newsman's condition. He reasoned that being the news was vastly different from just reporting it, and Butch was not adjusting well.

Nate cleared his throat. "How long have you and…"

"Teddy. Teddy Brandicourt. About three years." Butch answered while staring at Teddy. His voice sounded flat and distant.

Nate studied Butch's face. "Come relieve me Butch, my arms are starting to cramp."

Butch's head snapped toward Nate. His eyes focused. "You sure? Is it safe to move him?"

From near Teddy's knees, Mac cleared his throat, but Nate cut him off with a glance. "We're not going to move him. We're just gonna replace my hands with yours. It'll be good; your hands are probably warmer."

Butch took a stuttering step forward and reached out as if to grasp something valuable and fragile. His eyes locked onto Teddy's face.

"That's right," Nate encouraged. "Just place your hands here and keep his head straight." Nate squared his back and examined the scene. He heard the sirens getting louder, but realized they were still a few minutes out. He walked around the table and stood near Mac. "How's the leg?"

"We've got the bleeding stopped, but that bone's gonna have to be reset. Not to mention stitches." Mac knitted his brows and leaned closer to Nate. "You know, we probably have a neck brace in the kit somewhere."

"I know," Nate said, "but look at his face. This is the most human I've seen Butch in all the years I've known him. Besides, the medics will be here before I run up, find it, and get back down here."

Mac sighed. "I'd better release the tourniquet for a minute to get some oxygen to that lower leg. He's not losing that on my watch."

Nate stared up the hill when flashes of blue and red joined the amber and yellow strobe of the patrol unit parked on the side of the road. Listening intently, he heard Kiffin say, "They're down here." A few moments later, he saw Kiffin leading the paramedics down the trail. Nate noticed that the paramedics took the time to secure a safety rope near the trail to help with footing.

***

Nate and Mac sighed as they settled heavily into the electrically heated seats of the Jeep and watched the paramedics depart. With his eyes closed, he reclined against the headrest. Nate rolled his head toward Mac. "This is not how I planned my Thanksgiving."

"Speaking of, Sara's gonna want my butt for this. I promised her we would have the whole day together...no callouts. Oh well, huh?"

"Yeah, it's the nature of the beast."

Mac sat up and adjusted his seatbelt. "Let's go."

Nate grabbed the steering wheel with both hands and exhaled, making a fluttering noise like a horse's neigh. He inserted the key and the engine roared to life. Outside, the remaining news crew roamed around recording their shows for the evening broadcasts. Nate shook his head, shifted the Jeep into first gear, and slowly let out the clutch hoping to keep the vehicle from spinning out on the ice-covered road.

A tap on the passenger window startled them. Nate hit the brake. Butch Jensen's haggard face appeared. Mac lowered the window just far enough to speak through the crack. "Yeah," he said in a clipped tone.

"Ah...just wanted to say thank you.... You know, for everything," he managed.

"Well, it's what we do," Mac said.

Nate leaned forward. "No problem. Looks like he's going to be just fine. Thanks for pitching in back there, you were a real trooper."

"You guys were awesome. I'm just glad you hadn't left yet. We would have been pretty screwed. Know what I mean?"

Mac rolled his eyes. "It's like I said, it's what we do."

Nate elbowed his partner.

Butch straightened up, his face disappeared above the roof of the car. His voice floated down to them out of the darkness. "Mac, I'm sorry about that story I ran about your—about you. I mean about how it.... How I made you look." He stood silent for a minute before turning to walk away.

Nate punched Mac in the shoulder and jerked his head toward the window.

Mac cleared his throat. "Err, Butch...we're good. Just be more careful in the future, okay."

Butch halted. A halo of snow flurries backlit by the news crew's lights surrounded him. He turned toward the Jeep, his face lost in shadow. "Yeah. Right." His voice heavy with exhaustion. "Okay." Then he blended into the darkness.

Nate put the car back into gear, and the Jeep began to roll forward. "We might still make dinner," Nate said, checking his watch.

"What was that?" Mac said, jerking forward against his seatbelt.

"What—"

"Shhh," Mac said and turned up the volume on the police radio.

The repetitious beeping of the tone-alert filled the Jeep. The dispatcher's voice sounded calm as if she broadcasted disaster alerts on a routine basis. "...structure fire at 2411 Sugar Creek Court. Units to assist Fire?"

The rapid fired calls from responding units with their call-signs and ETA's burst from the radio. Nate slammed his fist against the switch in center console activating the emergency lights. Embedded in the grill and rear window of the Jeep, the emergency lights exploded into the altered nightscape as the vehicle accelerated, its rear-end fishtailing until the snow tires caught traction. The car lurched forward as the tires bit into the surface of the slick road.

Crystal Johansson's house was on fire.

CHAPTER TWENTY-SEVEN

FIFTY-EIGHT MINUTES LATER, Nate parked down the street from the remains of the single story house. Smoke billowed heavenward as the last sparks rose in lazy swirls into the night sky and disappeared. Mac jumped out of the vehicle and approached the yellow tape that kept the spectators back from the property and possible crime scene.

Nate scanned the crowd looking for anything that seemed out of place. Allowing his focus to soften, he glanced over the crowd looking for the odd thing, the peculiar person…anyone who appeared even remotely out of sort…anything more than the typical voyeuristic interest.

The red and yellow lights flashed across the curious faces of onlookers, coloring the scene with alternating shades of amber and ocher and back to inky darkness. Nate got out of the car and turned his back to the lights as he walked amongst the crowd. All at once the lights illuminated the face of a middle-aged man. Nate knew he had seen the man before, but when the light returned, the man was gone.

Nate stopped and searched the crowd, again, looking for the familiar face. About twenty feet further south, the man stood leaning out from behind a willow tree scanning the crowd with intense interest.

Nate strode toward the tree, determined at least to identify the man and what it was he was looking for. Their eyes met and held. Nate gave the man a two-fingered wave, then called him over.

Holding her collar pulled up tight against her neck, a young woman stepped in front of him. "Hey, aren't you the detective that was out here about a month ago?" The twenty-something reporter held a digital recorder up to Nate's face. "Would you care to comment?"

"What?" Nate stopped, dividing his attention between this new irritation and where the man had been standing. "Not now!" He tried to push past her.

"But Detective—"

"Not now," Nate said through gritted teeth. He sidestepped the reporter and fought to get through the crowd. Reaching the tree, Nate spun, looking for the familiar face. Nothing. The crowd closed in around him, trapping him on the island near the tree. *The perfect distraction.*

Nate slapped the side of his thigh and sighed, creating a faint cloud of steam around his face. He headed back to the burnt house hoping the crime scene unit would at least be able to find something in the mess.

Finding Mac, he stopped at his partner's side. "Where's Crystal? Julie has her safe, right?"

Mac turned to face Nate and dipped his chin. "Whadaya got? You see something over there?"

"Where's Julie?"

"She's en route. Crystal wanted to see the house. I wish you'd tell me when you're gonna just up and disappear like that. For all you know, I could have been over here crying because you left me all by my lonesome."

"Get on the air…. Give me your radio. What channel's our car to car?"

"What's going on, Nate? What did you see?" Mac eyed Nate, all kidding gone.

"What's Julie's call sign?" Then catching Mac's, "who you asking" expression, he keyed the mic on the hand-held. "Julie Pratt, go to four."

"Pratt on four."

"What's your twenty?"

"*Julie?* Somebody forget proper radio etiquette?" She responded with a hint of teasing in her voice.

"Do not stop at the fire. I'm not su-"

Julie stepped on Nate, cutting off his transmission by talking over him. "Richards! Break! Crystal just jumped out of the car! She's running toward the house. I repeat. She's on foot and approaching the house. I'm in pursuit."

Mac whipped around and sprinted toward the mouth of the inlet anticipating the frantic woman's approach. Nate keyed the mic again as he started running. "I saw a face in the crowd— looked out of place—didn't want to take a chance on her being targeted—in the confusion of the crowd." He spotted Julie jogging toward him and stopped mid-stride. She was alone.

She joined him and hooked her radio on her belt. "Where's your partner? Does he have Crystal with him?"

Nate rubbed his chin with the back of his gloved hand. "I was hoping she would be with you." Mac took off toward what's left of the foundation. Responding to her unasked question, he said, "This is his radio, mine's in the Jeep."

She rolled her eyes. Another hit on his tactical readiness. "Stay on channel four. Let's sweep the crowd staying near the inner perimeter. If I know her, she'll be trying to get to the house." She jogged off as Nate watched her disappear into the crowd.

After a moment's hesitation, Nate exhaled and turned in the opposite direction, splitting the difference between the way Mac had gone and where he stood now.

Ahead of him the night exploded. The compression wave slammed into him like a furnace blast shoving him backwards across the mud-slicked lawn. Glowing debris rained from the sky as pieces of glass and shrapnel pierced his legs and arm. Forcing himself to one knee, Nate grimaced as he plucked glass and wood shards from his shoulder. The crowd edged back toward the mouth of the cul-de-sac.

Nate winced and looked around the renewed circle of fire light, again, as the line of firemen and uniformed officers worked together to move the crowd backwards. Soon Nate realized he was standing alone like a crab deposited on shore after the tide retreated to the sea. Scanning the crowd, Nate saw Mac converging on a disheveled blond woman standing a little apart from the crowd, her blue dress smeared with mud and soot.

From the opposite side of the circle, Julie broke free from the crowd and ran toward Crystal. The woman stood statue-like in the glow of the fire and the alternating red and white lights of the emergency vehicles. Jarred into action, Nate ran forward, but he could tell that Julie and Mac would reach her first.

As the three officers raced toward the distraught woman, a smaller explosion rocked the night. Julie grabbed Crystal's shoulders, spun her around, and tucked her under her arm. Drawing her weapon to the low ready, she panned her eyes across the crowd and began pulling the mostly unresponsive Crystal toward the car.

As Nate joined them, the roof of the house began to cave in. A cloud of smoke and soot rose and then settled along the ground thickening the already heavy night air. They jolted and spun then watched as the building, as if in slow motion, folded in on itself.

Mac arrived and turned toward the fire as well. "Hey, let's get her out of here." Like a herd of deer, the three officers rotated and moved forward together shielding Crystal between them.

A shot rang out.

They fell in a heap, with Crystal beneath them. Firemen ducked to the ground and leaped behind equipment. The officers drew their weapons, securing a perimeter around the firemen as they tried to locate the shooter.

The crowd streamed out of the dead-end street like water from a broken main. Their screams echoed as they fled. The sound of additional units responding filled the air, like the haunting cry of birds of prey, as police units hurried past the fleeing masses. Cautious of the crowd, the backup units approached at a speed barely greater than that of the surge of pedestrians.

Looking at Nate with weary eyes, Mac sighed. "I hate it when you're right."

"Well, I'd rather of been wrong on this one." Nate pushed up to his knees and then stood. You ladies all right?"

Reaching his hand out to assist the women, he froze. "Oh God, no, not again!"

"Medic!" Mac shouted springing to his feet.

Nate lifted his face. "Medic! Man down! Man down!"

CHAPTER TWENTY-EIGHT

JULIE LAY FACE DOWN in the wet street; a dark pool of blood spreading from beneath her short brown hair reflected the brilliant lights of the emergency vehicles. Nate dropped to his knees, his breathing labored. Instead of Julie lying there, he saw Sabrina, his former partner who had been shot in the line of duty. An assassin's bullet had left her hovering between life and death for months before making a remarkable recovery and then retiring. The smells and sounds of the ICU came rushing back, and for a moment, he couldn't seem to focus.

"Get off me!"

Startled, Nate looked down, but didn't move.

"I said...get off me. I can't breathe." Julie grunted and pushed Nate in his chest. He fell backward landing on the seat of his pants, hands splayed beside him.

"What? Wait, you're okay?" Nate scrambled back to his feet and began helping the two women to theirs. The uniformed officers had drawn their handguns and formed a protective circle around them.

"Get down," one of the officers called out and pushed them back to the ground.

Nate found himself back atop of Julie. Beside them, Crystal lay in a fetal curve crying quietly. Mac knelt nearby with his gun at the low ready, scanning the crowd. "I think whoever it was is gone," Mac said.

Moments later, the paramedics finally arrived. The young medic lifted a blood soaked handkerchief from Julie's face. "Let me get a look at this," he said. "Not much more than a flesh wound, but you'll need stitches." He set his trauma bag beside him on the street and went to work closing the wound with a butterfly bandage before signaling to his partner to bring the stretcher over.

Julie looked at him sideways. "Who's riding on that?"

Mac chuckled and looked at the small pad he'd pulled from his pocket. Julie cut her eyes to him, her expression hard. He cleared his throat. "Eh-mm...the call came in at 1730 hours—"

"Who called it in?" Nate interrupted him.

"—by an anonymous male caller—"

"Did he say anything in particular?"

"—He said that he didn't want anyone innocent getting hurt, so—"

"So, was it our..."

Mac smacked Nate on the shoulder with the notepad. "You gonna keep interrupting me or you gonna let me read this thing to you?"

"Oh, sorry."

"Anyway, the caller said he only wanted the woman. Then he hung up." Seeing Nate's intake of breath, he raised his hand, stalling him. "And before you ask," he said hurriedly, "no, we did not get a trace. We assume it was a cell phone."

They were both quiet for a moment. Having moved about thirty feet from where the paramedics were finishing their treatment of both Julie and Crystal, Nate tapped Mac on the arm and said, "Let's go talk to Julie. I want to see what she has to say about all this."

***

Sitting on the bumper of the paramedics van, Julie looked up at the approaching detectives. Nate could see dark traces of smoke around her eyes and nostrils. Her face was smudged beneath the bandage covering the corner of her forehead. She coughed and shook her head from side to side, then winced. "Next time I'm taking the drug buy stakeout; you guys can keep the fragile-girl-babysitting duty. This stuff is gonna get me killed."

The paramedic chuckled but stopped when he looked at Crystal and pulled the stretcher closer. "It's for your friend. I don't think she could walk even if she wanted to," he said to Julie.

An hour later, Crystal lay resting in room 27 in the ER at St. Luke's West as Julie leaned against a wall in the hallway. A new patch covered the corner of her forehead. She smiled as she accepted a cup of coffee from Mac. She nodded her appreciation before speaking. "Looks like our guy is stepping up his game." She blew on the coffee before taking a sip.

Nate sighed, rubbed his face, and watched the ER floor-doctor go by with his assistant walking close behind him, typing notes into her pad as she followed. He rubbed his face again and looked up at the wall-mounted clock, *2030 hours. Mom would be finished with dinner and washing the dishes by now. I guess cold turkey is better than no turkey.* "We're missing something," he said out loud and took a drink from his own Styrofoam cup. Removing the cup from his lips, he frowned at the bitter beverage. "Look, it's been a long day. The doc is going to keep Crystal overnight for observation, and patrol will be with her until morning. Let's all get out of here, catch a good night's sleep, come back, and hit it fresh in the morning."

Neither Julie nor Mac answered him, but instead, pushed up from their various perches in the hallway. Julie walked over and shoulder opened the door leading into Crystal's room and disappeared behind the partially pulled curtain. Mac pulled out his cell phone, checked the time, and took one last sip of coffee before tossing his cup into the trash.

Soon Nate found himself standing alone in the hallway. He grunted, and then he too pushed away from the wall. Shuffling out through the ambulance entry door, Nate kicked at tuffs of snow welled up by tire tracks through the parking lot. He looked up holding his face exposed to the brisk night air, allowing fresh snow to caress his features before melting or tumbling free. In spite of his well-documented dislike of winter and all things cold, he had to admit that in moments like this, with virgin snow, things just seemed magical. Like anything could happen.

Retrieving the key-fob from his jacket pocket, Nate used the remote to start his Jeep, which sat covered in snow on the far side of the parking lot.

"You know you can do that from inside the building," Julie said coming up behind him.

Nate turned, looked at the bandaged warrior, and smiled. "Ahhh, yeah, I knew that." He chuckled at himself, suddenly at a loss for words. "You...ah...heading home for Thanksgiving dinner?" He finally managed.

"You always this funny?"

"No, usually not."

She chuckled. "Nobody at home to hurry back to. My family's all back east and near Minnesota. You?"

"Nahh," he heard himself say. "I mean, yeah. Yes-yes, I have family here, but dinner has long been over." He took a breath. "Want to grab a bite and get a decent cup of coffee somewhere?"

"I-I don't know," she stammered. And for the first time since he'd met her, she looked put off her game. "It's getting late and—"

"And you haven't eaten since you left my dad's church this morning. Speaking of which, how did all that turn out?"

She smiled and her shoulders relaxed. "Come on, I'll tell you over coffee."

***

"Where have you been? And not so much as a phone call. The way you just up and marched out of church this morning, you 'bout to worry your mother to death," Sherri Richards spoke through the open doorway.

"I don't know about worrying anybody to death, but if you don't close that door you sure gonna freeze your poor husband." The elder Richards reached past his wife and pulled Nate inside by the shoulder.

Nate laughed as he stomped snow and mud from his shoes, leaned forward kissing his mother's upturned cheek. "Sorry Mom…. Work." He scanned the room.

"She's upstairs," his mother whispered.

Nate met his mother's gaze and shook his head. "Mom, I told you that I wasn't pursuing a relationship—"

"You mean you're not pursuing Amber." She smiled at the awkward expression on her son's face.

Nate turned to look at his father, who smiled noncommittally before returning to his favorite chair.

"Maybe I should just…it's late, and I just wanted to say happy Thanksgiving." Nate rubbed his chin and looked at the stairs. His mother smiled and returned to her seat opposite her husband's. Picking up the magazine she'd been reading, she smiled.

Nate cleared his throat and headed for the kitchen. "Save me some sweet potato pie?"

His mother set aside the magazine and made as if to get up. "I'll make you a plate. You need more than just dessert."

Nate turned back toward the living room. "Mom, that's okay. Really." But she was already walking past him into the kitchen.

"As long as you're in there…" Reverend Richards called out from his chair. Nate could hear him getting up as well.

Before long, the three of them stood in the small kitchen warmed by the love they shared one for another. Nate pulled out a seat at the table as his mother sat a plate of food in front of him. Across the room, his father drew Sherri into his embrace and kissed her cheek. "I like my dessert before dinner," he said as he squeezed her.

"Is that turkey and cornbread stuffing I smell?" Amber stood in the doorway wearing a pair of skinny jeans and an oversized gold sweatshirt. She smiled and her face seemed to glow. "Nate, I didn't hear you come in."

"Maybe that's why you spent the last five minutes fixing your hair and touching up your make-up," Gracie said, coming up behind Amber.

Amber turned, her face flushing. "Grace Marie Fletcher." She swatted at the teen just as the girl ducked past her and headed for Nate, jumping into his lap squealing like a four year old.

"Nate, help," Gracie said laughing and clinging to him. Then looking up, she poked her tongue at a red-faced Amber.

Gathering herself, Amber made her way into the kitchen and slipped into the chair opposite Nate's. "Slice of pie, Mother Richards?" She smiled and pushed a loose strand of hair from the corner of her face and chanced a glance at Nate.

Nate cleared his throat and then smiled at her. "So did you enjoy the service this morning?" He asked with a knowing smile.

Amber giggled. "Yeah, sorry about that, but it was too perfect. Wouldn't you agree?" She smiled, and once again, Nate's heart sped up. The worst part was that he was sure she knew it.

Amber leaned forward, her chin resting on the backs of her interlaced fingers. "Well, Nate," she began and flashed her brightest smile, "you know how the saying goes, 'All's fair in love and—"

The doorbell rang. Everyone looked toward the living room, but no one moved.

The doorbell rang again. Nate glanced at the wall clock, noting it was ten o'clock, and then turned to his dad.

Someone began beating on the front door while repeatedly ringing the doorbell. Nate pushed back from the table and stood, causing Gracie to slide from his lap. "Let me get it, Dad."

Pushing his sweater back, Nate uncovered the handgun holstered at his side. As he approached the entryway, he could see a silhouette move across the frosted glass in the door.

"Wait, Son, this is still my house," Reverend Richards said, following Nate into the living room.

The small group all moved together toward the door with Sherri Richards following behind, still drying her hands on a towel. "Oh, move aside, you're all acting like a bunch of frightened children." Up ahead of them, Reverend Richards opened the door. As he did, a gust of wind driven snow danced in like a dust devil settling near the older Richards' feet.

On the porch all that remained was a set of footprints leading up to the porch and then away again. "Who would play doorbell ditch on a night like this," Gracie asked no one in particular.

Nate stepped past his father out onto the porch and looked around but saw nothing unusual. He was about to return to the house when a sudden movement caught his eye. Stuck beneath the driver side windshield flapped a folded sheet of paper.

Reverend Richards started to follow his son onto the porch, but Nate waved him back and then drew his handgun from the black composite holster at his side. He moved further from the door and pressed his back against the wall and looked around. A sudden gust of wind blew snow across the lawn and swirled in the empty street. There was no one there.

The roar of what sounded like a truck engine and tires squealing resonated in the still night air, then faded. With careful steps, Nate followed a set of fresh footprints leading from the porch to the curb. Holding his gun at the low ready, he stopped and listened for the sounds of movement.

After a moment, he slipped the Glock back into its holster and continued toward the street where his car was parked. Above him, the purple vault of night had cleared; a new dusting of snow had fallen. The hood and windshield of his Jeep lay beneath a half inch of new snow, all except for the driver's side of the front window. Someone, judging from the smudge pattern, had used a forearm and brushed the snow from the glass just in front of the driver's seat.

What Nate thought to be a folded sheet of paper, turned out to be an envelope. Folded and stuck beneath the windshield rested a large manila packet, the ends flapping in the intermittent gusts of wind.

Taking the envelope, Nate looked around again as he judged the weight of the packet in his hand. "What is it?" His dad called from the porch. Nate held the envelope up in his hand for his dad to see.

"Come on back in the house. Get out of this cold."

Nate looked around again, wondering after the sound of the vehicle speeding away in the distance. Slapping the packet against his thigh, he headed back to the house.

Once inside and standing near the fireplace, Nate lifted the small metal tabs holding the flap shut. His mother and Amber crowded around his shoulder trying to look past him to the envelope in his hands. Gracie stood by Reverend Richards, who was still looking out the window beside the front door.

Pulling a single sheet of paper from the envelope, Nate flicked his wrist causing the paper to unfold in his hand. Smoothing the page, he read the sheet out loud.

"'Nevertheless, if thou warn the righteous man, that the righteous sin not, and he doth not sin, he shall surely live, because he is warned; also thou hast delivered thy soul.'"

"Ezekiel chapter three…" Reverend Richards said perplexed, "from the King James translation."

Nate turned the paper around so his father could see it, then scratched his chin. "I don't get it." He accepted a cup of coffee from his mother who had walked up beside him. After taking a drink of coffee, he turned his attention back to his father.

Reverend Richards walked over to the table by his recliner. Picking up his worn leather Bible, he flipped open the pages to the Old Testament book of Ezekiel. "Strange passage to quote from," he said, tracing along the page with his finger. Taking out his reading glasses from his breast pocket, he licked his finger then flipped the page once more. "Yeah, here it is," he said without looking up.

Nate leaned against the mantel as his father read the passage out loud. He arched his brow as his father read the passage in context. "Is it a warning then?"

Reverend Richards closed his Bible and cleared his throat. "Yeah, the passage refers to a warning given to the prophet by the Lord. If Ezekiel failed to do the work God commanded him, in this case, to tell the people about their sin, God would judge them, but He would also hold the prophet as guilty for not doing what he had been commanded to do."

Sherri moved over and sat in her own chair next to her husband. A worried scowl furrowed her face. "Do you think this is some kind of warning for you, Nate?"

Both Amber and Gracie settled on the sofa. Nate looked around the small room. Everyone's eyes were on him.

CHAPTER TWENTY-NINE

JUST UNDER AN HOUR LATER, Nate dropped the folded note on the desk in front of Mac. "What is it with you and packages in the middle of the night?" Mac said sarcastically, referring to the very first case he had worked on with Nate where an unknown person had dropped off a box just outside his apartment door.

"Ha, ha," Nate said and sat on the corner of the desk. He lifted his foot and rested it on the edge of a chair then leaned forward and propped his elbows on his knees. "Sorry about your evening. How was Sara?"

"She'll get over it."

Nate cocked an eyebrow at his partner. "Really?"

Mac leaned back and crossed his legs at the ankles, a wry smile coloring his face. "Well, right after we get back from the coast, that is. I had to promise her a long weekend to get out of the doghouse on this one. As soon as this case is done, we're outta here."

Nate dropped his feet from the chair and stood up. "I had the paper both dusted and fumigated. Nothing. Whoever left that for me made sure it was clean. The thing that burns me on this is we're no closer than we were at the beginning."

Mac grunted but did not respond otherwise. He stood and began walking around the pod. Coming back to the desk, he grabbed the case folder and flipped it open. "What do we know?" he asked.

Nate stared at the open folder and then sighed. "First, we've got a serial killer targeting RSO's, and he's leading three bodies to none. The first shot with a PVC gun; the second, a twenty-two to the back of the skull; the third, a pickaxe to the temple, and a blond woman scared out of her mind. Did I miss anything?"

Mac grunted again. "Not much, huh?"

"Coffee?"

"Yeah, I need something. I should be getting ready for bed right now."

Nate walked over to the coffee pot and began to fill two cups. Looking through the open doorway he saw Lieutenant Haynes sitting behind his desk with his eyes closed. Nate could see that his computer was already turned off, undoubtedly ready to call it a night. After stirring in cream and sweetener, he carried the cups back to Mac's desk. "Maybe we've missed something. Let's go back to the beginning."

Nate handed a Styrofoam cup of coffee to Mac, then sat in front of the computer monitor. He brought up the master file and scrolled through until he found the file labeled Daily Log. He clicked on the folder, opening it, and paged back to the week of the first killing, then began reading. Most of the entries were mundane listings; car alarms, traffic accidents, then noted the call of the shots fired entry. He continued scrolling.

Most of CID had been scheduled off for the holiday. Only a few lucky souls were kept in on open cases with deadlines pending. Lieutenant Haynes was just one of those cops that liked being around the office.

Nate stared at the screen, holding the scroll button as several days' of entries passed by with nothing of particular interest catching his attention. He looked up at Mac. "There's nothing here."

Mac walked over and planted his palms on the desktop. "Go to the analyst page. Let's check the—"

"F.I. cards," Nate said interrupting him. He paged through the entries until he came to the date of the Sansome murder. There were six F.I. cards logged for that morning. Nate clicked on the entry.

The screen flashed and then the scanned image of the card enlarged. "Look at this," Nate said over his shoulder.

Mac stopped pacing. "What?"

Nate moved the cursor along the lines of the card. "On the morning of Sansome's murder, Officer Peters F-I'd an unidentified white male parked in the area about an hour or so before the body was discovered."

Mac reached past Nate and grabbed the file off the desk. "An hour…that puts it at just about the M.E.'s estimation of time of death." He dropped the folder back on the desk and pointed to the M.E.'s report.

Nate minimized the screen and brought up the RNQ mask and ran 10-28, a registration check, on the vehicle's license plate. The screen went dark, and after several long moments, the registration information began to flicker onto the screen.

```
----Tan 1989 Ford Ranger---
----Registered to...---Timothy L. Jackson Sr.
```

"This is taking too long," Nate said to no one in particular and picked up the phone. "Dispatch, this is TC9019, I need a 10-28 on…" he stopped, adjusted the screens and read the license information to the dispatcher.

"Are you on a call," this dispatcher asked.

"No, just checking some information. I'd appreciate it if you could hold me a hard copy of that, and I'll stop by and grab it on my way out."

"Copy that, no problem. Stand by one." The dispatcher left the phone and the muffled noises of the dispatch center filtered over the line as Nate waited.

"Richards."

"Yeah, go ahead."

"I show a tan, 1989 Ford Ranger registered to a Timothy L. Jackson Sr. Last known address is at 223 West Cherry Avenue in Meridian.

"I know you didn't ask for it, but I have his DOB showing, 03-15-27, six feet, 265 pounds, brown and blue. No wants, no warrants."

"Now, that's what I call service," Nate said with a chuckle.

"Nothing but the best for the lucky stiffs who have to work on Thanksgiving night."

"Happy Thanksgiving to you too," Nate said and hung up. "We've got an address for our guy in the truck."

"What's all this noise over here," Lieutenant Haynes said, leaning against the wall beside the desk.

"I think we've got a lead," Nate said, standing and grabbing his coat. Mac was already dressed and wrapping a scarf around his neck.

"Hold on there, Wyatt Earp," Haynes said, his southern accent growing deeper, "let's not get the horse out in front of the saddle. If you think this could be our guy, maybe we ought to make this a tactical approach, get SWAT involved."

"Come on L.T., it's almost 2300 hours" Mac said. "We're just going to knock on the door and say hi, just like we do a hundred times a day in this job."

"But it's that hundred and first time that bites you in the butt," Haynes said and crossed his arms over his chest.

Nate grabbed the file. "Look L.T., we'll just make contact and see what's what. The name on the registration is for an eighty-three year old man. We'll just make contact and see if anyone else has been using his vehicle. Nice simple citizen contact.

"Nice and simple—" Haynes began but the door closed behind Nate and Mac as they left the pod, cutting off the lieutenant's response.

***

Ten minutes later, Nate and Mac found themselves driving just below the posted speed limit as they passed 223 West Cherry. The entire neighborhood appeared dark, like everyone had decided to go to bed early on the holiday weekend. "I'm going to circle the block again, see if there's anything moving besides us," Nate said, without taking his eyes off the house on the south side of the street.

The Jeep's engine idled as he accelerated slightly and turned around the corner, leaving the house behind them. As they completed the lap, Nate pulled over to the curb and parked the car.

Mac looked at his partner and laughed. "I know you like to go in on foot, but you could have parked a little closer, its 37 degrees out there. And you say you don't like winter."

"Well, I just don't want to get shot trying to get out of my car," Nate said and laughed.

"What? It's just a simple citizen contact."

CHAPTER THIRTY

TIM JACKSON SAT OUTSIDE the St. Luke's ER and watched as the detective and the lady cop talked. He saw them laugh, and that's when he knew that the detective was being deceived. He had to warn, at least try to save him. Tim knew that at one time the detective had to have been a righteous man. A true servant.

He looked back at the sliding glass doors leading into the ER then he looked down at his watch. It was only 8:30. He still had time. But it had to happen tonight. The voice had said so.

Tim watched as the detective drove off in his Jeep with the lady cop following behind him in her car. He wasn't sure why, but he felt he needed to follow them, to keep an eye on them.

An hour later he watched as the detective went into a house. He figured from the way the people greeted him at the door it must have been his family. Tim flinched when the older man reached out, grabbed the detective's shoulder, pulled him into the house and then closed the door. Despite the cold, his truck's heater wasn't working. Tim was sweating.

You saw him. The *voice* said.

Tim nodded.

He's just like your dad, always touching, feeling, grabbing, hurting.

Tim began to shake.

You must save him. Don't let it happen to him too.

Tim grabbed the sides of his face and pulled at the loose skin. The *voice* got louder, demanding. *Do it now! Do it now!*

He lowered his forehead to the steering wheel resting in between his hands. The voices were getting louder; contradicting one another; demanding.

You have to do it now!

Save him! Warn him!

It's too late!

Do it. Do it. Do it! Do it! Do it! Do it!

Then everything stopped, and Tim knew he was alone...for now. Grabbing a towel off the seat, he wiped his face. Slipping on a pair of rubber gloves he used to mix cleaning chemicals, Tim slipped a single sheet of typing paper from a folder and wrote a note for the detective.

Walking carefully up to the front of the house, Tim looked into the plate glass window and saw the people moving toward the back of the house. Quickly, he ran back to the detective's Jeep and, using his forearm, wiped the freshly fallen snow from the windshield and clipped the note under the wiper blade.

He snapped his face from side to side, looking around. The neighborhood was quiet still. Crouching, he made his way back to the house and rang the doorbell, then began beating on the door before scurrying away and hiding in his truck, which he had parked just around the lip of the cul-de-sac.

Once he was sure the detective would get his warning, Tim headed back to the hospital. He only had two and a half hours before his time would be up, and *He* would come.

Tim stopped in the main parking lot of the hospital and watched the security guard sitting behind the large desk reading a news magazine. Tim used his hands to brush his hair back. With a jerk of his head, like a bird, he looked back up at the security guard. He pulled his collar tight around his neck. He checked the guard again. He slipped on his ball cap. He found the guard again.

Getting out of his truck, Tim walked with quick steps and passed through the rotating door without being noticed, just one more distraught family member coming in to check on a sick or injured loved one. The halls were mostly empty this time of night. Just a few groups of people huddled in front of the TV or entertaining small and tired, but over stimulated children.

Tim turned his back to the security guard station, walked out of the ER waiting room to the main hall, and pressed the elevator call button. He got off on the third floor, his best guess as to where the Johansson woman had been moved. He sauntered over to the waiting area and sat in the corner seat behind the large aquarium. Opening a Sports Illustrated magazine, he settled in to listen and wait.

CHAPTER THIRTY-ONE

NATE WALKED UP onto the small porch, the wood squeaking beneath his steps. A fine sheen of frost had formed on the wood where snow had melted and then frozen, demanding that each foot be placed with purpose to avoid slipping. Small drifts of snow piled up near corners and on the backsides of empty flowerpots where they had been protected from the gusting breath of wind. He looked at his wristwatch and then at Mac, who had stayed on the ground to provide cover if the need arose.

He pressed the doorbell.

After several minutes, the porch light came on and Nate stepped to the opposite side of the door, and Mac moved a step back under cover of shadow. The door swung open and Clara Jackson stood framed by soft light. "Yes," she said in a small voice. The woman was diminutive and looked frail. She wore a thin shawl wrapped around bony shoulders and stood with a slight stoop, like an animal that had been beaten once too often.

"Hi, Mrs. Jackson. My name is Detective Richards. I'm with the Treasure Valley Police Department. Can we come in and speak with you, please?" Nate signaled Mac, and he walked out of the shadow and joined his partner on the porch.

Clara didn't answer, but rather turned and walked back into her home. The temperature was the first thing Nate noticed. It wasn't much warmer inside than it had been on the porch. He followed her into the short hallway. Mac pushed the door closed behind them. As they made their way in, Nate noticed that the rooms were dark. The only light appeared to be coming from down the hall from the small kitchen.

Passing the stairs, Nate pointed two fingers at his eyes then pointed toward the stairs. Mac nodded his understanding, and posted himself so he could keep an eye on the stairs and the landing.

Nate cleared his throat and called to Clara, who still hadn't said anything, but had stopped and lowered herself on a small bench-like seat in the archway separating the kitchen from the dining room. "Mrs. Jackson?"

She looked up, but didn't speak.

Nate tried again. "Mrs. Jackson, is your husband home? I need to speak to him about his 1989 Ford Ranger."

She looked at him this time and seemed to focus on his face. "You're looking for Big Tim?"

"Yes, ma'am," Nate said, taking a step closer to her.

She smiled and then pointed toward the stairs. "He's in bed. Timmy put him to bed for me."

Nate looked back at Mac, who raised and dropped his shoulders. "Mrs. Jackson, do you think you could call him downstairs so we can talk to him?"

She smiled and reached out and patted the back of Nate's hand. "He's in the bed, dear. You can go up if you like." She raised a skeletal hand and, with palsied tremors, pointed toward the ceiling.

Nate fixed his gaze on Mac as he began, with careful steps, moving up the stairs. He looked back at Clara, who was muttering to herself in a low voice and appeared no longer to be aware of the two detectives. He joined his partner on the steps.

With each rise, the ancient steps creaked and moaned beneath the weight of the men. The odor of staleness and dust filtered up as they moved. The darkness hung like thick smoke on the upper level of the home. Each open door hid a threat. Around every corner violence waited. Both men carried their weapons at the low ready, communicating with hand signals, avoiding speaking out loud.

The landing opened onto a short hall, with two doors on either side, and one at the opposite end from them. Nate slid along the wall with his shoulder hovering just above contact. Across from him, Mac cut the wedge of the doorway, setting himself at a forty-five degree angle and giving him a clear line of fire.

Pulling out his flashlight, Nate illuminated the first room. A bedroom; it was empty. A few boxes and a broken chair made up the entirety of its furnishings. Sidestepping, Nate entered the darkened opening, careful to place his first foot down before lifting the next. Mac took position in the doorway with his back toward Nate and covering the hall and other open doors.

After checking the closet, Nate raised the four fingers of his left hand, signaling to Mac the code-four.

The men moved back into the hall, this time Mac taking the lead and Nate moving into the cover position. They checked the second bedroom and found it furnished, but otherwise empty. A third bedroom had a mattress tucked in one corner and several cardboard dressers, most of which were pulled open or missing altogether. Judging from the posters of young male rock performers, with their dark make-up and sparsely clad bodies pictured with vulgar gyrations and angry expressions, Nate figured the room belonged to a teenager. The flowers painted on the walls suggested it belonged to a teenage girl. The room at the end of the hall turned out to be the bathroom, also empty.

Nate pointed to Mac and then to the opposite side of the last bedroom door, positioning himself across from his partner. He pushed the door open and walked into the darkness. The odor of old decay assaulted him. Pulling up the collar of his shirt, he covered his nose and mouth and moved into the room. Leveling his gun at a figure he saw in the bed, Nate ordered the person not to move. "Treasure Valley Police. Let me see your hands."

Mac moved in quickly, moving away from Nate, getting an angle on the person lying beneath the covers and defeating a possible crossfire situation.

Nate gave the order again. "Show me your hands. Now!" Sidling up, he snatched the covers off the person and stepped back as Mac moved forward and took the contact position. "Freeze!" Mac demanded.

Mac covered his mouth then stepped back. Nate moved forward again and pointed his Surefire G2X mini-LED flashlight at the figure on the bed. Lowering his gun, he moved back with two quick strides toward the door and turned on the overhead light.

Lying on the bed positioned on its back as if asleep, rested a partially decayed body, a kitchen knife protruding from its chest. "What the—" Mac said and looked over at Nate. "What is going on here?"

The corpse appeared to have been in the bed for several months. The skin dried and wrinkled from exposure to cold air and time. Nate walked around to the far side of the bed and looked over the scene again, studying the bedding and items left on the nightstand. He pulled out his cell phone and called dispatch. "Dispatch, this is D9016."

"D9016, go head."

Nate advised the call taker of the discovery and requested the coroner and crime scene team. After that, he and Mac made their way back downstairs. They found Clara still sitting at her desk, still engaged in her one sided conversation.

Mac went outside to flag down emergency personnel as they arrived.

Nate stood over Clara and laid a hand on her slender shoulder. "Mrs. Jackson—Clara?" She didn't respond. He moved around in front of the woman and knelt down.

He tried again. "Clara, who is that in that bed upstairs? Is that your husband?"

"Yes, Tim is in bed. Timmy put him there for me," she said and smiled. Her eyes, a milky gray from what looked like untreated cataracts, seemed to focus on Nate's face, then soften. "Timmy came home to take care of his mother. He's a good boy, Timmy."

Nate looked toward the open doorway.

He stood and walked into the kitchen and noticed the dining table still set. One plate of dinner had been picked over, but not eaten. A second smaller plate lay in the sink, wiped out but not washed.

Nate turned and walked back to Clara. "Clara, where is Timmy?"

"Timmy's a good boy. He came back to take care of me."

"Yes, Timmy is a good boy, but where is Timmy now?"

She stood up and walked toward the kitchen. "I have to get his dinner ready. He should be home soon. He had to finish his work. He's doing God's work, you know?" She looked back at Nate, pride coloring her wrinkled face.

"What's his work, Clara? What is it that Timmy has to do?" Nate asked as he followed her into the kitchen. He caught her by the hands, stopping her busyness. "Clara, what does Timmy have to do for God?"

She smiled up at him. "He has to finish the cleansing. Those who hurt the children. They *must* be stopped, you know."

"Yes, Clara, but where is Timmy now?"

"He cleansed his uncles." She leaned toward Nate and whispered, "You know they weren't really his uncles, but they all did bad things. They hurt the children too."

Mac came in through the door. "Coroner's here—" He stopped when he saw Nate holding Clara's hands and talking to her.

Nate looked at his partner. "Get patrol in here. We need to get to the hospital."

***

Mary left the restaurant and noticed that it was almost nine o'clock. Three more hours, she mused. Standing just outside the door taking in the winter landscape, she felt refreshed, cleansed. After her conversation and prayer with the elderly priest earlier that morning, she was determined to see her life through a new and different lens. Only a few cars drove by, and the silence felt almost alive. The snow sparkled in the soft glow of moonlight, and the occasional zephyrs made wisps of white, lifted from drifts to rise and fall back on themselves like waves in water.

Feeling the odd weight in her purse against her side, she sighed and looked up at the silver globe hanging in the night sky. Pressing the fingers of her left hand against her temples, she fingered the scar, leaned against the wall, and began to pray, her lips moving in silent desperation.

"Hey, sweetie, looks like you could use some company tonight. If we play our cards right, we could both have something to be thankful for by tomorrow morning." The male voice broke into her reverie, reminding her of all the things she despised.

When she didn't respond, the man moved a step closer to Mary. His cologne, a mixture of stale beer, unwashed body, and the lingering fragrance of cigarettes assaulted her. He touched her shoulder. Her breath caught in her throat. Gasping, she stepped back.

"Hey now, don't be like that. We had such a promising start." He raised a dirt and oil creased knuckle, and brushed her cheek.

Startled, she turned to walk back inside the restaurant.

He grabbed her. "I said don't be that way!" He squeezed her shoulders and pulled her back against his chest. "Now, isn't that better?"

Mary screamed and spun, swinging her purse by the strap. The bag collided with a dull thud against the man's forehead.

He stumbled backwards.

Without hesitating, Mary reached into her purse, grabbed the small handgun, and pointed the short black barrel at the face of her attacker. "You like hitting women, jerk!? You think it makes you more of a man, don't you?" Shifting her thumb, she cocked the hammer of the gun with a soft click, shifting it into single action. The gun steady in her hands.

"Wait, lady! I'm sorry, okay. I'm sorry."

"Oh, you're sorry now. You're sorry that this time the woman has all the power, and you're the one begging not to be hurt, not to be used." Mary remembered the feelings of helplessness and fear as she had begged her ex-husband to stop hitting her. She had promised, had cajoled, but nothing penetrated the haze of anger and hatred that burned in his eyes.

"Please, lady…I'm sorry. I said I was sorry."

Focusing on the man standing in front of her, Mary adjusted her aim from his face to about two feet lower.

The man screamed, stepped backwards, stumbled, and began to whimper. "Lady, I promise you. Somebody help me!"

Speaking in a low steely voice, Mary walked forward. "Scream out again and I'll take what little manhood you do have." Ignoring the cold, the man began crab walking away from her, trying to put distance between himself and the woman with the gun.

"Please, lady, I'm sorry." He was crying now. He shuffled backwards again and his hand slipped on a patch of ice, sending him sprawling flat on his back. "Please…I'm begging you, don't shoot me."

She stared at him, and the rage inside her grew. More memories exploded into her mind. *Helplessness. Fear. Pain. Worthlessness.* Her sense of having no control and no say in what would or would not happen to her. They all came back to her in a rush. The anger swelled. Her finger caressed the trigger.

She focused on the man's eyes. They were wild with fear. Removing her left hand from the gun, she reached beneath the curls of her hair and felt the scar on her face. "You're just like him," she said in a hoarse whisper and lowered her hand back to the gun.

"Ms. Higgins?" It was Karrie from her counseling group. "Ms. Higgins, what's going on?"

Mary didn't look away from the man, but thought she heard someone calling her name. The voice called again. Finally, she looked toward the sound.

She focused on the concerned face staring at her. "Ka-Karrie…" she said in a halting voice. "Karrie, call the police. Hurry up. I don't know how long I can keep from shooting him."

"It's okay, Ms. Higgins. I saw what he did to you. I'll tell the police everything."

A few minutes later, Mary found herself sitting in the backseat of a police car. The door was left open, but the heat was on high, and she could feel it blowing against her face. In another car on the far side of the parking lot was the man that had assaulted her. The officer had told her that the man had several warrants out for his arrest, two for sexual assault.

The officer walked back to the car where he'd left her. She watched him coming toward her, his notepad in his hand. He'd just finished talking with Karrie and two other witnesses to the incident, an older man and his wife.

The officer leaned down, but was careful not to crowd her and not touch her. She was grateful for his consideration. "The witnesses all verify your story," he said. "If I can get a little information from you, we can get this wrapped up."

She looked up at him. She felt haggard and was sure she looked it. Running a hand through her hair and pushing it back from her face, she whispered, "I almost shot him...a part of me wanted to."

The officer stood up and looked at her again. "Mrs. Hig—"

"Miss, I'm not married."

"Sorry 'bout that. Miss Higgins. I think it might be a good idea if I get somebody out here to talk to you. To help you make sense of all this." He smiled at her. She figured he was trying to soften the effect of his statements. "But I'm gonna hold on to that gun for a while. I know your CCW cleared, but I don't think it would be a good idea right now for you to have that back."

"You think I'm crazy, officer? Well, I'm not. I'm trying to tell you that there was a part of me that really wanted to shoot that man. Not just for what he did to me tonight, but for all the men like him that are still free, hurting little girls and beating up their wives and girlfriends. You got somebody who can talk to me about that?!"

"Look, Miss Higgins, I'm just saying that right now is not the best time for you to be making any serious decisions. Let me get someone for you to chat with, just to make me feel better. Wha-da-ya-say?

She smiled at him, but it didn't reach her eyes. "Okay, just to make you feel better."

He turned to walk away, speaking into a mic clipped to his shoulder lapel.

"Officer," she called to him. He stopped. "Do us both a favor and get rid of that gun for me. I think it would be better for both of us if I just didn't carry that thing around with me. You know what I mean?"

He flashed his brilliant smile, and again, continued his turn away from her. She could hear him speaking into the mic, but could no longer distinguish his words. Leaning her head against the doorframe, she exhaled and, once again, looked up into the vaulted purple sky. "Thank You."

She couldn't explain it, but she knew God had somehow given her the answer she needed. All the years she had carried around her anger and unforgiveness for the injustice she suffered at the hands of her ex-husband. The feeling of being weighed down by the burden of shame. In the breath of a prayer, God had healed her.

She took off the glasses she wore to help hide the scar. Folding the arms, she laid them on the backseat of the patrol car, stood up, and walked away.

Karrie was standing near the front door of the restaurant, her eyes bright with wonder. The girl had been waiting for her. Coming closer, she smiled at the teen. "Have you had dessert yet, Karrie?"

"Um, no Ma'am. But…ah, Miss Higgins, that was awesome."

"Come on, it's on me." She draped a hand around the shoulders of the young lady, and together, they walked back into the diner.

RAY ELLIS

CHAPTER THIRTY-TWO

TIM JACKSON SAT LOW in the seat, his hat pulled over his eyes as if asleep. "I will! Stop pushing me. Okay?" he mumbled through clenched teeth. Tucked in the corner behind the large saltwater aquarium, the noise from the filtration system covered his occasional grunts and complaints against the voices, which urged him to do *their will*. "What! Don't you see the officer over there?"

Tim watched as the uniformed officer walked to the coffee stand and began pouring himself a cup of coffee. As the elevator door opened with a ring, he slouched lower in the seat as a second officer got off and began joking with the first. Straining, Tim could barely hear snatches of their conversation. "…3028, sleeping…no…hours…"

Stirring as if waking, Tim mumbled and stood on shaky, unstable legs. Then walking like he had purpose, he headed toward the men's room. Once around the corner, he darted through the double doors and began reading door numbers. "3021," he said rubbing the plastic doorplate attached to the wall. He hurried.

Near the end of the hall, the nurse's station was empty and a lone chair sat just outside room 3028. Without hesitating, Tim opened the door and slipped inside.

In the middle of the small room, a single figure, small beneath the covers, lay on its side facing away from the door. Judging from the deep regular breathing, he figured she was indeed asleep. The officer had been right on both counts.

Kill her! It's time for judgment. The voice demanded in his mind.

"I know," Tim said in a short angry burst of energy. He swatted at an unseen hand. "Stop pushing me!"

He inhaled, causing his chest to rise and then fall, letting the air out in a continuous stream through flared nostrils. He stepped toward the bed. Reaching inside his jacket, he pulled out a fixed bladed knife. The six inch serrated edge glowed yellow in the soft sheen of low light. Raising the dagger, he stood over the woman.

On the bed, the woman rolled toward him. Her eyes opened wide in fear. In the low light he couldn't see their color, but he knew they were blue. He pressed his hand over her mouth stifling the scream he read in her face. She grabbed at his hand, clawing into the dry calloused flesh. With detached interest, he studied her.

She trembled.

With slow deliberate motion, he brought the tip of the knife low, until its razor tip touched her cheek. He could see that she began to understand.

Turning to look over his shoulder, he tensed. He grimaced and then stretched his face as if in pain. His body spasmed.

Do it now! Do it… Do it… Do it… Do it!

"I will. Don't push me," Tim said and forced his focus back to the lady. *No. Not a lady, a…a child molester!*

She was looking passed him now staring at *Him.* Tim didn't want her talking to *Him.* He squeezed her face. "Don't… look…

at…*Him*." Tim ground her lips against her teeth, adding emphasis to each word. "You talk to me! You deal with me!" Tim pressed the blade into the soft skin of her cheek. A single burgundy streak made its way first into her hair then onto the white bedding.

"Okay." The woman mumbled against his hand. She was crying. She still had her hands on his but was no longer pulling against them.

She has accepted her fate. He studied her features again. She was pretty.

"You were made to be special…"

Kill her!

"Created to be a mother…"

Do it! Do it! Do it, now!

"You were supposed to be a protector of innocence." His voice was beginning to tremble.

Judge her!

He screamed at the illusion. "Can't you see I'm doing it?!" He paused as if listening. "She has to know why first."

***

Crystal knew her worst nightmare had come true. The man holding her mouth was crazy, and he held a knife to her face. *He's going to kill me. No, no….* She tried to shake her head. *I'm not ready to die.*

She trembled as she looked into the psychotic eyes of the killer and knew she couldn't reason with him, that begging would not help her. He would show her no mercy.

The cut on her face began to sting as her tears ran into the wound. *Who is he talking to?*

His hand pressed harder against her mouth. She could feel her teeth cutting into her lips. The old feelings were starting to reassert themselves. She was beginning to give up, starting to slip back into old patterns. Resolved, she stopped struggling.

Standing above her the man looked wild but conducted himself with purpose. "You know why you must die, don't you?"

She shook her head no.

"You are a sinner, and sinners deserve to die," he said, leaning close to her face. She could smell the odor of chemicals and an unwashed body.

She shook her head no. The man tensed, as if struck by her words. The cords in his neck stood out like taunt ropes, his finger dug into her face. White flecks of spittle jotted from his lips as he tried to speak. He drew the knife back as if to stab her. She snatched his hand from her face. "Yes. Yes, I'm a sinner," she blurted. Tears streamed from her eyes as she clung to her last desperate hope.

"Then you agree you deserve to die." It had been a statement; one he assumed she agreed with. He lowered his arm and his tension lessened.

Lord, help me. Pastor Richards said if I gave my life to You that You would always be with me. That You would be a present help when I needed it. Lord, help me now! "Yes, I am a sinner, but this morning I became a Christian," she said and took a shallow breath. "So, Jesus took away my sins. And I don't have to die for what I did wrong because Jesus died for me! Jesus died for me!" She rushed the words out, hoping he would listen, that he would hear her.

The man's eyes went vacant. "Stop, I can't think with you screaming in my ear. Give me a minute!" He stepped back from the bed and ran both hands through his hair, the knife still clutched in his fist. Crystal watched as the blade arced up and away from her face. He turned toward the door and bent over at the waist. He harrumphed and moaned as if he had been punched.

Crystal jumped up from the bed and pushed the emergency call button that dangled from the end of the control cord. She positioned the bed between herself and the assailant like a shield.

He turned back to face her. "You lied. You're a liar! You're trying to trick me!"

She could see his eyes focus on the flashing red light and then he screamed. He charged her.

She pushed the bed toward him and ran toward the door. The bed hit him just below his hips, and he fell forward across the mattress.

Crystal grabbed the handle of the door and began to pull it open, freedom only a few inches away. A hand gripped her shoulder, and she felt herself being snatched around like a child's play thing. He forced her against the wall. Her head collided with a thud that resounded in her ears and made her knees buckle. His hand closed around her throat. "Now, you will die for your sins." He raised the knife, and the last thing Crystal saw was the man's arm beginning its downward arc toward her.

***

The elevator door slid open and Nate and Mac came out in a sprint. They passed the uniformed officer as he sauntered back toward room 3028. "Why aren't you at your post," Nate yelled as he passed him.

Coming to the nurse's station, the duty nurse was just getting up heading toward the room when she saw the officers running toward her and she stopped. "The emergency button has only been flashing for a few minutes," she said in defense of herself.

Nate grabbed the handle to room 3028 and crashed into it with his shoulder. The heavy wooden door swung open and banged into something solid. With a shallow flash of reflected light, an object flipped into the air and clinked against the linoleum floor before sliding under the bed. Mac came in behind Nate and, without hesitating, slammed a hard punch into the nose of Tim Jackson.

Jackson did not fall, but released his grip around Crystal's throat and stumbled backwards. Nate rushed forward and caught the unconscious woman before she could collapse to the floor. Looking at the uniformed officer and the nurse who had followed them into the room, Nate passed the petit woman off before turning to join the fight.

In the short time it had taken Nate to secure Crystal out of the room, Tim had surged with psychotic energy. With an obvious broken nose and blood streaming from his face, he attacked Mac and fastened both hands around the detective's throat, choking him.

Raising both hands above his head, Nate dropped a double-fisted hammer strike onto Tim's forearms, trying to break the grip. Nothing happened. It didn't appear to have any effect.

Nate reared back and punched him in the face; once, twice, three times. Although the physical damage could be seen, Tim did not release his grip on Mac, or otherwise react to the blows. Mac's face was turning a deep shade of purple.

"Clear. Taser! Taser! Taser!" the uniformed officer said, as he rushed back into the room. Nate rolled to his left just as the officer fired.

A sharp popping sound erupted, followed by the crackling of 50,000 volts of electricity as it danced along the wires and to the probes connected to Jackson's back. He snapped into rigidity.

Grunting and moaning, the janitor tried to fight the spasms as he fell like a cut tree, crashing first against the wall and then to the floor. Five seconds later, the officer reinitiated the surge of power through the two points of electrical connection. "Cuff him, Detective," he said.

Recovering, Nate grabbed his handcuffs from his belt and pulling both Tim's arms behind his back, he secured him. "Throw me your cuffs," Nate said and thrust a hand toward the uniformed officer.

"What for?"

"Throw me the cuffs. You saw the way he took those punches. I don't want to be standing between him and the door if he comes out of that single pair of bracelets I just put on him."

The officer tossed the handcuffs, and Nate snatched them out of the air. After securing the second pair just above the first set, he rolled Tim Jackson onto his side.

Mac managed to get back to his feet, rubbing his neck. "He had me pushed up against the storage locker. I couldn't get to my gun. Thanks." His voice was gruff as if he spoke around his words, like his mouth was full of rocks.

"I don't know if I'd want to shoot in here anyway with all the oxygen running through this place," Nate said.

"I bet if I'd got my hand on my gun you'd of found out. I'd rather die 'cause I shot the fool and blew myself up with him rather than standing there and have him strangle me like a chicken." Mac continued rubbing his neck. "That hurt."

"Actually, it was kind of funny," Nate said and smiled.

"Yeah, funny. Get him out of here before I shoot him anyway." Mac turned and leaned a hand against the wall.

Two more officers had arrived, and the three uniformed men strapped Tim, his arms tethered to his ankles by a cord to a gurney, and were rolling it to the elevator. Medical staff followed.

The charge nurse had taken over the care of Crystal and already moved her to another room where the on-call doctor was treating her. Nate closed his cell phone and slipped it back into his pocket. "The VWC is en route. Patrol is escorting her, and they both will stay with Crystal," he said to Mac.

"Are we gonna try and interview him tonight?" Mac asked, and they both knew who "him" was.

"We are not doing anything. We are going to ER to get your neck and throat looked at."

"What? I feel fine."

"Yeah, until you get home and your throat swells up and you die in your sleep. No sir, not on my watch. Let's go."

"Are you serious? After all we put into this, I'm gonna have to miss th—"

"I won't start the interview until we get word on you first. Okay? But if you have to stay then—"

"Then you do your job." Mac pulled an empty gurney, which had been abandoned in the hall, toward him.

"What are you doing?"

"If I've got to go to the ER then I'm riding." He laid down.

Nate laughed, but began wheeling the bed toward the elevator. "I sure hope you appreciate this."

Mac leaned on an elbow and smiled. "Happy Thanksgiving, partner."

"Thanksgiving?" Nate looked at his cell phone, checking the time.

"Eleven fifty-nine. Happy Thanksgiving, Mac," he muttered. "Now lie down before I dump you off this thing."

CHAPTER THIRTY-THREE

NATE LOOKED UP from his computer console. "Hey, it's Black Friday, wanna go shopping?"

"Yeah, funny," Mac answered in a gravelly voice.

Nate pressed the pads of his fingers against his eyelids and rubbed, trying to brush away the gritty burning feeling that had built up there. "Wow, is this really over?" he asked rhetorically.

Lieutenant Brown walked around the corner of the pod. "Not until the paperwork's on my desk gentlemen."

"Morning, sir," both men said, looking up.

"I got the command-page and decided to come in and see what all the fuss was about. The school janitor, huh?"

Nate leaned back and kicked his feet up on the desk, and Mac sat forward resting his forehead on the backs of interlaced fingers. "Who would have thunk it?"

"Yeah, who would've thunk it," Mac echoed.

Brown harrumphed and then laughed. "Look, both of you had a long day. Go home. Get some sleep and be back at 1100 hours. We'll brief then and see what all we got."

"Yes, sir," they spoke together, again.

"Sir," Nate said stopping mid stance. "Did anyone take care of Mrs. Jackson and that mess out there?"

RAY ELLIS

"Oh yeah. Rosie's working the scene. Probably be out there all night. Adult mental health took Mrs. Jackson. I understand they're trying to locate an adult daughter who's supposed to be living in L.A. or somewhere in Southern Cal."

Mac grunted and cleared his throat. "That's good," he said, "maybe she can get some help." He shrugged on his jacket.

"They found five other bodies besides Mr. Jackson," the lieutenant said. He rubbed his face, pulling his bottom lip slightly before releasing it. "All men. All murdered."

***

"The uncles," Nate said as he entered the CID workstation, rested after a few hours of sleep.

"The what?" Brown asked.

"The uncles. The group of men Mr. Jackson shared his son with." Nate had used the first two finger of each hand to make quotes signs when he said the word *shared*. Stretching forward, he grabbed the mug of coffee and rubbed it against his face. The late morning sun, although bright, did little as far as bringing warmth to the valley. The Boise Foothills, to the northwest of the station, still showed a few patches of gray-green beneath the cover of winter white that crept ever further down its sides.

Mac backed into the briefing room, holding the door open with his hip as he balanced a stack of files in one hand and a cup of coffee in the other. Rosie came in next, followed by a variety of very tired officers, both patrol and CID. "What about the uncles?" Mac asked.

After swallowing a mouth full of the bitter liquid, Nate looked at the cup as if wondering what was in it. "I stopped by Adult Mental Health on my way in and met with Mrs. Jackson. It

276

appears that the uncles were…," he stopped and rifled through a pile of papers on the table in front of him. Finding the sheet he'd been looking for, Nate looked up making eye contact with Brown before he read the names. "Seventy-eight year old Jessie McClure, reported missing in June of last year; seventy-seven year old Brian David Grove, missing since August 2007; sixty-nine year old Robert Boone Bolster, missing since February 2005; seventy-one year old Laverne S. Courtney missing since last spring; and finally, seventy-two year old Brian Kemmerer. And of course you all knew about the elder Mr. Jackson. Or should I say Elder Jackson." Nate finished and dropped the paper back onto the file.

Rosie spoke next. Using the back of her knuckle, she pushed her glasses up her small nose. She swiveled in her chair to face the front of the room. "Well, apparently Elder Jackson was the leader of this small group; a house church they called it. The six families all took vows, giving Elder Jackson almost complete control over them."

"What about children?" Mac asked.

"From what I could find from the records, and they kept copious records, there were a total of thirty-seven children," she continued. "Looks like the good elder may have been the daddy to most of them."

Lieutenant Haynes walked in through the double doors and stopped beside Nate. Leaning down near Nate's ear, he whispered so only Nate and Mac could hear. "Records say there's a Tracee Gaythwaite on the phone. She said she was Mrs. Jackson's daughter." He arched a brow at Nate, then continued forward and sat next to Lieutenant Brown.

Nate smiled, checked the time on his cell phone, and stood heading for the door. Mac made as if to follow him, but Nate waved him off.

***

Settling behind his desk, Nate activated the call record system then answered the phone. "Detective Richards."

The voice was hard that emitted from the phone. "Detective Richards, this is Tracee Gaythwaite. I'm Clara Jackson's daughter."

"Good morning Mrs. Gaythwaite, I'm so glad—"

"Yes, I'm sure you are. Look Detective, it's been over 30 years since I've been to my father's house, and I have no intentions of ever going back there. You have no idea the hell we lived through in that man's house."

Nate looked down to make sure the conversation was being recorded. "We're starting to get an understanding—"

"Be that as it may, my father was an evil man, Detective. Anything my brother has done, I'm sure can be laid at the feet of Elder Jackson. He and the uncles physically and sexually abused us children from the time we were in diapers. They called it discipline. And to make their points stick, they would make the rest of us watch when one of our brothers or sisters was being disciplined." Nate could hear her moving like she was pacing as she talked.

"Mrs. Gaythwaite, I'm sorry that you had to live under those circumstances, but we'll do everything we can now to help correct the mistakes your father made."

"Mistakes?!"

Nate winced and snatched the receiver away from his ear.

"Those were not mistakes," she continued. "He would beat my mother and then make little Tim beat her while he and the uncles watched. Do you have any idea what it does to the mind of an eight year old boy who is forced to watch his mother being physically and sexually abused, Detective?" She inhaled sharply, the intake of air loud in the receiver.

"I think so," Nate said quietly.

She laughed. Not a happy sound, but one filled with bitterness and sadness; the laughter of one who has lost all hope. "Detective, I know my brother has done some very bad things, but he's sick, you know." The earlier ferocity dissipated from her voice now, replaced by heaviness. "He's a very sick man." She began to cry.

Propping both elbows on the desk, Nate rested his forehead in his hand as he held the receiver against his ear. "I assure you we'll take that into consideration, but he has to be held accountable for what he did. You do understand that, don't you?" Nate asked purposefully, injecting softness into his voice.

"Well," she giggled and this time it held a hint of sarcasm, "you go ahead and do whatever you think is right Mr. Detective, but from where I'm sitting all my brother did was get rid of the garbage that you and the system didn't have the guts to take care of."

"I—"

"Detective Richards, I don't mean you any offense, but when you've grown up with men like my father and the uncles, there's not a whole lot of sympathy for men like them."

"I…" he hesitated waiting to be cut off again. "I think I'm beginning to understand. Mrs. Gaythwaite, may I have your permission to call you back about this if I have any further questions?"

"No, sir, you do not. I made this call out of respect for the woman my mother used to be, but I don't have any desire to be entangled in her world anymore. So, in answer to your question, Detective, no, I will not be coming down for the trial. Nor will I be coming down to take custody of my mother. And as far as the house goes…burn it!" She hung up.

Nate looked at the phone receiver in his hand for a long moment before dropping it back into the cradle. He stopped the recording, selected the playback function, and listened for a few minutes, checking to make sure the conversation had been saved.

He rubbed his face, still feeling the effects of too little sleep. *Lord, six men and all of them fathers.* Nate stood and turned toward the window. A blue and orange passenger plane made its entry approach toward the Boise Airport, the bright colors standing in contrast against the soft blue-white snow on the foothills. "How many lives did they destroy, Lord? And for them, where are they now…. Receiving judgment?" *Is it enough?*

Nate sat on the edge of his desk and thought back to the night when the first body was discovered and wondered what anyone could have done different. Was there any way he could have helped Tim Jackson, the easygoing soft-spoken janitor he and Mac had bumped into in the school hall?

Shaking his head, Nate stood and made his way back to the briefing room. *How many more Tim Jacksons, Lord?*

Upon entering the briefing room, he locked gazes with Mac. He moved his head in a slow motion from side to side. With heavy steps, Nate made his way to his seat. Exhaling, he allowed himself to simply drop into the seat beside his partner.

"How does any of that connect with our guy?" Patrol Officer Chet Baraza had just asked.

"According to the records, the uncles were responsible for doling out discipline. The records don't say what the discipline was, but it records the child's name, the date, and which uncle administered the discipline," Rosie said, looking over the tops of her glasses.

Nate closed his eyes and let his head roll back as he thought about the conversation with Tim's sister. *They would make the rest of us watch when one of our brothers or sisters was being disciplined.... The sisters.*

Renae Gonzaga, the VWC, took up where Rosie stopped, her voice cheery for no apparent reason. "I spoke with Crystal this morning, and she seems to be doing just fine. I understand that she was able to give a good statement to one of the officers about what happened at the hospital. And she said she will definitely hang around long enough to testify against our guy. That's all," she said and closed her file.

"Anything else from the house?" Nate asked of the room, in general, his eyes still closed.

This time one of the other detectives answered. "We found a list in our perp's bedroom with the names of our victims listed in chronological order by date of their offense. Our three dead guys' names had been crossed off and Mrs. Johansson's name had been crossed off and re-written, twice. We also found the PVC gun in the bedroom along with pictures of the crime scenes: the park, campsite, and the apartment."

Mac leaned forward. "Search warrant?" he asked the detective. After receiving the affirmative nod, Mac acknowledged it with a dip of his chin, sat back in his chair, and began flipping through his folder. "What about Willaby, anything on him?"

"No, but we did find the same type of thumb-drive as was dumped with the Monarch body. It's a good bet Jackson is good for that one as well," Rosie said and folded her arms across her ample breast. "Besides, his name is on Jackson's list. No doubt in my mind who killed Willaby."

"Very good, Madam Prosecutor," Lieutenant Haynes said standing. He paused until everyone looked his direction. "Now, let's finish strong. Get the evidence to put this animal away for life. Beyond reasonable. On all counts. That's what I want, people."

CHAPTER THIRTY-FOUR

NATE WALKED OUT of the debriefing with a heaviness he could not explain. *The threat was over. The killer locked up, and the lieutenants are happy.* He slapped the file folder he carried against his leg and harrumphed.

"Who stole the toy out of your Cracker Jacks box," Mac said bumping him with a shoulder.

Nate started. "Oh, it's nothing...I guess."

They walked in silence for a few steps before both men stopped, leaned against opposite walls, and stared at each other. "Something just doesn't feel right," Nate said.

"Come on, can't we just say job well done, get a cup of coffee, and then go home for once?" Mac stuffed his hands into his pockets, his own eyes red. He looked tired.

"You're right. Let's get a cup." Nate smiled. "Don't worry this one's on me."

***

Nate leaned back in his favorite seat at the Library Coffeehouse and enjoyed the fragrance of fresh ground coffee.

The warm roasted smell of the beans wafted throughout the small shop, interlaced with scents of the season: pine, nutmeg, and cinnamon.

With his eyes closed, he hummed along with an instrumental version of George Handel's, The Hallelujah Chorus, when a new fragrance caught his attention. Inhaling, he sat up as a smile grew across his face. He looked up and saw Jackie standing above him. Her brown eyes seemed to glow as she returned his smile.

"Hello stranger."

Standing, Nate took her hand and kissed the backs of her knuckles. "Hello yourself." He pulled her into an embrace and held her there enjoying the feel of her. She was warm against him as she lingered there, making no effort to pull away.

"Maybe I should just leave," Mac said, but made no effort to get up.

Nate pushed her back to arm's length and looked into her eyes. "Join us."

"I guess I can take a minute." Her smile never left her face as she sat across from Nate. "So, how's the big case coming? Any leads?"

Mac raised his cup in salute. "Case solved. This is our celebration party."

Nate looked at his partner and smiled, but the heaviness he'd felt earlier reappeared. He shook his shoulder and adjusted himself in the seat, trying to shake off the feeling. Beneath the table, Jackie grabbed his hand and squeezed it.

"Yep," Mac said, "bagged the old boy this morning...the school janitor."

Jackie leaned forward and rested her chin on the palm of her right hand, the knuckles curled against her cheek. "That poor girl." She shook her head and took a sip from Nate's cup.

She turned and smiled at him. "Hey, that's good."

"Yeah, I know the girl that works here," Nate said, "I could put a word in for you if you like." He kissed her hand again. "What did you mean, 'That poor girl'?' Jackson's a guy; Tim Jackson."

"Oh, I know, but they—he and his daughter come in here at least once a week for coffee. I think it was a daddy daughter kind of thing. They didn't talk much; just sat over there and finished their drinks." She nodded her head toward the rear corner.

Nate sat up and drew her hand back to the tabletop. Jackie reacted to him and sat forward, pulled by the gentle motion. "What is it?"

"You starting to freak me out, partner," Mac said, also sitting up. "What's going on? What do you got?"

"Do you know the daughter's name?" Nate asked.

"Why? What's going on?"

Nate didn't answer but stared into her eyes.

She cleared her throat. "Renae or Carrie or Kay…. Something like that. Is she involved or something?"

He stood and started toward the door, stopped, came back to the table and kissed her, a quick soft kiss on her upturned mouth. "Gotta go. I'll call you."

"You'd better." She waved at his retreating back.

"Kiss-kiss," Mac said, hurrying to catch up. "I'll call you too." He put thumb and pinky finger beside his face like he was talking on the phone.

***

Once in the car, Mac turned to face Nate. "What's going on?"

Nate didn't look up, but kept his eyes on the ice slickened road. "Karrie Jackson. The girl in the hallway outside that teacher's door, on the morning we bumped into Jackson."

"You think she's his daughter?"

Nate turned onto Fairview from Main and had to slow down as a delivery truck sped by the access lane. The resulting spray of dirty ice water covered the Jeep's windshield; forcing Nate to wait for several seconds before he could see clear enough to pull into traffic.

Mac took another sip of coffee from his travel mug. "So what? Just because she's his kid doesn't mean that she's in on this."

"It's something Tim's sister said. The uncles' always made the children watch when the discipline was being handed out. I think he made her watch."

"You think she's gonna try and finish the job her dad started?" Mac sat his mug into the cup holder and pulled his cell phone from his jacket pocket. He dialed.

"Dispatch, this is TV9016," Mac said into the phone. Nate looked at him out of the corner of his eye trying to hear dispatch's response.

Mac continued, "Can you get me a landline into the ER at St Luke's West or a cell for the officer on duty there with the witness?" A few seconds passed and it seemed like an hour.

Nate passed the Fred Meyer's at the corner of Locust Grove and Fairview, and again, had to slow down as a semi and trailer pulled out across lanes. He activated his emergency lights and crossed into the westbound lanes, fishtailing slightly on the slick surface. Accelerating, he pulled back into the eastbound lane, ahead of the truck this time.

"What?!" Mac said and acted as if he would throw the phone away. "Thank you," he said, then flipped the phone and closed it, slipping it back into his pocket.

"What? Don't leave me hanging."

"Uniforms cleared. Johansson's checking out and unescorted."

Nate pulled into the turn lane and headed south on Eagle Road. The early morning traffic usually ran slow and moved at slightly more than a jog when the roads were bad. He pulled into the center lane and urged the vehicle faster. On both sides of the road, cars slowed and pulled to the right of the street. Nate accelerated.

As they approached the Pine Street intersection, Mac reached forward and changed the pitch of the siren from the standard whaling cry to the two-tone "Ewhew-Ewhew" of the British police car.

Seeing that cross traffic had slowed, Nate entered the intersection. Just as he pressed the gas pedal, a green mini-van flashed across in front of him. Pulling the wheel hard to the right, Nate dropped the Jeep into a lower gear and accelerated.

The Jeep began to spin, its tail end whipping around, and the vehicle began to slide side-ways toward oncoming traffic. Nate looked up into the face of a wide-eyed woman with four children in the car as she lifted her hands from the steering wheel and screamed.

Nate down shifted again and turned the Jeep into the spin, bringing the nose back around until it faced south. The two vehicles passed with only a few inches of space between them, and Nate accelerated back in the center lane and headed toward the hospital.

They finally reached the parking lot after what seemed like forever, and Nate brought the Jeep to a sliding stop near the large revolving door of the ER waiting room. Mac leapt from the car and ran through the spinning door. Nate headed toward the lobby at the hospital main entrance, a few dozen feet ahead.

Choosing not to draw their weapons, the men entered the long hallway where the elevators opened. Nate looked over the heads of the various people in the hall and made eye contact with Mac. Pointing two fingers at his own eyes, he then pointed down the long external hall, which led back toward the medical suites and pharmacy. Mac nodded and turned to check with hospital security to give a description of the teen girl.

After a few minutes, Nate came back around the corner and waved Mac to him. "She checked out about ten minutes ago, but was supposed to be heading to the pharmacy to fill a prescription."

The men hurried down the hall, scanning the faces of the people in the crowd as they went. Rounding the corner into the main lobby, they stopped. The area wasn't overly crowded, most people being off for the day after Thanksgiving, but a few dozen souls wandered around. Broken in to small groups, the people clumped together in various locations around the large room.

Ahead of them to the right was the pharmacy, and just coming out, still dressed in the casual pants suit she'd worn the night of the shooting, Crystal Johansson walked out, her head down and unaware of her surroundings, looking into her bag.

As the lobby opened up before them, the men separated, each walking near opposite walls. Nate made eye contact with Mac and pointed toward the double glass doors, which led from the lobby to the west parking lot. Mac quickened his pace, hurrying around the information booth manned by the two gray haired grandmother types assisting a harried patron. He swung around to get in front of Crystal while Nate continued his approach from the rear and slightly to the side.

As Crystal approached the automatic doors, she stopped and looked up as if she heard a sound. She started backing away from the door; Nate could see fear in the woman's face. He started to call out to her, but stopped when a tall man wearing a long overcoat walked right past the woman, never looking her direction.

Crystal let her arms drop to her sides and sighed, the bag banging against her leg. For a long moment, she did nothing. Then gathering herself, she took a breath as if resolved and started toward the door. This time she did not stop.

As she passed through the electric doors, a young lady of about fifteen or sixteen approached her. She smiled and Crystal smiled back. As the teenager passed by her, she suddenly stopped and spun back toward the woman and screamed. She attacked.

***

When Crystal turned, she looked into the eyes of madness. She had seen that look once before, earlier that morning. The girl leapt at her, snarling like a feral cat. Flecks of yellowish-white spittle gathered at the corners of the girl's mouth as she brought the dagger down toward Crystal's breast.

Feeling like she had nothing left to give, she resigned herself to death. As if everything was happening in slow motion, Crystal watched as the rusted blade arced downward toward her. She could see the wild look in the girl's eyes and knew she was screaming but couldn't understand what the sound was that was being made.

She felt her arms go up and her hands splay out in front of her and knew she should run but could not. She watched as her new bottles of meds slipped from her hands and fell toward the floor. She wondered if the pills would have helped. And then the blade fell.

Crystal felt a force hit her from behind, knocking her to the floor and then an oppressive weight holding her there. She could hear a voice, this one vaguely familiar, telling her that everything was all right. That she was all right.

Suddenly everything returned. The lobby was filled with the sound of people screaming, and she could hear what sounded like children crying. The weight on her chest lifted, and she looked into the face of Detective MacGilvery.

He smiled. "We've gotta stop meeting like this," he said and some part of her thought it was funny, but she didn't laugh.

The detective helped her to stand. About ten feet away, the other detective, Detective Richards, sat beside the crying girl. She was lying on her side. Crystal wondered why the girl was lying on the floor crying. Her mind was foggy; she couldn't get her thoughts to coalesce.

***

Nate grunted and rolled the crying teen to her side to take the pressure off her cuffed hands. He looked up to see Mac escorting Crystal back to the waiting area near the pharmacy and uniformed officers rushing into the lobby, their weapons drawn. He waved a four-fingered salute to them, indicating the situation was code four and that they could stand down.

Beside him, the girl was still crying as she rocked herself back and forth on the floor. "Sorry, Daddy. I'm sorry, Daddy, I tried. I tried. Will *He* leave us alone now, Daddy? Will the *voices* stop?"

Nate rested his hand on the girl's shoulder. "It'll be okay now, sweetheart. It's over now."

The girl stopped rocking and looked over her shoulder at Nate. Her face was placid, and her voice was calm when she spoke. "No, sir, there's seven more names on the list." She smiled and began rocking again.

CHAPTER THIRTY-FIVE

NATE STOOD NEAR THE MANTLE in his parent's living room, a cup of coffee in his hands. For long moments, he said nothing but simply looked into the fire, watching as red and yellow flames danced along the surface of the logs and wisps of smoke made its way up the flue.

"Penny for your thoughts." A voice sounded from behind him.

He turned to see Amber watching him from across the room. She had her hair pulled back from her face and tied in a loose braid at the nape of her neck. She smiled and he felt the effect of it in the pit of his stomach.

He returned her smile, and she walked over to stand near him. She was wearing Roots Spirit. Its cedar-woodsy fragrance smelled fresh and light, like she just showered in a wash of spring flowers. It was his favorite fragrance on her. She reached for his cheek, and he caught her hand and held it against his face. Their eyes met and held.

The crackle of the fire burning and soft hum of the heat being vented through the house was the only sound besides their breathing. Neither of them moved. Nether wanted to be the first to speak.

Finally, Nate waved his hand toward the sofa, and she turned to walk toward it. He watched her move and marveled at the way she made such a simple act into a thing of art. He'd forgotten how much he loved just looking at her.

They sat facing each other. She had one leg curled beneath her; the other foot dangled just above the carpeted floor. Their knees touched.

Nate cleared his throat. Outside the sun was setting, casting long shadows across the street. The first stars were just starting to rise in the deepening night. "I love this time of day," he said, looking past her to the window.

She didn't respond, but folded her hands in her lap and looked down at them. She chewed her lip.

Was she nervous? Nate cleared his throat again and she looked up. "Ah...we need to talk."

"Yeah," she said, her voice so soft he had to concentrate to hear it.

"Look, Amber," he grasped her fingers into his, "a lot has happened since you left. You've changed. I've changed. We're both very different people than we were a year ago. You're my best friend."

She began to cry.

"Come on now, don't do that." He reached forward and brushed away her tears. "Don't cry, please."

"It's not that easy when my heart feels the way it does."

"Look—"

"Nate, let me. I know I messed up. I don't know why I acted the way I did." She stopped and pulled her hand free of his. "No, that's not true. I do know. I was afraid. I'd loved you for so long and then when you finally told me that you loved me too.... I know I should have been happy, but all I was...was scared."

Nate started to speak but she placed a hand on his lips.

"Please, Nate." He sat back.

She stood and walked back to the fireplace. With her back to him, she continued to talk. "Jackie's a nice girl; a very lucky girl to have won your affections."

There was a long pause where she didn't say anything, didn't move. Nate began to feel uncomfortable. He looked at the darkened stairs, glad his parents had gone out. He adjusted his leg, straightening them out, rubbing stiffness from his thighs and calves.

Finally, she turned and faced him. This time she made no attempt to hide her tears. "Nate, I still love you. I will always love you. I don't know what will happen, but I want you to know, I walked out on you once, this time you'll have to be the one to leave."

Nate stood and walked over to where she was standing. Reaching out, he grasped both her hands in his. His thoughts swirled. He remembered all the times he and Amber had shared and the sadness he'd felt turned to anger as he thought again of her abandoning him. He recalled the earnestness he'd seen in her eyes as they shared breakfast a few days ago. And then, he remembered Jackie.

They were still standing this way when the door leading from the garage opened, and his parents walked into the kitchen. Gracie ran ahead of her foster parents as they laughed and began to unload the bags gathered during their Black Friday shopping spree. "What's going on in here?" she asked, coming into the living room.

Nate's parent followed her in, and the moment he'd shared with Amber was gone. He smiled at her. His father walked near the fire and held his hands up to the flames. "Hey, Son, you want to have dinner with us?"

Nate grabbed and squeezed his father's shoulder. "Somebody's been working out," he teased.

His dad flexed a bicep and leaned conspiratorially toward him. "I've got to keep your momma interested, you know."

"I hear you over there, you old goat," his mother called from near the kitchen door.

"So, what do you say, Son, you going to go to dinner with us? My treat."

Nate looked at Amber, but he spoke to his father. "No, Dad, I'm gonna have to take a pass on this one."

His father laughed. "You mean you gonna walk out on a free meal? I must have done something wrong when I raised you, Son." He laughed again, and turned back toward his wife and began talking about where they would go for dinner.

"So, are you going to walk away from this one?" Amber asked.

Nate dropped his gaze for a moment then looked back up. "Yeah. At least for right now." He picked up his coat and scarf and walked over to give his mother a kiss. Gracie began pulling out packages and showing them to Amber who was only half paying attention, but smiled at the younger lady.

"How about you, Amber," Sherri called. "Where do you want to go for dinner?"

Nate reached the door and began to open it when he looked back. Amber caught his gaze as she spoke to his mother. "You know, Mother Richards, you guys go ahead and go, I'll just wait here until you get back."

Nate stared at her and watched as the solitary tear streaked across her cheek, and he understood what she was saying. He pulled the door closed behind him and wrapped the scarf tight around his neck. Walking out into the snow, he chanced one look back and saw his mother laughing as she spoke with Amber. He tucked his chin deep into his collar and walked into the darkness alone.

THE END... BOOK TWO

A Note from the Author

Thank you for reading *D.R.T.* *(Dead Right There)*, the second installment of the Nate Richards Seasons series. Now that you've finished this book, I would love to hear from you. You can email me with your thoughts on the book or friend me on Facebook. You can even sign up for my newsletter, which will give you updates on upcoming releases and all the other craziness going on in my corner of the world.

If you would like to help this story succeed, please tell others about it. You can loan your copy to a friend, and ask your local libraries and bookstores to order it.

In addition, if you post a review on **amazon.com**, **goodreads.com**, or **shelfari.com**, it would be very helpful.

My email address is:
   ray@rayellis-author.com

You can download discussion questions or follow my blog entries at:
   http://authorray.blogspot.com

Please visit my web site at:
   http://www.nccpublishing.com/rayellis.html

Follow me on Twitter at:
   Twitter@RayEllisNHI

Acknowledgments

As with any project of significance, it is never completed alone and without assistance. This is no less true of *D.R.T.* First, I'd like to thank God for His grace and the gift of His wonderful Son, Jesus. Without Him, none of this would ever have been possible or necessary.

Secondly, I'd like to thank the ladies of the Tully's Critique group: Angela, Cheryl, and Ruth. Without you three, I would still be stuck on "rain fell in sheets and chilled him to the core..." It's an inside joke, but I know my ladies will get it.

Next, I would like to say thank you to the many talented people who gave me their time and effort to help bring this project to launch: Judy Marker Simmons, a very special thanks to Debbie Sloane, and of course, my wife and children who have lived with Nate and Amber as guests in our home for these last few years.

Thanks to my wife especially for believing in me when I began to doubt myself. And finally, thanks to my church family at Nampa Christian Center for its prayerful support, and lastly thanks to Aaron Patterson at StoneHouse for believing in me just enough to give me a chance. And thank you to my readers.

About the Author

Ray Ellis is a veteran law enforcement officer, former Marine, and ordained Christian pastor. Ray began his career in law enforcement with the Orange County Sheriff's Department in the city of Orange, California in 1989. After working for a number of years in the maximum security facility, he transferred to patrol, working along Orange County's coast as well as the inner canyons and barrios.

After eight years in Orange County, Ray moved to Idaho and continued his law enforcement career where he has served as a patrol officer, detective, and officer instructor for the Idaho POST Council. In 1999 Ray was appointed as a primary instructor for the Idaho POST Academy Police Training Institution for Idaho, instructing on subjects of arrest control, cultural diversity, and instructor development. From 2007-2011 Ray served as the lead sex crimes investigator for the agency where he works.

Ray is active in the writer's community in Idaho and has recently served as the president of the Idahope Writer's Group. In 2011, Ray was selected as one of the *Top Fifty Authors* in the state of Idaho.

Ray was first ordained into the ministry while living in Orange County and now serves as the Associate Pastor in his home church in Nampa, Idaho. Ray has been happily married to his wife, Sharon, since 1983 and has three grown children: two sons and one daughter. Ray currently lives with his family in Idaho.

More by this author:

- N.H.I. - No Humans Involved (A Nate Richards Novel - Book One)
- "I" – A Short Story (Released as eBook by NCC Publishing)

Coming Soon

I.A.I.

INTERNAL AFFAIRS INVESTIGATION

By Ray Ellis

A Nate Richards Novel - Book Three

After two successful investigations, Detective Nate Richards is feeling secure in his new position. That is, until he is summoned to the office of the assistant chief. An accusation is made, charges leveled and Nate finds himself suspended, the focus of every cops fear…the Internal Affairs Investigation.

For the first time, Nate finds himself the subject of a criminal investigation. All the resources of the powerful machine of the law enforcement world, once his to command, have been turned against him. His name and honor called to question, and Nate finds himself in a position where he doesn't know who he can or should trust. With friends turning away from him and being cut off from his normal systems of support, the question is, will Nate's faith be enough? Where do you turn when you're a cop and the attack is coming from the inside, the I.A.

CHAPTER ONE

"PUT YOUR BADGE, I.D., and gun on the desk."

Detective Nate Richards looked at the man sitting across from him, and then back at the plainclothes officer standing by the door, certain he had not heard him correctly. He replayed the last sentence in his mind and cleared his throat. "You're taking my gun...?"

Assistant Chief Terry Lawrence of the Treasure Valley Metro Police Department stared at Nate, his eyes boring into him. "Nate, I need your gun...and your I.D....and your badge. I need them now." The Assistant Chief, the A.C., had taken a breath between each phrase, making each statement hard. Nate felt each word as if it had been a blow. "From this moment you are on administrative suspension pending the outcome of the I.A." His gray eyes fixed on Nate, unflinching. Muscles in his jaw flexed and then relaxed.

The assistant chief stood, his face hard. His broad shoulders strained beneath the fine tailored dress shirt as he moved. Clipped in place by a diamond-accented tiepin, the designer silk tie swung free beneath the pin bouncing off of his perfectly flat stomach. With careful precision, he placed his large hands on the desktop. Like a defensive-end preparing to attack a quarterback, he rocked forward, pressing the color from his knuckles.

His office was a pictorial representation of the man himself. It was compact and had no windows or natural light. Clean white walls held mementos of youthful acquisitions and memorials of manhood. Patton, MacArthur, Doolittle, and John Wayne, posted in solid wood frames, looked down from their respective perches over the A.C.'s shoulders, and all of them seemed to be staring at Nate. "Until further notice," Assistant Chief Lawrence began, "you are restricted to the same movement in this building as any other civilian."

Nate frowned and shook his head, trying to clear away the fog of emotions settling into his mind. Any other civilian?

"You will have no contact or communication with any employee of this department without my direct approval."

He took my badge... my gun? Why?

The assistant chief, known to the troops as the A.C., turned to the only other person in the room, the witness. "Sargent Swift, escort Mr. Rich—"

Nate jumped to his feet. "You don't really think I did this, do you, sir?!"

The assistant chief turned a wary eye on Nate. Taking a breath, he seemed to deflate, then lowered himself into the large black leather armchair. For a moment the two men stared at each other. No one spoke or moved. Then the assistant chief exhaled, long and slow then leaned back in his seat. He rested his hands palms up on the desk and shook his head in short quick movements. "I don't know, Nate."

Nate sagged. "It would have hurt less if you'd slapped me, sir."

Sargent Swift stepped forward and touched Nate's elbow. "Com'on, Nate, let's get you out of here. We can stop by your desk on the way out."

Nate started toward the door, but stopped and turned back to the assistant chief. "Sir—Terry, you've known me for over ten years. Have I ever given you a reason to believe this of me...that I am even capable of—" his voice broke and he looked away, "of raping someone?"

I.A.I. - Internal Affairs Investigation, by Ray Ellis is due out by winter of 2012.

RAY ELLIS